BLURB

Once upon a time, I was nothing more than a bad boy seeking all the tail I could get ...

Something happened to change all that.
Suddenly, chasing women turned into chasing the dream of becoming a doctor.
Hard work and determination had me meeting my dream a hell of a lot sooner than most.
And with the title of doctor came ready and willing women, set on landing themselves a wealthy physician.
Little did they know that I would readily give them some hot, steamy memories to keep, but my heart belonged to someone else. Someone I didn't want to share with anyone.
But then she came along, claiming what had always been only mine.
And maybe she would claim my heart as well ...

CHAPTER 1

Zandra

Cold wind whipped around me as I climbed the stairs up to my apartment, which I shared with four roommates. Unfortunately, they were four of the messiest and most immature individuals I'd ever had the misfortune of meeting.

I'm met all of them while working as a cocktail waitress at Underground, a nightclub in Chicago, and we'd gotten along well enough to decide to live together. Little did I know that all four of them were very different people at home than they were while working with the public.

Being a few years older than any of them, at twenty-six I supposed I was just growing up a bit. That had to be the reason behind my budding impatience with the people I'd lived with for the last year.

It seemed like just yesterday that I was right there with them all, dumping clean laundry onto the floor instead of putting it in my closet, making a mess while trying to search for just the right thing to wear. Or even leaving dirty dishes in the sink with the hope that someone else would get disgusted enough with the mess to feel the urge to clean up. Yes, I was once just as filthy as they were, but things had changed in the last few months.

I had changed. Now all I wanted was a clean apartment to live in.

Is that too much to ask for?

Walking back into the quiet house after having a morning coffee at the small café down the street, I headed toward the one bathroom the five of us shared.

I would've loved to have been able to go to the bathroom without having to clean the damn toilet first. Two of my roommates were guys who had a habit of leaving trails of pee in places that didn't make sense. Along the edge of the tub, around the floor near the toilet, and once even by the door, for some odd reason. And they never seemed to notice their mishaps either, leaving them for someone else to deal with.

I'd begun carrying around a little container with convenient small towelettes covered in peach-scented bleach that I would use to wipe things down. It seemed I was becoming more like my mother in this regard, a realization I disliked very much, but had no clue how to push away so I could go back to not giving a hoot about cleanliness.

In retaliation to my impending maturity, I'd gone to the salon to get my dark hair done in a more fun, youthful fashion. The new dark blue streaks might just be a visual representation of my attempt to cling to my youth, but so what? I liked them.

But even as I looked into the bathroom mirror after wiping the entire room down, I could see a new maturity in my blue eyes that hadn't been there even a few months ago.

Yes, the streaks in my hair were the same color as my eyes. A girl likes to match, you know.

Staring disconnectedly into the eyes of the person looking back at me, that empty feeling I had at times started to creep in. Most of the time I could ignore the emptiness, but now and then it would find me and linger for a while before letting up and allowing me some relief once more.

Whenever it hit me, my life would temporary turn into a hellish existence. My dreams would turn into nightmares, and all I could do was drink coffee to keep me awake, trying to keep the bad dreams away. Wishing the feeling wouldn't last more than a few days this time, instead of the week-long agony that had nearly drowned me the last time it hit me, I closed my eyes.

When I opened them up again, I saw myself staring back at me once more. A young woman, no longer the girl I had been. I needed to face things instead of trying to ignore or forget about them.

I had a bad past. So what?

Lots of people had bad things happen to them in their lives. Who did I think I was?

Was I invincible? Was I too good for anything bad to ever happen to me? No, I wasn't. And I had to stop the internal berating that came along with every bout of depression.

Leaving the now-clean bathroom, I went to the bedroom I shared with the other two girls in the apartment. They were sprawled out on their little twin beds; one of them had her head at the wrong end of the bed.

I fought the urge to move her into the right position, a motherly urge that only proved to make the depressed feelings inside of me edge closer to the surface.

Tears began to sting the backs of my eyes, and I left the room to go to the kitchen and clean some more. Cleaning was fast becoming the outlet I turned to whenever the emptiness tried to claim me.

And with this crew of slobs, there was plenty of cleaning to do. The dishes needed washing, so I did the sink full of them. The floor needed to be swept and mopped, so I did that too. The fridge needed to be cleaned out, the leftovers tossed, and the entire thing wiped down with one of my handy bleach wipes as well.

By the time the first roommate woke up and dragged his ass out of bed, the kitchen sparkled, and everything smelled peachy. Standing there in his not-so-white, tighty whiteys, Dillon rubbed his brown eyes with the back of one hand as he yawned loudly. "What the hell are you doing, making all this noise on a Sunday, Zandy? We didn't get in last night until four in the morning. Are you insane?"

Am I?

I wasn't sure how to answer that. I felt it best to ignore his question. "I'm cleaning, Dillon. A thing the rest of you must not have learned how to do yet. I'll try to be quieter, so you guys can sleep. Sorry about that." Apologizing for doing chores shouldn't be something anyone should have to worry about.

I found resentment building up inside of me. *These ungrateful kids should have to live in filth!*

As Dillon walked wearily back to the bedroom he shared with the other guy who lived with us, I looked at the clean floor and wondered what the hell I was doing there.

My parents lived just outside of town. But I would never go back to live with them. I only talked to my mother when she called incessantly, and then only for a very short amount of time. I would let her know that I was alive and fine, but nothing more than that.

She didn't deserve to know any more than that. Not after what she and my father had done to me.

Their evil deed had left a hole in my heart. A hole that I knew could never be repaired.

Going out the front door, I took a seat on the top stair outside our apartment. The wind still blew a thousand miles an hour, making my hair fly all around me. The cold air chilled me to my bones, as I'd come out once again without so much as a sweater on to keep me warm. Only an old sweatshirt and a pair of jeans covered my body. It wasn't enough to keep the cold out.

Fiddling with a hole in the knee of my jeans, I made it even bigger. The image of a baby made a brief appearance in my brain before I successfully pushed it aside.

No, I didn't ever let things like that take up any space in my head. But when I fell asleep, those thoughts and images would sneak in, taking my dreams and turning them into nightmares.

Two days had already passed with little sleep. Waking up with tears on my pillow, I would get up and do anything I could to make myself stop thinking. Thinking only made it hurt worse.

Ten years have passed. Why does it still bother me so much?

Looking down at my left arm, I still couldn't believe that I'd gotten so drunk three nights earlier that I'd gone and gotten a tattoo on the inside of my wrist.

Why did I do this to myself?

Why would I purposely do anything that would be a constant reminder of the one thing I tried desperately to forget about? Why would I put that on my body?

For the rest of my life, I'd look down and see "05/03/2008" written in baby blue ink multiple times a day. Why would I do such a hurtful thing to myself?

Only God knew why I would do such a thing, no matter what amount of alcohol I'd consumed. Or the devil. I wasn't sure which had the strongest hold on me.

At times, it sure felt like the devil was the one who'd laid out the path my life would take.

Is there a way to change my path, or is it too late? Can there be a way out of this emptiness?

If there was, I knew now that I wouldn't find the answer in Chicago. Of that much, I was sure.

I'd been dragged there against my will when I was just sixteen years old. When I left my parents' home on the day I turned eighteen, I could've gone anywhere. I had ten thousand dollars that I'd inherited from my grandmother. She'd died when I was twelve, and the money had been left in a bank account in Charleston, South Carolina, where we'd lived most of my life.

When I turned eighteen, I gained access to that money and hauled ass out of the house I'd essentially been held captive in for two long-as-hell years. Without any other plan, into the big city of Chicago I went.

The bank card from the Charleston bank had come in the mail a few days before my birthday. It had my name on it. The accompanying letter said that it would be activated on the date of my birth and would be ready to use that very day.

I used it to buy myself a birthday present—a cab ride into town and then a week in a cheap motel. I found a job that very night at Underground.

My first roommate was a girl named Sasha who'd been working at the club for a few years. At twenty-five years old, the older woman took me under her wing, teaching me everything I needed to know in order to bring in big tips by being flirtatious and sexy.

A couple of years later she met some guy and moved out to live with him. She also quit working at the nightclub. That's when I met a new friend. Taylor had come to work at the club when she was just eighteen, too. I was a little older by then and took her under my wing, letting her stay in Sasha's old room.

Taylor didn't need much coaching. She seemed to be a natural at flirting. And it didn't hurt that she had absolutely no problem sleeping with any guy who wanted her.

I had issues with sex. My past made me it very hard for me to have any kind of eagerness for the act. It was sex that had gotten me into trouble in the first place.

As sexy as I dressed and as flirty as I was, it was all a performance. An important one, that helped me keep a roof over my head, food in my stomach, and a car under my ass to keep me going to and fro on my own.

Following the same routine for nearly a decade can grow tiresome. And boy, did I feel tired. Tired of looking at the same old buildings. Tired of driving down the same old streets. Tired of living with a bunch of overgrown adolescents.

The back pocket of my jeans vibrated, so I pulled out my cell phone. A smile broke the no-doubt forlorn expression my face must have settled into. As if by magic, Taylor's name appeared on the screen.

She'd left a year ago, sparking my need to get a new roommate. I didn't recall exactly why I kept letting people move in, but I had. I hadn't heard from her in a good while.

"Hey, you," I answered the call.

"Hey yourself, girlie. What're you up to these days?" she asked me.

Shoving my hand through my hair, then holding onto it so the wind couldn't blow it around, I sighed heavily. I didn't know what to say. I had been up to the same old dreary thing. But to say that out loud seemed just too pathetic. "Not much. You?"

"Just working at this badass club in Charleston called Mynt," came her enthusiastic reply.

"Mynt?" My mind wandered back to Charleston. The home I'd had to leave when I was just sixteen. Barely sixteen, really, as my mother was constantly reminding me.

Mom would remind me far too often that I was barely above fifteen when I'd gotten myself into what she liked to refer to as "the situation." A situation, she also reminded me, that had forced her and my father to uproot our little family and move far away. Life had never been the same after that move.

"Yeah, Mynt," Taylor said, pulling me out of my reverie. "And you want to know what I think, Zandy?"

"What do you think?" I chewed on my long fake black-painted fingernail as I waited to hear what she had to say.

"I think that you should come on down here to the South and work with me." She paused to let that sink in as I thought about it. "I've got a very nice two-bedroom apartment that my roommate has just moved out of. I could use a new roomie, and who better than you to fill that role?"

Yeah, who better than me to fill that role?

Charleston sounded nice. Going back to what I had always considered my home sounded like a fantastic idea. *Why not go back there?*

Even if I saw anyone from my old life, it wasn't like anyone knew why we'd left all of a sudden anyway. What harm would it do to go back to my hometown?

"And the pay at Mynt?" I asked. "Is it pretty decent?"

"Let's just say that I make enough money to pay my bills, eat what I want, when I want, drive a nice car, and even splurge on shopping now and then with what I'm bringing home." She laughed, the pitch high and shrill but still pleasant, as only Taylor could make it. "Please tell me that you'll come. I've already talked to the boss about you. He thinks you'll fit right in with our little family at Mynt. It's lots of fun,

Zandy. You'll love the atmosphere. I promise you that we'll have a great time."

She made it sound like a great idea, and it wasn't like I had anything holding me in Chicago. A change might be just what I needed to get the emptiness to go away. At least for a little while.

Another gust of frigid wind hit me, and I got up. My hand balled into a fist at my side; I was ready to make the big change. "It's a miracle that you called me right at this moment, Taylor. I've been in a funk lately. Change is exactly what I need in my life right now."

She sounded hopeful. "Does that mean you'll come?"

"Yeah, I'll come." I went back inside to get out of the cold. "When do you want me?"

"Yesterday," she said with light laughter threading her high voice. Taylor was the closest thing to a fairy a human woman could get, and it was utterly charming. People often called her Tinkerbell.

"Then I'll pack up my things and give my notice at work. Then I'll get into my car and come your way. Text me the address, and I'll be there as soon as my wheels can get me there."

Change was important. It's what I'd been missing in my life lately, and without change life could be one long, dreary existence. I wanted to leave dreary behind me. Hopefully, Charleston would see to that.

CHAPTER 2

Kane

THE CRACK of the bat connecting with the baseball made my heart swell with pride. "You did it, Fox! Now run, son!"

On my feet as soon as the ball started soaring, I clapped as my ten-year-old son threw the bat down then ran to first base before anyone could get a hold of the ball. "Go to second," I called out to him, seeing that he looked a little confused about what he should do.

The coach shouted, "Go on, Fox. This could be a home run!"

My son's first home run!

Standing, watching, not daring to breathe, I crossed my fingers, hoping that he would make it. Moments later, he slid into home base. All the parents on the bench let out a cheer, as my son run had earned his team, the Bears, the one point they needed to take the lead against their biggest rivals, the Tigers. "Way to go, boy!"

Fox waved at me with the biggest grin on his face I'd ever seen. "I did it, Dad!"

"You did!" I knew I had to be beaming.

With a nod, he headed back into the dugout where his teammates gave him high-fives and pats on the back. He'd earned them too.

Taking my seat again, I looked over at the man sitting next to me, my Uncle James. He and my Aunt Nancy, who sat on the other side of him, always joined me to watch Fox's games.

My mother and Aunt Nancy were sisters. I owed everything to Aunt Nancy and Uncle James. They'd done the biggest favor anyone could do for another person, and they'd done it for me. They'd found the girl I'd accidentally knocked up in high school and had adopted the baby.

If it hadn't been for a friend of mine, Bess Peterson, who'd lived next door to the Larkin family, I wouldn't have ever known that I'd gotten Zandra Larkin pregnant. Bess had overheard the awful shouting that had taken place when Zandra's parents had found out that she was having a baby.

Zandra and Bess weren't friends. Zandra was mostly a loner, probably because of her parents' strict religious beliefs. Those beliefs were probably what had put them into panic mode, whisking their only child away a few weeks after Zandra and I had hooked up at a party one night.

I'd always thought Zandra, who was a year younger than me, was pretty. Her long, dark hair, deep blue eyes, and pretty pink lips had caught my attention more often than they hadn't. But she was shy, reclusive, and kept to herself.

That one night at that party, which I'd found out one of her few friends had dragged her to, had given me the chance to get to know her. And boy, did I get to know her!

She didn't give me her phone number before she left me that night in my friend's bed. I fell asleep, and she took off without waking me up. It was the end of summer, so there wasn't any school the next week. And knowing how strict her parents were, I wasn't about to just show up at her house unannounced.

Everyone knew how strict her mother and father were. I was afraid I might get her into trouble if I just showed up. I planned on catching up with her when school was back in session. But I never got that chance.

It was Bess who came to me when school started again. She'd

seen Zandra and me together at that party, and she was pretty sure that I'd been the one to do the deed that had put Zandra's family in such turmoil.

It seemed that Zandra's mother kept track of her periods, and when Zandra failed to start on time, she took her to the doctor. Bess told me that she overheard Zandra's parents screaming that she wasn't going to get to keep the baby and blaming her for ruining all of their lives. They repeatedly asked Zandra for the name of the boy she'd been with, but Zandra refused to tell them a thing.

Some other boys in that position might've counted themselves lucky that they didn't have to deal with any of it. Instead, I went home and told my parents what I'd done. I told them that I knew Zandra had been a virgin before me. She'd told me so, and the fact that she'd bled told me she hadn't lied about it.

I'd gotten her pregnant the very first time she'd ever had sex. Along with that, I shared the responsibility of her being taken away from her hometown. It wasn't fair, and I knew that. I also knew it wasn't fair to give our baby to strangers.

Mom had called her sister right away, knowing she had the connections that would make tracking the baby a possibility. Aunt Nancy and Uncle James did the investigative work, and our son was given to them in a closed adoption. Neither Zandra nor her family even knew the names of the people who adopted the boy. And they would never know it was my family who took him.

"Handing custody over to you was the best thing we could've ever done for Fox," Uncle James said as he bumped his shoulder to mine. "We're damn proud of you, Kane. We're very proud of you for finishing your doctorate last year and earning that position at the clinic. Twenty-seven is pretty young to be so well established and settled down."

"Well, Fox was all the incentive I needed to grow up quick." I had to sigh as I watched my son cutting up with his teammates. "From the moment you guys brought him to see me when he was just a week old, I knew I would live my life for him. I just wanted to make sure I could be the father he deserves."

I clapped my uncle on the back. "Thanks for always letting me be there with him, you guys. I can't thank you enough for giving a seventeen-year-old kid the chance to prove that he could be a stand-up father. Letting me take custody of him and actually make him mine last year was a dream come true for me."

"And for Fox," Aunt Nancy added. "That kid has always loved you, Kane. It was only fair that he be with his biological father."

Nodding, I thought about the fact that my aunt and uncle had decided from the start to have Fox call them aunt and uncle. They'd told him I was his father right from the start. It made things easier when I finally had a home to bring him to, making the transition a smooth one.

Fox knew the whole story, now that he was old enough. We never planned on hiding the truth from him, so it was just a matter of waiting until he could understand. His mother was only sixteen when she got pregnant. Her parents made her give him up, and we jumped in to make sure we never lost him.

"He's looking more and more like his mom every day," I commented as I looked at my son. "His dark hair is the exact same shade as hers was. And those freckles across his nose come from her too."

Uncle James asked, "Do you think you'll ever try to find her, Kane?"

Shaking my head, I answered him truthfully. "No. I have no idea if she wanted to give him away or not. The fact is she went along with the adoption—and a closed one, at that. She may have wanted it that way too. I won't find her and tell her about something she may not want to hear about."

Aunt Nancy had always leaned more toward contacting Zandra one day. "He just turned ten last week. Fox is a bright boy with tons of curiosity. I know he doesn't talk to you about his mother nearly as much as he talks to me about her, but he does ask about her a lot. I think you should start thinking some more about finding her, Kane. It might be what's best for Fox."

Pushing my hand through my hair, I felt that nagging feeling coming over again. The feeling always lingered when I thought about the reality that Zandra might not want anything to do with our son, or me, for that matter.

"But what if she didn't want him? It might have started out as her parents' idea, but what if Zandra wanted to get rid of him too, in the end? How would she react then if I tried to pull her into his life when all she wanted was to be rid of him?"

Uncle James smiled at me with that expression of pure wisdom on his face. "What if she didn't want to give him up and was only doing what her parents made her do? What if she's still as shy as she was when she was sixteen and doesn't have a clue how to find her son? What if she's hurt by what she was made to do and thinks about him every day?"

God, the man knew how to pull at a person's heartstrings!

Even still, I wasn't sure about anything, other than that she had given him up in a closed adoption. No authority, other than her parents, had made her do that. "She could've told the adoption agency that her parents were making her give the baby up and that she didn't want to."

Aunt Nancy shook her head. "I was there when she gave him up, Kane. She had no idea I wasn't a nurse, Kane, and that girl was heartbroken when I took that baby away from her that day. She told him that she loved him more than anything. She told him that she was sorry for what she was doing, but that he would have a much better life without her or her parents in it."

Aunt Nancy had told me this a million times. And as many times as I'd heard the story, I had never understood why Zandra would've gone through with giving him up if she truly loved him. And I'd never understood why she'd never tried to contact me about the pregnancy.

It wasn't as if I was some lothario who had slept with countless girls. I'd never intended to just sleep with her and then drop her. I'd thought about her a lot after the party. I'd thought about how I would approach the shy girl when school was back in session, about how I would bring her out of her shell again, just as I was able to that night.

The fact that she never seemed to even try to get in touch with anyone, not even the few friends she'd had at school, had me thinking that she wanted to forget all about that part of her life.

I stayed in Charleston. With my parents' help, plus my aunt and uncle's, I raised Fox. Everyone we knew was aware that I was that boy's father and that Zandra Larkin was his mother. Everyone. Even Zandra's friends knew about it.

So why hadn't Zandra ever tried to contact any of her friends?

Each one of the girls I talked to back then told me that Zandra had their phone numbers, though Zandra's number was no longer in service after the move. And even at Fox's tenth birthday party, one of his mother's old friends stopped by to wish him a happy birthday and give him a present. She told him that if his mother were around, she'd be very proud of him. And she also told him that his mother was a very private and shy person, but she was sure that she still loved him, as she was also a very nice and loving person.

I recalled the smile that spread across my son's face that day as he and his mother's friend talked. He nodded. "I'm sure she does love me. I love her, and I don't 'member meeting her ever in my life. But Aunt Nancy said that she held me for a little while before she had to say goodbye. And that she told me that she loved me too. I know that someday I'll see her again. And then I'll be old enough to 'member her."

Most people seemed sure that one day Zandra would try to find Fox. I was one of the few who didn't think that day would come at all. And I prayed that our son wouldn't be hurt if the day he was so hopeful about never occurred.

And I wondered how I would react to her if she did come looking for him. Would I be angry with her?

As understanding as I'd tried to be about her situation, I had also been mad back then. Mad that she hadn't told me what was happening. Mad that she'd planned to give our child to strangers. Mad that her parents thought they could take my son's future into their own hands.

Zandra may have been intimidated and controlled by her parents, but I never would've let them control me too. I would've taken care of Zandra, had she told me about the situation.

Looking at the ground, I knew my thoughts weren't healthy. I'd been a seventeen-year-old kid at that time. Zandra had been a minor; her parents had still been in control of her life.

In reality, I couldn't have taken care of her. My parents could have and would have. But only if Zandra's parents allowed that to happen. And we all knew that they would never have allowed that.

The sound of cheers pulled me out of my internal reverie, and I looked up. My son's team had won the game. The boys were jumping up and down with triumphant joy.

"Looks like we're going to get to go to a pizza party, Kane," Uncle James said. We all got up to join the kids on the field to congratulate each one of them and to tell the kids on the other team that they'd played a great game too.

"We did it, Dad!" Fox shouted as he ran to me.

"You sure did, son!" Putting my arm around his narrow shoulders, I pulled him close to my side. "Your home run was the game-winner, too."

"Hey, Fox, catch," the coach called out.

He tossed the ball to Fox, who caught it easily. The smile he'd been wearing grew even bigger. "I get to keep the game ball?"

"It's yours, kid," his coach told him. "At the pizza party, you can get everyone to sign it for you."

"I'll get you a little case to keep it in, Fox," Uncle James told him as he pulled him away from me to give him a hug.

"Man, this is like the best day ever!" Fox shouted as he held the ball up. "We won! Woohoo!"

Man, I bet his mother would love to see him like this.

CHAPTER 3

Zandra

"CUTE OUTFIT," the manager of Mynt said as he looked me up and down. "Nice legs. It's good to see you don't mind putting them on display." Wearing a short black leather skirt with a white button-down top, I had tied my shirt in a knot in front to show off my belly button piercing. I was the epitome of hot nightclub waitresses everywhere.

"Yeah. I've been doing this waitress thing since I turned eighteen. I've pretty much got it down pat now." I pulled the long braid I'd put my hair in over my shoulder, stroking it as I looked into Rob's gray eyes. His pupils got big, telling me he liked what he saw.

By now, I was used to having my body raked over by men's eyes, and it didn't bother me to be the center of attention. As long as the scrutiny came with a paycheck, I could suck it up.

Rob trailed his long fingers along one of my shoulders. His dark hair was parted low on the left side. Some type of product made it shiny, helping him keep it slicked back. He wasn't my type at all. He was the kind of guy most people would call a guido—maybe not to his face, though.

"And how many years have you been doing this now?" he asked.

"Eight years." Placing my hand on my hip, I defied him to say something about my age. Though I was still young and as fit as any one of the younger waitresses, I knew a lot of managers liked to stick to the under-twenty-five crowd when it came to their waitresses.

"Twenty-six," he mused as his eyes met mine. His lips pulled up to one side. "Your body might not give it away, but you can see it in your eyes, Zandy."

"Well, it's a good thing no one will be looking at my eyes, then, isn't it?" Sashaying my ass, I walked away from him, earning a wolf-whistle. The sound made me smile. That whistle meant money, and money was all I cared about.

"Does that mean she's got the job, Rob?" Taylor chimed in.

I turned around to look at him as he answered. "If she can start tonight, she does."

"I can." Hurrying back to them, I found myself grabbed up by Taylor, and the two of us jumped up and down in our sky-high heels. "Yes!"

Now I had a nice apartment with a bedroom all to myself and a job that Taylor promised would make me lots of money. More money than what I'd been making in Chicago.

On the drive back to the apartment, the two of us chatted away excitedly about being able to work together again. Taylor stopped at a light then screamed, "Yes! Together again! We're gonna rock Charleston, Zandy!"

"We rocked Chicago," I agreed. "I know we can rock this place too."

Looking to my left, I thought I recognized a guy from high school. That had been so long ago, it seemed. He looked right at me, gave me a wink, and then Taylor took off so fast that I didn't get the chance to even wink back or see if he recognized me.

I was pretty sure he hadn't. I no longer looked like the bookish, shy girl I'd been back then. Nearly eleven years had passed since I'd been in town, since I'd been that person. I didn't expect anyone to recognize me.

And I prayed that one man, in particular, wouldn't. If he was even still in the around—which I highly doubted.

The blue streaks in my hair would offer me a bit of protection, should I happen to encounter someone from my old life here. This hair choice was something I never would've done when I was a teenager. And I wore a lot of makeup now, too. It was what waitresses did. I didn't make the rules; I just followed them.

Revealing clothes, too much makeup, hair that stood out—I was dressing for the job I wanted. And I was pretty certain not one of the people I'd known back then would come to the club I'd be working at. Even if they did, no one would ever think the sexy woman who waited on them was the same mousy junior from high school who'd left town without saying a word to anyone.

"Did it piss you off when Rob said he could see your age in your eyes, Zandy?" Taylor asked me as she drove too fast down the street.

"No." I pulled a pair of dark sunglasses out of my purse and put them on. "I can see it too. There aren't many ladies in my age group who still do this sort of thing. Being twenty-six, many women my age have already hung up their heels. And have replaced their Mustangs with minivans, yuck!" We laughed uproariously at my little joke, which wasn't too much of a joke at all.

Taylor zoomed around a corner, making us both lean to one side, laughing like hell all the way. "So why haven't you settled down, Zandy? I mean, you haven't even dated any guy seriously. What's up with you?"

Where to start?

Pain. Anguish. Guilt. Along with a healthy side of resentment and regret.

I'd never told anyone about my unexpected pregnancy, or any of the life-altering events that followed. Maybe it was time I did. Maybe talking about it would help me begin to heal from it. If anyone could truly heal from a thing like that.

Even though I wasn't sure how Taylor would take it, I decided to spill my guts to her. "Dating would mean giving someone a chance to get close to me and taking a chance of falling in love. And when two people fall in love, they eventually decide to procreate. And I've done that already. It ended badly. And I don't want to do it again."

"You had a miscarriage?" she asked as she took another hard left.

The Nissan Altima felt like it had tilted onto only two wheels, making me scream with a mix of terror and excitement. "No! Shit, girl. You're a crazy driver!"

"So I've been told." She laughed menacingly, making me smile. I loved living dangerously. Why not live that way? What did I have to live for anyway? "So, no miscarriage. Did you lose the baby after it was born?" I could hear the sympathy in her voice, mixed with caution. Taylor knew me well enough to know that revealing so much about myself wasn't easy for me.

"Kind of." I grabbed the dash as she made an abrupt stop at a stop sign that seemed to have crept up on her.

"Kind of?" She narrowed her pale blue eyes at me. Her tiny nose was pointy and turned up at the end. Taylor really did remind me of Tinkerbell. Only, her short blonde locks were pulled into spikes, and each one was dyed a different color on the ends. "How is that an appropriate answer, Zandy?"

"I had a baby. And my parents made me give him up for adoption," I clarified my answer.

"Made you?" she asked, then hit the gas hard enough to make a jackrabbit take off.

Clutching the bar above my head, the one I called an "oh-shit bar," I went on, "At barely sixteen I lost my V-card to the boy I'd had a crush on since I was about twelve. He had dirty blond hair, all-American good looks, and eventually, a killer body. The first hint of attention he gave me made me putty in his hands."

Zipping up to the parking space in front of the apartment we shared, she stopped right next to my red Mustang. Her head swiveled to look at me. "So, you gave it up to this guy who you weren't dating but you'd been crushing on for years, and you ended up preggo? On the first go?"

"Precisely." Getting out of the car, we made our way to the front door.

The whole complex was made up of ground-floor apartments, another thing that made me like this place better than the place I'd been living for the last eight years. No stairs to climb and no one living overhead, making noise all the time. The apartment was perfect.

Taking a seat on the expensive leather sofa and loveseat, Taylor asked, "Your crush didn't want to do the right thing by you, Zandy?"

Shaking my head, I said, "I never told him about it. I never told anyone about it. My mother was totally up in my personal business. She kept track of her periods on this calendar that she called the "menstruation keeper." When I got my period when I was around thirteen, she began adding mine to it. She said she did it so I would know right when I was about to start so I'd never be unprepared."

"So you'd put some tamps in your purse then, stock up on Midol," she said with a knowing grin.

"Most of the time, yeah." Chewing on my lip, I thought back to that time when my period hadn't come. "Well, anyways, suddenly, one month, my period didn't start."

"And when it didn't show up, what did you do?" Taylor asked with wide eyes. "I mean, I've never had a pregnancy scare at all. My mother trotted my ass down to the clinic right after my first period when I was fifteen. She made me start getting the shot as soon as I could, and I've been on it ever since."

"I tried to hide the fact that it hadn't started." I remembered how hysterical I felt when I was late. "I lied to my mother about having it, telling her it was right on schedule. Only I didn't think about one important thing."

Nodding, she said, "You forgot to plant evidence, didn't you?"

"Yep." My chest rose and fell with a heavy sigh.

She shook her head sadly. "Rookie mistake, Zandy."

Shrugging my shoulders, I said, "I was a rookie. And I wasn't ready to handle anything, never mind what would happen when my parents found out. I figured I'd have at least a few months to figure something out and eventually talk to the guy about it. I had no idea if he wanted anything to do with me after we'd slept together. We didn't do a hell of a lot of talking before we got naked together."

"He must've been so hot," she mused. "'Cause you're a really gorgeous girl, Zandy. You could have your pick of anyone."

"I was plain back then, and my parents were really strict. I wasn't allowed to wear any makeup at all. Everyone else was, but not me. And my mom cut my hair." I cringed, remembering the horror that was my hair. "I had these straight, very short bags. The rest of my hair was one length that went down to the middle of my back. My clothes were all purchased by my mother, too. Needless to say, they would have looked very appropriate on a teenager in, say, 1950."

"I don't suppose you've got any pictures," she said with a wry smile.

I threw a little pillow at her, smacking her in the face. "No, you jackass."

"Thought as much." She tossed the pillow back at me, and I caught it. "So, what happened next?"

"Mom took me to see our doctor. He told her I was pregnant. I was only a couple weeks along and already my parents were making decisions about the little baby I carried." The tears sprang up on cue as his tiny face made a brief appearance in my head. No matter how many years passed, I knew without a doubt that I'd never forget the sight of his perfect little face.

Taylor got up and came to sit next to me. Her arm around my shoulders was meant to comfort, but it didn't help at all. There was just no way to comfort someone who'd had their child taken away. "They made you give it up?"

Nodding my head, I let the tears flow freely. "We left that night to go stay with relatives in Chicago. Mom and Dad took me out of school. I had to finish high school online. Dad had a cell phone, but other than that we had no other phone because they didn't want me to be able to talk to any of my friends—the few that I even had. When I was on the computer doing schoolwork, my parents would watch me, making sure I didn't get a chance to contact anyone. They never wanted anyone to know the shame of what I'd done."

"And the father of the baby never knew?" she asked as she patted my shoulder, trying to reassure me that everything would be okay. It wouldn't ever be okay. I'd already accepted that fact.

"He doesn't know a thing." I wiped my eyes with the back of my hand, seeing black smudges from my makeup. "He never will. The adoption agency arranged a closed adoption. My parents and I were never given the names of the people who adopted him. And the guy's name wasn't on anything—I never even told my parents his name. That was the one thing I refused to do. I didn't want them saying anything to him or his family about it. It was all my fault, anyway. I was the stupid girl who, when he asked, told him he didn't have to use a condom."

"Wow." Taylor sat back, looking stunned. "That was dumb."

Nodding, I had to agree. "Yeah, it was."

"All that happened a long time ago, Zandy. Why let it keep you from getting close to anyone now? Or let it stop you from having more kids when you want them?"

I rubbed my fingers over the black smudges on the back of my hand, trying to make them go away. "It wouldn't be fair to that little boy if I had more kids. I gave him away. How could I ever expect him to understand that I had to give him up and then go on and keep any other kids? Like I just replaced him like he was nothing."

"I doubt he'll ever know you, Zandy." She took me by the chin to make me look at her. "He will never know if you get married someday and have kids. Stop thinking that way."

"I just ... I can't do." I shook my head. "And there's no way I could ever let a man into my heart anyway, Taylor. There's an enormous hole there, where my little boy is supposed to be. My heart can't hold a damn thing in it. I can't keep anyone in my heart for long before they just leak out."

"Therapy," came her answer. "You need some help, honey. And there's nothing wrong with that."

Her calling me honey just made me mad. I got up and went to the kitchen, rubbing at my eyes one last time, making sure all the tears were gone. "I'm making celebratory margaritas. I've got a new job, a slamming apartment, and I get to work with you again. Life has never been sweeter."

Taylor got up to follow me. I could feel her eyes staring a hole through me. "Zandra, seriously, you need to deal with this. It's a big deal. I'm not even smart, and I know it's a big deal."

"Yeah," I agreed. "And it always will be. Whether I talk to a shrink or not, I will never get to see my son. I will never know if he's okay or not. I will never, ever feel him in my arms. Mostly, I will never forgive my parents for what they made me do. Now, let's get wasted, take a nap, and then get up and get ready to go to work tonight."

It sounded like a solid plan at the time.

CHAPTER 4

Kane

MY BEST BUDDY, Rocco, called to invite me to his family's traditional Italian restaurant in downtown Charleston. Seeing as it was a Saturday night, and my aunt and uncle had taken Fox to Florida to spend the weekend at their vacation home in Miami, I accepted his offer.

The vino flowed like rain, his huge family refilling the glasses all night. One long table ran along the back of the dining room, and close to closing time the family would always eat dinner together, letting the staff take over what was left of the customers.

Rocco and I had been friends since grade school, and I felt like a part of his family. His father clapped me on the back as he filled my glass with red wine. "So, what are you two handsome devils going to be doing after closing tonight, Kane?"

"Going home and getting some sleep," came my quick answer.

Rocco shook his head, his dark eyes peering into mine. "No. We are not doin' that, bro."

"I don't know about you, but that's been my plan all along. I'm stuffed and getting soused from all the wine. I think bed sounds like an amazing idea." I took another drink of the fruity wine, which had a nice, crisp finish, savoring the flavors that burst inside my mouth. "Oh, Papa, this one is delicious!"

"Glad ya like," he said with a nod. "That one came straight from my cousin Sal's vineyard in Italy. He brought me a case when he visited last month. Mama and I are taking a trip to see them all in the summer. You should bring Fox, and we can make a real trip of it."

"That sounds awesome. I might just take you up on that offer." I thought about Fox getting to see Italy and a real working winery. He'd get a kick out of it, I was sure.

"Please do, Kane." Papa jerked his head toward his son. "And we'll take the meatball there too."

Shaking his meaty fist in the air, Rocco growled, "The meatball would love to come with you, Papa." He kicked the leg of my chair as he sat across from me. "For tonight, though, I've got plans for you, my best bud."

Not in the mood to go out at all, but deciding to humor him anyway, I asked, "And what are these plans, Rocco?"

"Mynt," came his one-word statement, which told me nothing at all.

"Mint?" Crossing my arms over my chest, I leaned back to think about what mint could possibly be. "Is that like a dessert shop of some kind? Because I can tell you right now, I cannot possibly eat another bite of anything."

Loud laughter peeled through the air as he cracked up for some reason. "No! Ha!" Then he stopped laughing. "Unless you consider gorgeous females a dessert, then yes."

"Gorgeous females, huh?" I still wasn't convinced. I had no desire to hook up with anyone after the brutal week I'd had. I'd taken two shifts for another doctor who had been fighting a losing battle with his allergies. On top of that, the clinic was overflowing with sick patients each and every day. All I wanted to do was sleep.

"Very beautiful women, Kane. And God knows you could use a woman." Kicking the leg of my chair again, he wiggled his dark brows at me. "You get what I'm throwing out there, man?"

His cousin Louisa came up behind him. She'd had a crush on me for years. Her slender hands ran down her cousin's arms as she looked at me, both things seeming rather inappropriate to me. "Don't go throwing things like that at my man, Rocco."

"He ain't your man, Louisa," Rocco corrected her.

Louisa was drop-dead gorgeous—she had the face of a super-model and her body was round in all the right places. But beauty on its own wasn't enough for me, and I'd always found that her brand of aggressive sexuality just didn't work for me.

"He ain't my man yet, Rocco. One day he'll see that I'm the woman for him, though." She licked her ruby red lips. "One day."

"Don't wait on me, honey," I told her.

"Like she's waiting," Rocco said with a chuckle. "This one here went out three times this week. Once with the guy who delivers our tomatoes, once with the man who delivers the beer, and once with the guy who comes in to ask if anyone wants their cars washed."

I couldn't help but laugh. The woman certainly liked variety!

Red cheeks blazing, she hit Rocco upside the head then turned to leave. "Idiot!"

Shaking his head, Rocco added, "I might be an idiot, but I ain't lying."

We laughed even harder. I wasn't usually a jackass, but that woman had been coming on to me forever. But then again, she came on to every man within a 10-foot radius. Either way, I was getting sick of her not being able to accept my disinterest.

"So, this place with the gorgeous women. Tell me about it," I conceded. I wasn't saying I would go, but I did want to know what the hell it was.

With a flourish of his massive arm, he told me, "Mynt is one badass nightclub. The beauties are endless, the drinks keep on flowing, and the chances of not getting any leg are slim to none."

My friend often used slang from the age of the dinosaurs, though I had a pretty good idea of what he meant. "Leg, Rocco?"

One hand came up to cover the left side of his mouth, hiding it from his mother, who sat only two chairs away from him on that side. "Sex, moron."

"Ah!" I didn't need or want any of that. "Nah. I'll pass."

"Pass?" His brows raised, his expression changing to one of absolute confusion. "Who says no to that?"

"A tired doctor," I let him know. "I told you about my week, Rocco. Don't look so stunned."

"Well, here's how my week went." He banged his fist on the table, making the wineglasses shake, "Grandmama's arthritis flared up, so I had to make meatballs every day this week. On top of that, it was my week to clean the damn fryer. That is one bitch to clean, mind you. I've worked three double-shifts this week and closed one night, then opened the next day. Now that is one hellacious week, and one that I need to end on a positive note." His hand came up to cover the left side of his mouth once again. "And that positive note is sex, my friend. As much and as nasty as I can get. And I need a wingman, if nothing else."

"And you want me to be said wingman, I suppose." My drink sloshed as I picked it up. I was just about tipsy. Maybe the rest of the wine would make my decision for me—either take me home to bed or out to play wingman for the man I considered my very best friend. Downing the rest of it, I looked at Rocco. His eyes pleaded with me. "Can I go home and change first?"

"Hell, yes, you can!" With a snap of his fingers, his young cousin Giovanni came to Rocco's side. "Give Kane a ride to his place so he can change. Then come back here and get me. I'm gonna clean up a bit in the kitchen, then I'll be ready to go. You're gonna drive us to that nightclub you were telling me about earlier."

Minutes later I was sitting in the passenger side of an old Buick as the kid drove me home. He stopped abruptly in my driveway, making me grab the dashboard. "Okay, we're here." I got out of the car then looked back. "I'll be right back."

Going into the empty house, I immediately felt the absence of my son. I hated when he wasn't home. But he'd really been looking forward to the trip to Florida, so I had let him go.

Walking past his bedroom, I stopped and pushed open the door. I hadn't stopped by the house when I left work; I'd gone right over to Rocco's restaurant. I saw that Fox had left his drawers open in his haste to pack. The maid would have to clean up his mess on Monday.

Closing his door, I pulled out my cell to call him. He answered the phone with an excited, "Hi, Dad!"

"Hey there, son. How was the trip down to Miami?" I went to my bedroom and took a seat on the bed, pulling my shoes off.

"Pretty long and mostly boring. I slept most of the way. Uncle James kept teasing me that I was farting in my sleep." I heard him laughing.

Then the voice of my uncle came in the background. "He was farting up a storm."

I couldn't help rolling my eyes. "Well, doesn't that sound like a fun trip." More like a nightmare that I was damn glad I hadn't been a part of.

"Nana and Pawpaw are coming up tomorrow, Dad," Fox said. "They wanted to surprise us. But now they're only going to be surprising Aunt Nancy, Uncle James, and me."

I'd had no idea they would be going too. And now I felt bad for not being there. "Well, dang. I wish they would've told us something. I definitely would've come with you guys if I'd known. Do me a favor and give them some kisses and hugs from me, buddy."

"Sure, Dad." He laughed. "Nana will smother me with her kisses anyway. She always does."

Mom and Dad had moved to Napa Valley, California, a couple of years back. We only got to see them once, maybe twice a year. As the newest doctor at the clinic I usually got the worst shifts, and my busy schedule made it hard for us to get out there to see them much. And they didn't like to travel, so seeing them was difficult. The fact they'd gone to Florida was odd.

"Tell them I'll call tomorrow," I said as I got up to take my pants off to put on a nice suit.

"Whatcha doin' tonight, Dad?" Fox asked.

I didn't want to tell him too much about the little outing Rocco had planned. "Not much. Just going out with Uncle Rocco for a while."

"Oh, man!" Fox laughed and shared my news with whoever else was around him, "Dad's goin' to hang out with Uncle Rocco tonight."

"Don't do anything I wouldn't do, lover boy!" Uncle James called out.

I wasn't some horny teen anymore who needed a scolding. Having a son before you turned twenty could be a real wake-up call. "I shouldn't have mentioned anything about my night. I can see that now."

"Nope, you shouldn't have," Fox told me. "Be good, Dad. And please, don't do what you did when you were in high school. I'm not ready for a little sister or brother yet."

"Gee whiz," I whined, not used to getting sex and relationship advice from a ten-year-old. "Love you, son. Be good. Mind your aunt and uncle and be careful, please."

"You too, Dad. Love ya." He ended the call as I sat back down on the bed.

Being so open and honest with my son didn't come without a bit of a backlash sometimes. It had been Rocco's party where I'd finally gotten to know young Zandra Larkin better, making my little boy in the process. And no one ever seemed to forget it.

Sitting on my bed, I found myself thinking about that night. I'd had no idea she was a virgin until she told me so. I'd been hot for her, but when I'd heard that softly-spoken confession, my cock had taken over completely.

I'd never had a virgin before. Not that I'd even had that many girls at seventeen—I'd had three, to be exact.

If I'd been more mature, I wouldn't have taken her virginity that night. I would've done things differently. Maybe spent that night talking more and kissing less. Maybe I would've taken her on a few dates before even going past first base.

If I could go back in time, I often wondered if I would do it all over again. After all, if things had gone differently, I wouldn't have

Fox, and he was my entire world. Would I have ruined that young girl's life to have my son?

Would I have taken that sweet cherry away from her if I'd known that she would get pregnant and that her parents would react as they had?

Shaking my head, I knew I wouldn't do that to her again if I could go back. If I'd only known how much that two hours of passion would take away from her, I wouldn't have done it.

My heart began to ache a bit. With no idea how Zandra had fared after all of that, I wondered from time to time what she was doing with her life.

Being a doctor, I knew what the loss of a child could do to a person. Even if she'd wanted to give our son up, that decision could've had some serious repercussions on her mental state. Every woman reacted to that decision differently.

Is she okay?

Had she moved on with her life? Had she gotten married? Had more children?

With no idea what Zandra Larkin, or whatever her name was now, was doing, I had no way of knowing how having our son had affected her. All I knew was that if I hadn't ended up with our son, then I wouldn't have been okay.

I'd gotten lucky. I had family who believed that blood ran thick. We would never give one of our own away. Come hell or high water we'd do everything we could to keep our family together and safe.

Our families were clearly very different. Hers had made her give up the baby. Mine had searched relentlessly until they found him and made him ours.

What would it do to a person to have their own blood turn on them like that—to not only not support them through a difficult time, but to actively make them give the baby they'd carried inside of them away to strangers?

I knew that some babies were better off with adoptive parents. Some people just didn't have the capacity to care for a child. And there were others who were more than capable of caring for that baby. But in those cases, the biological mother and father came to that decision.

I'd been left out of the decision. And for all I knew, Zandra had been left out of it too.

Before we knew whether we'd be able to get my son, I'd felt empty and lost. Afterward, the relief of knowing he'd be with me forever—that he'd have a loving family for the rest of his life—had been the best feeling ever. Sure, there was the underlying fear that I wouldn't be such a great father, but I knew I had great role models and that my family would help me learn along the way.

Poor Zandra clearly didn't have that same support system. How would that have made her feel? And how would she feel about that, so many years later?

And most of all: is she okay?

CHAPTER 5

Zandra

THE DOORS HADN'T EVEN OPENED YET, and Mynt already felt electric.

"Damn, did you see that line? It goes all the way around the block!" Taylor asked me as we hurried to help the bartenders get ready for the onslaught of patrons who would soon be inside the club.

Out of the corner of my eye, I could see the manager, Rob, staring at me. I wasn't sure if that was because he wanted to see how I handled my first big crowd, or if he just liked watching me. Either way, it made me feel more than a little bit uncomfortable.

Taking a deep breath, I settled into my waitress attitude and turned to look at Rob. With a wave of my hand, I broke his silent stare. "Hey, boss. Don't worry about me. I'm used to busy Saturday nights."

Jerking his head toward the entrance, he shouted, "Let them in!" His eyes still on me, he added, "Let's see if you're up to a Charleston Saturday night, Chicago."

He'd nicknamed me that from the first night. I'd only worked three shifts so far, and they'd been easy enough. Rob got a kick out of trying to intimidate me with what he called "the largest crowds in history" that graced his club on Saturday nights.

From the line I'd seen outside when we came in, I was sure that the place would be packed, and we would have a hard night coming our way. But it wasn't anything I couldn't handle. "I've got this, boss."

With the doors finally open, the place filled up in record time. I helped people find tables and got their drinks to them before helping more patrons. It was a fast pace, but I liked to be busy rather than bored.

On the other side of the packed room, I caught sight of a couple waitresses up on the bar, dancing. People cheered as they watched the two shaking their asses.

Taylor came up behind me as I took a moment to watch. "We should show those girls a thing or two, Zandy."

Being no stranger to ass shaking, I nodded. "Okay. As soon as I get these three tables set up, I'll meet you at the bar on this side."

"It's a date," she said with a smile as she went to serve her customers.

The club had barely opened, and already I was forced to head back to my locker to put away the cash that filled my pockets. In this business, Saturdays were always the most profitable nights, but I was already on track to have one of my best nights ever.

When I left the locker room, I found Rob standing in the doorway of his office. He seemed to have been waiting for me. "How's it going so far, Chicago?"

"Not bad at all, boss." I made sure to keep calling him that, as the way he kept looking me up and down made it clear that he wouldn't mind taking our relationship into something more personal than employer and employee. And I was not interested in that at all.

Taking a step back inside his office, he offered, "You want something to help make the night go better? A little boost?"

"The night's already been pretty good so far. As a matter of fact, the tips I've already gotten tonight are enough to cover my car payment this month. I'm hoping the rest of the night will pay the rest of my bills." I laughed as I kept walking. Going into his office alone didn't seem like a great idea to me.

"Come on," he said as he reached out, taking me by the arm.

I didn't want to overreact, but the way he tugged at me had my alarms going off. Taylor's appearance did much to ease my anxiety. "Hey. They're playing our song, Zandy. Come on."

Rob's hand left my forearm. "You two going to dance on the bar?"

With a nod, I took off. 'Yep."

To my disappointment, he followed right behind me. "This, I've got to see."

Normally, tension didn't mess with me too much, and with Rob eager to watch me dance, tension had definitely settled in. By the time I got to Taylor, she had noticed my body language. "Maybe a shot first, then we dance."

Nodding, I couldn't think of a better way to help me chill out. Except if Rob would stop watching me, of course. "Yeah, how about a tequila shot?"

Rob's warm breath moved past my ear as he shuffled in close behind me. "I'll get you the good stuff," he whispered.

Slipping behind the bar, Rob poured two shots that Taylor and I downed.

My heart was pounding in my chest as Rob offered me his hand to help me up on the bar. People were already crowding around the bar, watching me and shouting words of encouragement as Taylor was helped up by one of the bartenders. She made some sign to the DJ and the music changed to something sexy and slow.

Ignoring Rob and his gray eyes that bored into me, I looked at Taylor as I moved my body in slow, sexy waves, undulating toward her then toward the crowd, who was cheering us on.

The drinks were flying as men took advantage of grabbing the alcohol-filled glasses from between our legs. The female waitresses all had to wear short black shorts with hot pink shirts that were tied up between our tits, which overflowed from the low-cut tops. Our bellybuttons were to be exposed at all times, and any customer who ordered a body-shot got one.

As the song and our dance came to an end, the men in the crowd started calling out the different shots they wanted to drink from our navels. Rob once again took my hand, this time to help me to lie on top of the bar. He filled my bellybutton himself, watching closely as men took turns slurping the liquid off my body.

Body-shots were just part of the territory of serving in these kinds of clubs, and never once had I felt an ounce of the shyness that had plagued me as a teen. But tonight, that shyness seemed to be coming back, and at lightning speed, too.

My cheeks heated as one hot guy after another took their turn. Turning my head, I looked at Rob. "I think that's enough. My tables are waiting, and I bet they're thirsty."

"You're right." Rob announced the end to body-shots, much to the dismay of the men who were waiting for their turn. Groans of disappointment filled my ears as I got off the bar, once again assisted by Rob. "If you need a boost, just come to my office, and I'll make sure you get one."

Following Taylor back out to the floor, I asked her, "What's this boost that Rob keeps going on about?"

She winked at me. "Blow."

"Cocaine?" I shook my head. "I'm not doing any of that. You know I'll drink just about anything, but drugs? No way."

"I know." She bumped her shoulder against mine. "I'll tell him to leave you alone. He's just totally crushing on you, that's all."

"I can tell. And I don't like it." I looked over my shoulder to see him leaning over the bar, talking to some young girl who was making sexy eyes at him. "He's got plenty of tail available to him. He can do without mine."

"He can," Taylor agreed. "But will he? That's the real question now, isn't it?"

Squaring my jaw, I wanted to make sure Taylor knew I wasn't about to roll over for that guy. And if he even thought about pressing the issue, I'd hit him with a sexual harassment suit that would make his head spin. Since being on my own, I'd never been one to take much shit out of anyone. Not after everything I had taken from my very own parents.

"Over here, Zee," some woman called out to me. I'd made sure that only Zee appeared on my nametag. I didn't want anyone to use my real name. Zandra wasn't exactly a common name, and I didn't want anyone who knew me from before to realize who I was. I knew there would be loads of questions. And I didn't want to answer any of them.

For only a split second, that tiny baby's face filled my head again and it stopped me dead in my tracks. "Zee?" Taylor asked as she came up behind me. "You okay?"

Am I?

Shaking my head to clear it, I said, "Yeah. Just a little lightheaded is all. I guess that tequila shot finally kicked in."

"Be careful, girl." Taylor took off to deal with her own customers as I tried to focus on the task at hand, forcing the memories as far behind as I possibly could.

Reaching out to take the empty glasses off the table full of young women who'd called me over, I asked, "Do you girls want more of the same?"

"How about we go with something different this time, ladies?" the girl who'd called me over, the apparent leader of the pack, asked her friends.

The group agreed and then they all looked at me for some suggestions. "You were drinking mojitos, so how about trying cable cars? They're both rum-based. The key to avoiding a killer hangover is to drink same-base liquor all night, but you can mix up what you drink it with."

The leader gave me a huge smile. "Aren't we lucky to have you as our guide for the night? Cable cars it is, then. Thanks, Zee. With age comes wisdom, right?"

A curt nod answered her question. As I left their table to get their drinks, it occurred to me that my twenty-six years seemed to be years apart from the early twenties of seemingly everyone else at the club.

Not even the blue streaks in my hair are making me look younger!

But did I really want to be a young twenty-one or two-year-old? I'd learned and grown a lot in the last few years, and I wouldn't go back for anything.

My expression must've given my inner thoughts away. "Feeling a little overwhelmed, Zee?" the bartender asked.

"No." I wasn't about to tell him that I was feeling old. "Five cable cars, please."

I put the dirty glasses in the washer while I waited for him to make the drinks. He eyed me while he made them up. "You're doing well tonight. I've got to admit that I thought this might be harder for you than it is."

"And why is that, exactly?" I had to ask him, thinking I already had a few ideas of what he might say. My age. A lack of experience with large crowds. The shyness I'd overcome in Chicago, but that seemed to be creeping back in now that I was back in Charleston. Any one of those things could be the reason behind his words.

Pouring some Captain Morgan into the shaker, his lips pulled up into a cocky smile. "You're new here. It takes most people about a month to get to where you are now. Impressive."

"So, it was my lack of experience that made you underestimate me," I said wryly, though truthfully I was happy to know it wasn't my age.

And when the hell did I get so caught up with my age?

It wasn't as if I was some dinosaur, after all.

"Yeah," he admitted. "I mean, I knew you'd been a waitress in Chicago, but I had no idea that you'd been such a good one." He jerked his head at the big glass jar under the bar, which was filled with cash. "Those body-shots earned us a heap of tips. We'll be split-ting them at the end of the night too, like always."

Dollar signs flashed in my head, and I couldn't help but smile. "Hell, Saturday nights alone seem to be helping me meet my bills. The rest of the week will be gravy for me."

Finishing the drinks, he placed them on a tray. "And you'll get Sunday and Monday to recoup for next week's fun. Have you made any plans for your days off yet?"

"Nah. I'm gonna just play it by ear." I picked up the tray and headed off to make the girls happy.

The night just kept getting wilder and wilder with the tips coming at me left and right. Taylor came over to me as I walked up to the bar with a bunch of empties in my arms. "Hell, this is one hot night, don't you think?"

"I've made enough money to do more than pay my bills, Taylor," I said, leaning in so no one else would hear. "Thanks for calling me and asking me to come work here. This is a godsend."

"I know, right?" she asked with a huge smile. "I knew you would clean up here."

Laughing, I felt like I was on some kind of a high, knowing that the change I had made was definitely worth it. "I see a brand-new car in my future."

With an exchange of high-fives, Taylor and I parted ways to tend to the club's guests and see how much more cash we could attain.

On my third trip to the locker room to put away more cash, I passed Rob's office again. His door wasn't all the way open, just a bit ajar, but I tiptoed across anyway, hoping he wouldn't hear the sound of my heels clicking against the tile floor. Unfortunately, my attempt to go unnoticed was in vain.

"Hey, Chicago, come here, will ya?" he called out to me.

A loud sigh escaped me. As I pushed the door open, I made sure I didn't go fully into the room. Leaning on the door frame, I asked, "Yeah, boss?"

"Making bank, I see." His feet were propped up on his messy desk, his hands linked behind his head as he rested it on them. He seemed to be relaxing after doing very little at all.

Back in Chicago, when the club was busy, everyone was busy, including the managers. But Rob didn't work that way. It seemed he liked to sit back and watch other people work.

"I'm doing well." Looking over my shoulder, I went on, "And I should get back to it. It's busy as hell out there."

"Yes, it is." He sat up, taking a more managerial position. "You can take a half-hour break now. There's a little café around the corner if you're hungry."

"I never eat when I'm working. It slows me down too much. I always eat after work." Turning to leave, I added, "Thanks, but I don't need a break, boss."

"Take one anyway. I don't want people thinking I overwork my staff. Catch some fresh air for a little while." He chuckled. "That's an order, Chicago. Take thirty and take it now. It's eleven-thirty, and we always get another surge of people at midnight."

"'K, boss." I wasn't about to argue with him.

After putting my money away and making sure it was locked up tight in my locker, I walked to the front to go outside and take in some cold night air.

Rounding a corner to go through the entrance hall, I stopped short when my eyes caught sight of a man I hadn't seen in years.

Dark blond hair, longer on top than on the sides, caught my eye. Green eyes sparkled as the large chandelier's light danced in his eyes. His tall, muscular frame moved with cat-like grace.

I faded into the wall, hiding behind several of the bouncers as I watched him walk through the hallway and into the interior of the club.

My breath caught in my throat as I whispered to myself, "Kane Price ..."

CHAPTER 6

Kane

THE POUNDING bass of the music matched my heartbeat as we walked into the packed nightclub. "This is insane," I had to shout for Rocco to hear me.

"Off the chain," he shouted back at me. "Right?"

"I guess so." I wasn't in the right frame of mind to enjoy the place. To be more precise, I had full use of my mind. That made it impossible for me to just go with the flow the way everyone else seemed to be doing.

Scanning the room, which was filled with undulating bodies, I couldn't help but notice that half the girls here were hardly wearing enough to cover those moving bodies. One girl raised her arms in the air as she swayed her ass, the little bit of black material covering her nether regions flashing out, and she looked like she just didn't give a damn.

Rocco noticed it too, jabbing me in the ribs with his elbow. "Whoa, check out the barely-there underwear on the chick at two o'clock, will ya?"

"Rocco, you know that's somebody's daughter, don't you?" I asked him as he openly gawked at the girl.

"She ain't yours, so why are you even thinkin' about it, Kane? You need alcohol, and you need it stat." He led the way to the nearest bar. "Give me a couple of Godfathers, please."

So, whiskey it is, then.

It seemed my friend was going to try to dull my senses with a stout mixture of bourbon and amaretto. Unfortunately, I'd have to disappoint him. My mind wasn't into it, and my drinking would be limited.

Everywhere I looked, I imagined I saw things in a much different light than most of the other patrons. To my left, a group of four men was laughing and drinking. One of them had droopy eyes, his glass hung loosely in his hand, and he had to lean on the bar to stay upright. He'd had too much to drink, and his companions took no notice of that fact at all.

To my right, a girl who was most likely barely twenty-one danced with a man who looked like a serial killer. His hands were all over her, and he was looking down at the top of her head with a menacing stare that told me he'd like to take her outside, push her up against the side of the building, and bone her until she couldn't see straight. Then tie her up and throw her in the trunk of his car, taking her away forever.

"Drink this," came Rocco's demanding voice.

Taking the glass from his extended hand, I took a small sip. "Thanks."

With a nod, Rocco took a sip as he looked around the room. "Over there, see those two chicks dancing with each other?"

"I do." I had no idea why he would point them out. Tons of girls were dancing with each other, some in large groups even.

"Let's cut in," he continued. "I get the blonde. I know you prefer brunettes."

I wasn't up for that at all. "You go ahead. Take them both. I'll be right here when you're done."

One heavy sigh let me know he wasn't happy with my attitude. "Come on, Kane. Loosen up, man."

"I am loose. Go on. Go dance, Rocco. I'll be fine." My attention was taken by the mass of drunken people anyway. I would be thoroughly entertained just watching them.

Finally, he seemed to accept that I wasn't going to get out on that dancefloor and we parted ways. Now I could focus my attention on people-watching.

When I saw a girl stumbling off the dancefloor, heading to the bar, I couldn't hold the doctor inside of me back any longer. I reached out, taking her by the arm. "Hey, where you headed?"

Her blue eyes were glazed over, and she had trouble focusing on me as she wobbled in her high heels. "The bar. I need a drink. Care to buy me one?" she slurred.

"How about I pay for your cab ride home, instead?" I offered as I put my drink down on the bar.

"What?" She shook her head then stopped. "Whoa. I'm kinda dizzy."

"So, how about that cab?" I slipped my arm around her narrow shoulders, moving her toward the exit instead of the bar.

"Are you trying to take me home?" she slurred, then her head bobbed. "'Cause that's okay if you are. I'm up for it."

"Good to know." She wasn't up for shit. "But I'm not taking you home. I'm sending you to your home. You do know your address, right?"

"Fifteen fifteen, um ..." she hummed as she tried to recall where she lived. "Blue Ridge Trail. Yeah, that's it." Pride filled her eyes as she looked up at me. "See, I knew it."

"Great job. Do you know how many drinks you've had?" I pushed the door open and we stepped outside, the cool air hitting us in the face. It didn't seem to affect her much at all.

"I didn't count them," she said, and then hiccupped. Looking over her shoulder, she looked lost for a second. "Um, I should go back and tell my friends I'm leaving."

Her cell phone was in her hand, and I took her by the wrist, raising her hand so she could see it. "Why don't you send them texts while you're riding in the cab?"

"You're smart," she said with a giggle before another hiccup popped out of her mouth. "Has anyone ever told you that?"

"Yep." Snapping my fingers, a cab pulled to the curb, and I helped her get inside. "Fifteen fifteen, Blue Ridge Trail please." Handing the driver two twenty-dollar bills, I added, "Please see this young lady gets there safe and sound, will you?" The fact that the driver was a woman in her fifties gave me confidence that the drunk girl would meet no harm in her vulnerable condition.

"Will do," the driver said with a smile.

The girl reached out, trailing her hand over my cheek. "You're, like, my hero. I should get your number."

"Nah. But do yourself a favor and drink some water when you get home. And watch your intake of alcohol next time—it's time to stop when your head gets light. And if your words start to slur, you're already drunk. Got it?" I knew she probably wouldn't retain a word I said, but I had to say them anyway.

"'K." She kissed the palm of her hand and then blew it my way. She had no idea how terrible her breath smelled. "Thanks, hero."

Closing the door, I waved goodbye before heading back inside. One of the bouncers nodded at me as I went back in. "That was nice. Don't see a lot of good deeds like that going on in my line of work."

"Yeah, well, I'm a doctor, and I couldn't just watch that poor girl get another drink." With a shrug, I went back inside. I didn't feel like a hero at all. I just felt like that had been the right thing to do.

Maybe it was the fact that I had a ten-year-old at home, but suddenly all the people around me just seemed like kids to me. At twenty-seven, I wasn't much older than the majority of them, but I felt eons older—and wiser as well.

Some rambunctious shouting drew my attention to another bar. A waitress lay on the bar, a line of men waiting to take shots out of her navel. Not one of them cared about the fact that their lips were touching the same place another man's had been just seconds earlier. On top of being disgusting, it wasn't sanitary either. "Yuck."

Rocco came up behind me, clapping me on the shoulder. Jerking his head toward the men I watched, he asked, "Thinkin' about getting in that line, lover-boy?"

"There's not a chance in hell that that's what I was thinking, Rocco. And as your physician and best friend, I can't allow you to even think about doing that either. Do you have any idea how many germs are now on that poor woman's body?"

Shaking his head, he said, "The alcohol kills all the germs, Doctor Price. It's perfectly safe, and it's sexy too."

"You're as crazy as the rest of them." I shoved my hands into my pockets before looking elsewhere, as that scene made my stomach uneasy. "I could use a drink. And not the kind you gave me. I wonder what kinds of wine they serve here."

"You've got to be kidding me." Rocco huffed. "At least have a beer, Kane. Shit, you can act like such an old geezer sometimes."

He was probably right, and I knew it. But it wasn't something I particularly wanted to change about myself. I was a father first and foremost, and prided myself on acting like one. But he was right about ordering wine in such an establishment. "I'll get a beer then. I don't want to spoil your bad boy rep by acting like a geezer." Spotting a waitress not too far ahead of me, I called out, "Can I get a beer over here, please?"

She paused for only a moment before hurrying through the crowd. I knew she had to have heard me—she had stopped, after all. Following after her to get her attention, I noticed the swell of her hips, the dip of her waist, and the way her long dark hair was twisted into one braid that hung down her back. Dark blue streaks ran through it. Normally, I didn't particularly care for unnatural colors in a woman's hair. For some reason, I liked it on her.

Just as I was about to catch up to her, she placed the tray of empty glasses she carried on the edge of the bar and then disappeared behind it, going straight through a door into the back.

Disappointment welled within me. I just wanted to see her face.

"What can I get ya?" the bartender asked me.

"A beer," I said, my eyes still glued to the door she'd gone through.

I crossed my fingers, hoping she'd pop back out of it before I walked away.

"What kind?" he asked me, taking my attention away from the door.

I looked at the names on tap. "Michelob Ultra."

Another waitress came up next to me, putting empties on the bar as she rattled off, "Two gin and tonics, a blue spruce, and three bloody Marys."

The waiter placed the beer on the bar in front of me. "That'll be seven fifty." He looked at the blonde waitress with a frown. "What the fuck is a blue spruce, Taylor?"

"Fuck if I know." She shrugged. "This guy said he wanted one. I figured you knew what it was."

"I'll have to look that one up, I guess." The bartender got to work making the drinks, and the waitress looked at me.

Raising my glass to her, I said, "Here's to you, and every other hard-working woman in this bar."

"Thanks." Her smile was sexy as she asked, "You having yourself a good time tonight?"

"Would it offend you if I said I wasn't?" I took a sip of the cold beer as I looked the little thing over. With pale blue eyes that sparkled with good humor and pixie-cut blonde hair that was pulled into spikes that were each dyed a different color at the tips, she reminded me of a fairy—small, with a fiery look in her eyes.

"Not me personally." She put her hand on her hip. "But can I ask you what might make your night more enjoyable?"

With a chuckle, I answered, "Being at home with my son, watching cartoons or playing video games with him."

She cocked her head to one side. "Then why aren't you doing that?"

"He's out of town this weekend." I found Rocco and nodded in his direction. "My friend made me come out with him tonight. I'm not very good company though."

She looked over at Rocco just as a girl approached him. "Looks like he'd be fine on his own." Her eyes came back to mine. "I've got a break coming up. Maybe I could make your night more pleasurable. Say, in the back room, where no one would see us."

Now ain't this some shit!

Nearly choking on the beer I'd taken a drink of, I shook my head. "No, thank you."

"You married?" she asked with one dark brow cocked.

"No." I couldn't believe she'd think the only reason I'd turned down her generous offer was because of a prior commitment. "I just don't make a habit of screwing women I don't know, is all."

"Shame." She picked up the tray of drinks and gave me a wink.

"There's no drink called a blue spruce, so I made up something blue for the idiot." The bartended watched her go. "Good call not picking up what she put down."

"You think so?" I asked as I took another drink, watching her as she swayed her ass on purpose, trying to entice me into changing my mind.

"Yeah. She's a sweet girl, but she gets around." He got back to work, and I nodded.

Yeah, I can tell!

Waiting at the bar until I finished my beer, I was disappointed that the woman I'd been after hadn't come back out. Placing the empty mug on the bar, the bartender came back. "Want another one?"

"No. What I'd really like is to know when that waitress who went through that door a few minutes ago is coming back." I couldn't believe I'd said that. It wasn't like me to stalk women. But there I was, stalking away.

He looked back at the door then shook his head. "I've got no idea who went back there. I can tell you this, though. If she's been back there since you came up to this bar, then she's with the boss. If you know what I mean."

"Oh." Now I really felt disappointed. "I'll be heading out now, then. She's the only one her who's snagged my interest, and if she's not available, then I think I'm just wasting my time here."

With a nod, he said, "Yeah, if she's been back there that long, chances are she isn't available."

Hands back in my pockets, I had to fight myself from letting my head hang as I went to tell Rocco that I was leaving.

I must've had an even worse week than I'd realized if I was getting down in the dumps over not getting to, at the very least, see that waitress's face.

What the hell is wrong with me, anyway?

CHPATER 7

Zandra

WATCHING Kane through the two-way mirror behind the bar, I couldn't understand why he was waiting there instead of going back to the guy he'd come in with. I recognized that man as his friend from high school, Rocco. The way he kept looking at the door I'd gone through gave me chills.

Does he know it's me?

After Kane left the bar, with what I thought looked like a dejected expression, I came out. "Did that guy say anything to you?" I asked Patrick, the bartender.

With a smartass tone, he answered, "Which one, Zee? There're tons of guys here tonight."

"The guy with the dark blond hair. Black suit, green eyes." I sighed quietly, thinking that he looked even better than he had the last time I'd seen him.

"Ah, the beer drinker who asked about the waitress that went to the back. That guy. I see it much more clearly now. Were you the one who went back there, Zee?" He handed change back to some woman, who stuffed it in her bra.

"Yeah, that was me. Did he ask about me or what?" My heart began to pound with the idea that after all this time, he'd recognized me.

It hadn't crossed my mind at all that Kane and I might meet up. I didn't know why that was. He and I had both lived in Charleston growing up. I guess I just assumed he'd be on to bigger and better things than our small hometown.

Boy, was that a mistake.

And now he's found me.

"He did ask about you, as a matter of fact."

My heart stopped. "Did he know me by name?"

A slight laugh left his mouth. "No."

"Good," I sighed with relief. "So, what did he ask?"

"He wanted to know when you were coming back out." He went to help a customer. "What'll you have, partner?"

"Jack and Coke."

I went with Patrick as he started making the drink, so I could hear more. "Did he say why?"

"He said you were the only one who'd made his juices run or some shit like that. He told me he was leaving." He smiled at me with a wicked grin. "I told him that if you were back there that long, then you were with the boss. Like—with the boss. You know what I'm saying, Zee?"

"He thinks I was back there with Rob?" I was horrified. "God, no!"

He looked confused by my exclamation. "So, you weren't back there with the boss then?"

"Hell, no!" With long strides, I left Patrick behind and went to see to my customers. With the news that Kane had left, I could finally get back to work. Hiding from him had set me back, and I was sure the tips wouldn't be nearly what they had been.

Not only had I hidden from him, but I'd also spent a good chunk of time before that watching him from afar. When he put his arm around that drunk girl, my insides had gone hot with jealousy. I hadn't experienced anything like that before.

Sneaking along through the crowd, I followed them all the way to the exit. I couldn't believe he would just randomly grab a girl out of the crowd and so easily take her home. She looked like she was all for it, too.

I couldn't hear what they said because the music was too loud. But I could see that he was taking her outside. Then he snapped his fingers and a cab pulled up.

I couldn't even breathe as he opened that cab door. When the cab pulled away without him, I understood that he'd simply made sure that the drunk girl would get home safely.

Hell, maybe she was the sister of a friend of his. There had to be some rational explanation. I mean, no one was that damn nice, to make sure a drunken stranger got out of a club and back home safely for no reason at all.

Unless he's some kind of a saint.

Taylor saw me then and came up to me. "And where the hell have you been?"

"Hiding." I kept walking to get to my customers. "There was a guy here. You talked to him at the bar. I know him from the past."

"I've talked to a lot of guys here." She grinned at me. "You'll have to be more specific."

"Dark blond, green eyes, rocking body." I picked up the empties from the table full of girls. "More of the same, ladies?"

"Yes," came their enthusiastic answers. "More!"

"Oh, that guy." The way her eyes twinkled gave me a sinking feeling in my chest. "You know him?"

"Yes." Making my way back to the bar, I found a few more people holding up empty drinks and grabbed them as I went. "I'll be right back with refills, guys."

"I'm on break right now," Taylor told me. "I'll help you play catchup."

"Thank you." I needed the help at that moment. My head wasn't in the game after my unexpected reminder of my past.

She picked up more empties as she walked around with me. "He wasn't in his element here. He wanted to be back home with his son, who he said is out of town right now. I didn't spot a ring on his finger, and he even said he wasn't married, but my bets are that he is. Maybe he just didn't want it getting back to the old ball and chain that he was out, I bet."

"He's got a son?" I felt that stab of jealousy again.

"That's what he said. And when I offered to liven up his night while on break, he didn't take me up on it." She placed the empties on the bar as I got behind it to load them in the washer while spouting out what I needed to Patrick.

"Liven up his night, huh?" I mumbled. I knew what that meant. Taylor was still as forward as she'd always been. I should've expected as much. "It would please me very much, if you ever see him again, if you don't offer him any of your favors, Taylor. He's special to me in a way."

"Wait a minute." She stared a hole in me. "Is he?"

I didn't want a soul to know that Kane was the father of the boy I'd given up. "No. That's not him. He was just this guy who I messed around with once, that's all. And if you and he did anything, it would upset me." The lie came out so easily that it scared me.

"I see." She didn't seem completely sure of what I'd said. "He wasn't into me anyway. And I doubt he'll ever come in here again."

I prayed he wouldn't. "That would be nice. If he is married with kids, then I don't really want to know that anyway."

"I don't see why not." Taylor took one of the trays full of drinks while I took the other.

Going to serve the drinks, I said, "It's just better to leave him the way he's been in my memories all these years. Single, young, and still hot as hell."

Placing the girls' drinks on the table, I felt the tray slipping on the palm of my hand. "Oh, shit!" one of them shouted as she shot up to get out of the way.

Three of the glasses hit the table, splashing liquid and shards of glass everywhere. It all happened so fast that it stunned me. Taylor pointed at me. "Your hand!"

Looking down, I found a few small cuts and one big one on my palm. Blood poured from it. My head went light, and then all I saw was black.

"Hey, wake up, Zandy," Taylor's voice came to me. There wasn't any noise in the background, so I had no idea where I was.

Opening my eyes, I saw Taylor and Rob looking down at me. "What happened?"

"You fainted when you saw the blood," Taylor told me.

"You should go get stitches," Rob added. "That's a pretty deep cut. The club will pay the bill. Don't worry about that."

Picking up my left hand, I saw a white bar towel had been wrapped around it. There was only a little bit of pink color to it. "I'll be okay."

With a sigh, Rob walked away. "Well, I can't make you go to the ER, but I can make you go home. See you on Monday. Hopefully with stitches on that hand."

"You're making me leave?" I sat up, then felt woozy, so I laid my head on the back of the sofa they'd put me on.

"Yes," he said with a nod. "Go home. Come back on Monday."

Taylor looked a little concerned. "Do you need me to drive you?"

"Nah. I can make it." I got up. It was easy to do when I thought about what kind of crap might be on Rob's sofa. "I'll see you at home later, Taylor. See you on Monday, boss."

The ride home passed in a blur as all my thoughts were focused on one man.

Kane Price.

He was there. In Charleston. And he was most likely married. He also had a son—that much I knew for sure.

A son.

What would he do if I told him that he had more than one son? He had a son that I had had to give away. He had a son, and I had no idea where that son might be. He had a son, but I couldn't tell him if that son was okay—because I didn't know the answer to that myself.

No. If I ever did run into Kane, I would never tell him about the other son he had.

The apartment was dark as I walked in. I left it that way as I walked past the light switch, heading straight to my bedroom then to the attached bath. A nice bath would help soothe my sore hand and jagged nerves.

After putting a bandage on my hand, I soaked in the tub. And as I soaked, the memory of that night so long ago filled my mind ...

"HEY, aren't you in my chemistry class?" Kane asked me with a sexy grin on his gorgeous face. His dark blond hair hung in waves to his broad shoulders. His green eyes danced, making me weak in the knees.

"I am." I looked away to find the girl I'd come to the party with. "Have you seen Ann around?"

"Nope." His index finger trailed along my bare arm, leaving the oddest sensation behind. Heat mixed with cold—it was outstanding. And the way it made my bottom half pulse excited me.

"I should go look for her." Slowly, I looked up at him, and his index finger moved up to trace a line along my jaw.

"Why?" he asked as he looked into my eyes. "What's wrong with talking to me for a while?"

Everything.

"Nothing, I guess." Shyly, I looked off to one side.

With just that one finger, he drew my head back to look at him. "I've always thought you were pretty, Zandra. Did you know that?"

I tried to speak past the shock clogging my throat. "How could I?" He'd never said more than a couple of words to me the whole time we'd been in high school together.

The smile he wore faded. "Yeah, how could you have known I thought that?" He brushed my hair back, away from my face. "I haven't exactly been upfront with you, now have I?"

I shook my head. "No, you've never been upfront with me." I had never been upfront with him, either. I'd had a crush on the guy since I was in seventh grade and he was in eighth.

"So now I'm being upfront." His hand moved down to rest on my shoulder. "I like you."

"You don't know me, Kane." I looked down at my feet, biting my lip. I wasn't sure why that had come out of my mouth, but it had.

"Not well." He nodded then leaned in close to whisper the rest. "But I'd like to."

"I'd like that too." I thought in that moment that I'd never like anything more than that.

When his lips touched mine, I felt my whole world change. No more shyness. No more inhibitions. Nothing.

When he ended the kiss, which had taken me away to a place I hadn't known existed, he took me by the hand and led me up the stairs to a bedroom. I didn't ask any questions; I just let him touch me, kiss me, make me crave him.

My clothes came off without me realizing it. Then his did too. Naked, we lay on the bed, facing each other. When he ran one hand between my breasts, over my stomach, down to my pulsing sex, my body became tense. "It's okay, Zandra." His lips pressed against mine again, our tongues tangled, and I let him explore me more intimately.

One finger slid into me, and I gasped at the odd feeling. It didn't hurt at all, but it felt good—very good. I didn't know anything could feel as good as his finger pumped into me over and over again. His thumb rolled in circles over my clit, which I could feel swelling with arousal.

My body heated as he played with it. Moans came out of my mouth involuntarily as he moved his finger inside of me. His lips left mine and he smiled at me. "Can I kiss you down there?" he whispered.

My body got even hotter, and I couldn't believe what came out of my mouth. "Yes." It was too late to take the word back, not that I wanted to, deep down.

Our eyes locked then a smile curved his lips. "You won't be sorry,

Zandra." His eyes stayed on mine as he kissed one nipple then bit it playfully.

"Kane?" I bit my lower lip as I thought about what I was going to say.

"Yeah?" He went back to nibbling my tit.

"I'm a virgin. I just wanted you to know that about me." For some reason, shame filled me. I felt my cheeks go red with embarrassment.

Moving back up my body, his lips met mine again. "Thank you for telling me that." He kissed the side of my neck as he played with one tit, guiding my body so I lay underneath him. "Do you want to give your virginity to me, Zandra?"

"I do." I couldn't believe what I'd said. But I meant it.

He made a sexy groan then bit my neck. "Good."

Gripping his biceps, I arched up to him, feeling his hard dick press against my sex. I just wanted to feel it inside of me—feel him inside me. I couldn't think of anything else.

"Easy, baby. I want to make sure this is something you'll always remember with fondness." He pulled his head up to look me in the eyes. "You just relax and let me do all the work, 'k?"

I nodded. "'K."

His green eyes grew serious for a moment. "Should I use a condom?"

I shook my head. "No."

One word was all it took to change my life. One damn word that would change me forever. What a goddamned fool I was.

CHAPTER 8

Kane

"HELLO?" I sat up when I heard my cell go off. "Shit." It was five in the morning, the Sunday after my night out, and even though I'd gone home relatively early, I was a bit out of it. Picking up the phone, I saw that it was another doctor from the hospital I worked at. "Hey, Jack. What's up?"

"Me. With my sick daughter. She's puking everywhere, and her mother's out of town. I've got the day shift at the ER today, but I'm going to need to stay here to take care of her. Do you think you can go in for me today?"

"Yeah." I was always one to help out others. "I'll do it. You just take care of your little girl, Jack."

"Thanks. You're the best." He hung up, and I rolled out of bed.

One hot shower, a cold blueberry muffin, and a hot cup of coffee later and I was on my way to the hospital. There weren't any cars in the ER parking lot. Most Sundays were easy. I wasn't worried about being swamped.

Heading in through the sliding glass door, I walked past the nurse's station, calling out to the blonde who sat at the desk. "Buzz me in, please."

"Good morning, Dr. Price. I thought Dr. Friday was scheduled for today," she said just before I got to the door.

Grabbing the handle and pulling it open, I nodded. "Yeah, he was. His kid got sick, and he asked me to take this shift. How's it been so far?"

"Quiet. A typical Sunday." She went back to reading a book, and I went into the back.

An office had been set up for the doctors on duty. I went to it, using my key to open it. The smell of cleaning products stung my nose. I should've been used to it by now, but I didn't think it'd ever be easier to smell. The scents were just so pungent.

Going straight to the coffee machine, I started up a pot before opening the computer to see what had happened the night before. "Gunshot. Stab wound. Rabies?" I had to look at that entry again. "You've got to be shitting me."

Pulling up the results, I found that a man had come in with a bite from his pet bat.

Who the hell owns a pet bat?

I found there were a few patients who'd been admitted to the hospital for their conditions, and the man with possible rabies was one of them. I had to go meet this guy.

Heading out of the ER to go up to the rooms, I crossed paths with one of the men who worked in laundry as he was pushing his heavy cart along the hallway. "Hey, Gerald. How's it going today?"

"It's going, doc. How're things with you?" He stopped as he got to the staff elevator. I decided to ride up with him.

"Well, I'm on my way up to see a man who was bitten by his own pet bat," I answered after stepping on the elevator with him. "He's worried about rabies."

"No shit?" he laughed as he shook his head. "The things people do, huh?"

"Yep." The patient was set up on the third floor. "Here's my stop."

"I think I'll get off here too and go on ahead and pick up the dirty linen on this floor," Gerald said with a grin. "I've got to take a gander at this gentleman."

Heading to room 352, I tried to gain control over my expression. I didn't want to bust out laughing or anything like that. A light tap on his door and Mr. Jim Jones croaked, "I'm up. Come in."

Pushing the door open all the way, I was ready to see some kind of character. Imagine my surprise when a normal-looking older man sat up in the bed to welcome me in. Gerald was right behind me with his laundry cart. "Well, I'll be. You ain't what I was expecting."

The old guy laughed. "Yeah, I know. Who owns a bat as a pet? And a vampire bat, at that."

"A vampire bat?" I asked as I wondered how one even acquired such a thing. "Is that even legal?"

The old guy shrugged. "Not sure about that. You don't suppose your hospital will tell on me, do ya?"

I truly had no idea. "Let's hope not. Imagine the fine for owning a vampire bat. Well, let's move past that. Was the bat—um." I had no idea how to put it. The thing was the man's pet, after all.

"Murdered?" he asked me with a straight face.

"For lack of a better word, yes," I said.

"Yes. I had to kill Herman." He raised his hand up high, then it came down swiftly. "I took my shoe and WAP! Right on the head. It was quick."

I didn't see a bandage anywhere that was visible. "And the bite is where?"

When his cheeks went red, I began to wonder. When he threw back the blanket, I really had to wonder. When I saw the lump underneath his hospital gown, I knew this wasn't going to be easy to take. "On my junk, doc." He pulled up the gown and there he was, stark naked except for the bandage wrapped around the end of his penis. "I know how this looks."

"Yep," Gerald said. "You were letting that bat lick your cock, weren't ya? And he bit it, didn't he?"

The old man shook his head. "It ain't like that. And it wasn't a he-bat. It was a she-bat. But it's not what you're thinking. You see, I'd fallen asleep in my lounger." He might've look like an unassuming old guy, but it turned out he was a bit of a character after all. Seemed he wasn't shy about sharing all this with a stranger—I could understand him telling me, a doctor, all this, but he seemed more than happy to tell Gerald all about it too.

"And what's a lounger?" Gerald asked. "Is that some kind of a bat/man sex chair or something like that?"

A laugh came right out of my mouth before I could stop it. "Gerald! Please refrain from asking my patient any more questions." I clapped him on the back. "Let me do that, 'k?"

With a nod, he said, "Sure, doc. Go on. Ask him about the lounger and what it's for."

Mr. Jones ran his old wrinkled hand over his face. "A lounger is what I call my old recliner rocking chair that I sit in when I watch television in the living room. You see, I was doing laundry. Now, when I do laundry, I like to do it all of it at one time. That means I strip down to nothing while it washes."

"I get it now," Gerald said. "So, there you was, just sittin' there mindin' your own business when this lady bat came at ya and started biting your junk. So you're not some kind of freak after all!" He looked at me. "Thank goodness. I was startin' to get real worried there for a minute or two."

Mr. Jones looked right at me. "I feel asleep in the chair, and the door on Herman's cage must not have been shut right. She got out and bit the tip of my junk for some reason. I woke up, found her there, licking up the blood, and jumped up, grabbed my shoe and murdered her right then and there." He pulled his gown down and the blanket back up to cover himself. "It wasn't easy taking old Herman's life. But she'd never done anything like bite me before, so I thought she might've gotten rabies or something."

Nodding in agreement, I had no idea what to say. But Gerald did. "If she was a girl, why'd you name her Herman?" He put his hands on his hips, still looking a bit skeptical about the whole story. Despite what he'd said, it was becoming clear to me that Gerald still thought the old guy was some kind of a weirdo.

Mr. Jones clarified things for the laundry man. "When I first found the bat, I thought it was a male. I named it Herman after that guy on that old television show, *The Munsters*. You know, the vampire?"

"Ah hah!" came Gerald's quick reply as his finger shot up into the air. "Herman Munster was no vampire. He was a Frankenstein. It was Grandpa who was the vampire, and so was Herman's lovely wife, Lily. Their son, Eddie was a werewolf, and their niece Marilyn was the only one who was left out of the monstrous pack."

Things were getting out of hand. "Okay, Gerald. Get the dirty laundry and get going while I check Mr. Jones' bandages and his wound."

I'd been curious about the story but had had no idea just how crazy this rabies case would be.

The wound was small and clean, without a hint of infection. "So you've received the vaccine and now we're waiting on the results of the test. The vaccine should do its job, and you should be able to go home once we get them, Mr. Jones. It's a good thing you came in right away. Tell me, do you have any more bats at home?"

"Nope," he said with a toothy grin. "But I did find myself a little snake out back. I call it Thelma and keep her in the house too. She stays in the bathtub. I don't ever use it. I shower outside, the way God intended."

"A word of advice, sir," I offered, "maybe don't take anymore wild animals into your home. And that snake isn't going to stay put in that tub either, I bet."

"Shit!" he sat up and shouted.

"What?" I asked, not having any clue what he was going to say next.

"You're right, doc!" He wore a worried expression. "I bet it was Thelma who let Herman out of her cage."

And with that, I started making my way out of his room. "Yeah, probably. See ya, Mr. Jones."

As I walked down the hallway, back to the ER, my cell rang. I saw that it was Aunt Nancy and answered it. "Hello."

"Hi, Kane. We're almost there. Just wanted to let you know," she told me.

"Ah. I took the dayshift at the ER. I forgot to text you guys." I felt bad about forgetting that Fox would be coming home.

"Dad, can I come up there and hang out with you today?" I heard him ask in the background.

"Seems he heard me." I loved when he came to work with me. "Sure can, buddy. Can you drop him off here, Aunt Nancy?"

"Yeah," she said. "We're a few minutes away. I'll call you when we send him in, so you can meet him in the lobby."

"'K." I heard my name called over the speaker system and ended the call.

Hurrying to the ER, I found a nurse waiting in my office. "Hey, Dr. Price. We've got a twenty-six-year-old female in room one. She's got a laceration on her left palm. It's approximately one inch in length and fairly deep. She said she got it at work last night."

"Last night?" I asked.

"Yes, sir," she replied with a nod. "She wants stitches, but I told her that we probably couldn't do them now. It's just too late."

"So, what's the problem?" I took a seat in my chair, thinking there wasn't any reason for me to see this patient at all.

Her hands went to her hips, clearly annoyed. "The problem is that she wanted me to ask a real doctor."

"And you looked at the laceration, right? If you think it's too late, then go back there and tell her that a real doctor has told you that stitches can only be done within a few hours. After that, all we can do is use butterfly bandages on the wound." I opened the computer to get back to seeing what had happened the night before.

"Will do, Dr. Price." She left the office, and I went back to checking things out.

Not five minutes had passed when my aunt called me back, telling me to go to the lobby to meet Fox. Hopping up, I went to get my son, happy that he was back and would be spending the day with me.

When he spotted me, he ran my way. "Dad!"

"Hey, you!" I went to him, grabbing him up and hugging him before putting him back on the ground. "Boy, you got some sun." More small freckles peppered the top of his nose, and there were some on his cheeks now too.

"Yeah, I did. We played at the beach all day yesterday. It was fun." He followed me as we headed to the office. "And I saw a shark too."

"You did?" I asked with enthusiasm. "Up close?"

"Nah," he said as he waved his hand in the air. "It was really far away. And it was just the fin. Uncle James said it was probably a dolphin, but I was pretty sure it was a shark. I got out of the water to be on the safe side."

"Good thinking. Better safe than sorry, I always say." We turned the corner to the ER wing, and I pushed the double doors open.

"I know that." He laughed. "That's what I told everyone when they laughed at me. I said, better safe than sorry. What if it had been a shark? Bet no one would've been laughing then!"

"Smart thinking." I noticed a young woman up ahead at the nurses' desk. Bent over, she looked like she was signing papers. "So, what else happened in Florida, Fox?" I couldn't seem to take my eyes off the woman.

"Well, I walked on the beach and found lots of seashells." He tugged at my white jacket to make me look at him. "Don't worry. I brought them all home to put in our shell collection outside."

"Great." I looked away from him to look at the woman again. "We can add them to the garden outside when we get back home this evening. Doesn't that sound like fun?"

"Yeah, it does." He tugged my jacket again, and I looked down at him. "Can we maybe cook some hotdogs outside too? I really wanted a hotdog this whole weekend, and Aunt Nancy wouldn't let me. She says they're nasty and she won't feed me nasty food."

"Well, some of them are. But the ones I buy aren't. We can make some hotdogs on the outdoor grill." I looked back at the woman, who had by now straightened up and shook out her hair.

Long dark hair cascaded down her back. Dark blue streaks ran through it.

It's her.

It had to be the waitress from the bar.

She was talking to the nurse and raised her hands as she said something. There was a bandage wrapped around her left one.

The patient with the cut. The hand she'd cut at work the night before.

It has to be her.

"Dad, the door's right here!" Fox shouted, as I walked right past it in my distracted state.

The woman turned around at the sound of Fox's shouting. The world around me seemed to stop as our eyes met.

Zandra Larkin!

CHAPTER 9

Zandra

LIKE A DEER IN THE HEADLIGHTS, I stared at Kane Price.

This cannot be happening!

It had to be a dream. Or more precisely, a nightmare.

I had never, ever wanted to see this man again. Not after what I'd gone through because of him.

Not that it was his fault, really. I'd been the one who'd told him there wasn't any need for him to use a condom, even though I hadn't been on any type of birth control. I'd never faulted Kane, or myself, for that matter, for what had happened to that baby boy we'd made.

Seeing him again, with his muscular body that showed just how much he'd grown up, sent chills through my veins. I knew that body rippled with every little movement he made.

Kane Price is standing perfectly still, staring into my eyes, and I can't move or even blink.

My mind went back to the night he'd changed my life.

∿

HIS EYES HAD BEEN GLUED to mine as he pushed his hard cock into my virgin pussy. Gasping with the intrusion, pain ripped through me. And that pain would stay with me—not in my pulsing body, but in my heart—forever.

A few small tears fell down my cheeks. He kissed them away, soothing me with his body and his whispered word. "Hush now, Zandra. The hard part will be over soon. It'll feel good in a minute, you'll see. You can trust me, baby."

No one had ever called me baby before. The way he said it stirred something inside of me. "I trust you, Kane."

"Good girl." He moved slowly, pulling his cock almost all the way out before pushing it back in with one smooth stroke.

Biting my lip as I tried not to think about the white-hot fire that blazed in my most sensitive parts, I got lost in the green depths of his gorgeous eyes. "Kane, has anyone ever told you that you're really beautiful?"

The way his lips curved into a sexy smile made my heart pound. "No. No one has ever used that word to describe me. How about you? Has anyone ever told you just how beautiful you are?"

"No." I ran one hand across his back, feeling the tight muscles there. "Are you telling me that you think I'm beautiful, Kane Price?"

His lips barely touched mine as he whispered, "You are more than beautiful. I'm finding it hard to find the right words to describe the way I think about you, baby."

I didn't want to think about Kane and how many girls he'd been with before, but the fact was, he was kind of known as a flirt. "I bet you say that to all the girls."

Pulling his head up, his lips pressed together, forming a straight line. He moved his cock with ease now, and I was feeling more pleasure than pain. "Zandra, I don't think about you the way I think about anyone else. You're different."

Feeling embarrassed, I closed my eyes. "I know I am."

Brushing his lips across my cheek, he said, "In a good way. A great way." He gave me one long kiss that sent electricity through me.

Somehow, my body heated up even more, and we moved together now, my body finally having adjusted to his size.

Although I had never been intimate with anyone before, I found myself moving in ways I didn't know I could. My body just knew what to do. My legs moved to wrap around him, holding him close to me. My hands wandered to every place I could touch.

Moving his mouth away from mine, he kissed a line straight up my neck before finding the spot just behind my ear. His teeth grazed my soft flesh before biting down, gently at first and then harder as he moved faster.

With no idea how just a little bite in that place could affect me so much, all I could do was moan with how wonderful it all felt as he moved his hard cock in and out of me.

"Kane!" I gasped as my body began to shudder. "I think I'm about to ..."

"Do it, baby," came his growled words. "I want to feel you come all over my cock. I'm aching to feel your tight pussy clenching all around my hard dick. Give it all to me, baby. Just like you did when I ate your sweet pussy. Give me all you've got, Zandra. I want it all. Every last drop. And then I'll give you mine."

Shrieking with the release—the second orgasm he'd given me that night—I let it all loose, just like he'd told me to. At that moment, I would have given him anything he wanted. I was his for the taking. As long as he wanted me, I would belong to him. He'd owned me then.

I had no idea just how much he actually would own me—or how much of my past would belong to him, at least. No idea of what was to come for me and the little boy we were in the middle of creating.

WITH THE THOUGHT of the baby I'd given away, my memory faded quickly.

On Kane's left stood a boy. Dark hair covered his head, and green eyes looked at me.

Kane's eyes.

I watched as the two came closer to me as I stood there frozen in place.

"Is that really you?" Kane asked me.

All I could do was nod. A lump had formed in my throat that made it impossible for me to say a single word. My eyes turned to the boy who walked next to him.

"Hi, I'm Fox." He waved at me as they came my way.

Light freckles spread across the bridge of his nose, much the same way mine had back before I started using sunscreen every day to keep my skin freckle-free and hopefully wrinkle-free. The boy reminded me of someone, but I couldn't quite place him.

Swallowing the lump down so I didn't seem like such a freaking idiot, I tried to smile at the boy, who looked to be about the same age as the one I'd had to give up.

"Hi there, Fox. That's a cool name." I looked at Kane. "And is he yours?"

He nodded. "He is."

Well, wasn't he just a procreation machine. He must've gotten another girl pregnant about the same time he'd knocked me up. And by the looks of Fox, the mother must've looked a bit like me too. Seemed I hadn't been as special as he'd said I was that night—clearly, he just had a type.

Before Kane had fallen asleep that night, he'd held me in his arms. He'd told me he wasn't about to let me get away from him. But when he'd fallen asleep, I'd gotten up, dressed, and left him there on the bed he'd told me was his best friend Rocco's. The bed we'd made our son on. The son he had no idea existed.

"Leave it to you to come up with such a cool name, Kane." I thought better about what I'd said. "Or perhaps it was your wife's creative thinking?"

"My dad's not married. He's never been married." Fox looked up at his father. "It's just him and me. That's the way it's been for a while now."

Kane put his hand on his little boy's shoulder. "Well, it's not exactly just you and me, Fox. We've got Aunt Nancy and Uncle James too, you know."

"But they don't live with us," Fox said as he shook his head.

Kane looked back at me. "I saw you at Mynt last night. The back of you, anyway. The blue streaks in your hair gave you away today."

"You did?" I asked, acting like I didn't know. "Why didn't you come say hello?" I felt a little guilty for lying, but I didn't know what else to do. I couldn't tell him that I'd seen him too and had hidden from him.

"First of all, I had no idea it was you." Kane shifted his weight then crossed his arms over his chest. I could see the outline of some pretty massive biceps and felt wet heat pooling in my nether regions.

"You didn't?" I asked, as if I hadn't known that already either. "Well, then no wonder you didn't say anything to me."

"But I wanted to." He smiled at me, and I nearly swooned with desire for him.

Oh, if I could only have one more night with this man!

"You did?" I asked as I clasped my hands in front of me to keep them from shaking. "And why is that?"

That smile turned from charming to sexy with one easy move that I was certain he could make millions off of if he knew how to teach it. "There was just something about you that piqued my interest. But you walked into the back, behind the bar, and never came out. I waited and waited, and then I finally asked the bartender where you'd gone. He told me if you were still back there, then you were with the manager. Like, *with* the manager." He paused for a second, looking me up and down, and I felt that look from the tips of my toes to the roots of my hair. "So, are you?"

"Am I what?" I'd gotten a little lost in his eyes while he talked.

That heartbreaking smile got wider. "With the manager?"

"Oh, God, no." I shook my head. "He's not my type."

You know my type, Kane. My type is you.

"No?" he asked, then nodded. "Good to know. So, what brought you back in Charleston? Better yet, where have you been all this time? And why did you leave in the first place?"

I knew he would ask the hard questions!

"Long story." My brain hurt as I tried to think of what to say. "Another time, maybe."

"Definitely," he said with a nod. "Come back to my office with us. I want to catch up. And you're not getting out of here without giving me your number, either."

He wants my number!

"I don't know." I looked at the clear glass sliding doors that would lead me outside.

I should really get away from him before I blurt out the secret I've kept from him and everyone else for nearly eleven years.

"I do." In typical Kane fashion, he reached out and took my hand, tugging me along with him. "You're not getting away from me as easily this time."

Fox trotted right along with us on the other side of his father. "So, how do you know my dad?"

With no idea how to answer that question, I looked at Kane, who helped me out. "School, Fox."

"Oh, I get it now. You went to school with Dad." Fox nodded, looking much older and wiser than his young years. "Did you know my mom?"

Kane patted his son on the back. "Let's not go there, Fox. Not right now."

Kane had to have gotten another girl pregnant right around the time he'd gotten me that way. I knew that now without a single doubt. And she'd gone to the same school as us too, apparently.

Now I really didn't want him to know about the son we'd made.

How humiliating!

"Is his mother still in the picture?" I whispered to Kane as we went through a door that took us to a long hallway.

Shaking his head, Kane said, "Nah."

I found his answer pretty vague. But how could I say anything about that when I was being so vague too? "Oh."

Fox opened one of the many doors that lined the hallway. "Here's the office the doctors use when they work here. Dad really works at the clinic next door."

"I can't believe you're a doctor, Kane. That's such an amazing accomplishment. And you're still so young, too." I was thoroughly impressed, and a bit envious, too.

What could I have become had I not been shamed by my own parents, called an evil sinner every day for two hellish years, and made to give up our son?

Kane gestured to a chair, and I took the seat he'd offered. "Well, I found motivation in my son here. He came into my life at a young age, and all I wanted to do was accomplish my career aspirations as fast as I could. That way I could take care of him the way I thought he deserved."

"I had no idea you were on becoming a doctor." I crossed my legs, bouncing my foot to help release some of the nervous tension that had built up with our meeting.

This was never supposed to happen. Yet there I was, sitting in his office, looking at the little boy he'd made with someone else—and had been able to keep and raise, too.

He could've been a father to our son. But my fucking parents had taken it all away from him and me both. He had been a standup guy. He had taken on the responsibility of having a baby. And he'd made something of himself too.

We had both been robbed, and so had our son. And all because my godforsaken parents thought what we'd done was evil, impure, and one of the biggest sins one could commit.

It only served to make me hate them even more than I already did.

"Do you have any kids?" his son asked me as he sat on a sofa, smiling away at me.

"No," came my quick reply.

Kane took over the questioning, "Married?"

"No." I shrugged. "No one has ever asked."

"So, never married." Kane nodded as he leaned back on the desk, not six inches away from me. My body craved his. Every last part of me wanted him.

"No. And have you ever gotten close to getting married?" I asked as I tried not to look him up and down, very aware that I shouldn't be looking at him with so much lust in front of his young son.

"Nope." His reply filled me with the hope that I might get to feel his body all over mine again. How would he feel against me now that he had the body of a man?

"Never?" I asked as I went ahead and let my eyes wander over him.

My God, I want him!

"Not ever." He reached out, taking my chin in his large hand. "Will you be staying in Charleston long?"

Now that I knew he still lived here, I had no idea if staying in Charleston was a smart thing to do. "I'm not sure. I'm kind of a drifter."

Furrowed brows only served to make him look even hotter. "And why's that?"

Because if I'm around you, I might spill the beans and you'll end up hating me, that's why not.

But there was no way in hell I'd say such a thing. "Can't say. I just like to see new places, I guess," I said instead.

The drifter thing wasn't true at all. I'd spent my adulthood in one place—Chicago. I'd worked in one club, Underground. I had no idea why I'd told him that lie.

But the truth sounded so pitiful; I couldn't bring myself to tell him about the sorry existence I'd lived for the last eight years. An existence that had been caused by that one fiery night when I'd given him my virginity, and he'd given me a baby that I'd never had a chance of getting to know.

I should've run away from my parents. Straight to Kane Price.

CHAPTER 10

Kane

ZANDRA LARKIN SAT HALF a foot in front of me, and I couldn't believe it.

Our son looked at us from his seat on the couch, completely unaware that the woman I had yet to call by name was his mother. Unsure of what to do if she told Fox her name, I decided to wait and see what happened.

Fox knew the name of his mother. But how would he react if he found out this woman was her?

With his wellbeing at the front of my mind, I asked, "As a drifter, where have you lived?" I wanted to know if Zandra Larkin had become a person that shouldn't be in Fox's life. I was praying that she hadn't changed too much, that she'd be exactly right for his life.

I knew the attraction that I'd felt for her all those years ago was still there. It was simmering under the surface, urging me to hurry up and grab her, to pull her into my arms and get her into my bed. The way she looked me over told me she felt pretty much the same way I did.

Her blue eyes darted back and forth, telling me she was having a hard time coming up with the answer to my question, which I found odd. Finally, she said, "I've only lived in Chicago. I don't know why I said I was a drifter. I'm not. I guess you make me nervous, Kane."

The answer reminded me so much of the Zandra from my memory that my mind went back to that night.

WATCHING her from across the room filled with wild teenagers, I liked the way Zandra sipped from the red Solo cup filled with beer. Her cute little nose wrinkled with each tiny drink she took. I knew she would never finish that cup of alcohol.

Two other girls stood with her, talking quietly as they looked around at the others now and then. One of them said something that made them all laugh. Zandra's laugh sounded melodic and magical. Her sweet smile made my pulse speed up.

I didn't know a lot about the girl, except that her parents were the strictest people on the planet, supposedly. But Zandra was out for the night. I'd overheard that she'd gotten to come to the party only because her friend had told her parents that they were going to some kind of a lock-in at her grandma's church in Beaufort, a town a couple of hours away from us.

Apparently Zandra wasn't opposed to telling a little lie so she could have some fun, and that told me she just might not be opposed to what I wanted either.

Taking notice that Bobby Franklin was coming up to the girl I'd already pegged as mine for the night, I was shocked by the spark of jealousy that shot through me.

"Hey, Zandy, how'd you escape?"

Her pretty blue eyes went straight to the floor, her shyness taking over again. "I'd rather not say, Bobby."

But her friend didn't mind letting him in on the secret. "She lied to her parents for the first time ever!"

Zandra's cheeks turned beet red. "Hush, Stacy." She pulled the cup to her lips and took another sip, wrinkling her nose again. "I don't want anyone thinking I'm a liar."

Bobby nudged her shoulder with his, and I saw red for a second or two.

My girl.

He whispered something in her ear, so I had no idea what he said. But the blush on her cheeks went a shade deeper, and the red haze of jealousy came back to cloud my vision.

Time to make your move, Kane.

A TUG on my white coat pulled me out of my reverie.

"Hey, Dad. Can I run down to the nurses' station to see if they've got anything good to eat? They always have cake or something down there."

"Yeah." I looked at Zandra. "You want him to bring you anything back? The cake is always good."

She shook her head. "No, thank you." Her eyes went to Fox and followed him as he walked out of the office, leaving us alone. She looked back at me after he closed the door behind him. "It's good to see you, Kane."

"You too." My hands itched to touch her. But I didn't dare, not here. "I would really like to take you out sometime."

"No." Her answer came way too quickly. Her hair flew around her shoulders as she shook her head, adamant. "I can't."

"Why is that?" Purposely, I reached out, taking her hands into mine. "You'll have to come up with something good, you know. You did take off on me that night. I think you owe me a date or two. Or I owe them to you, rather. I've never forgotten you—I want you to know that." It wasn't a lie. She came into my head pretty often.

"Kane, things are different now." She tried to pull her hands away, but I held onto them. "I'm different now." Her eyes bored into mine. "I'm not that same little shy girl you knew back then. I've grown up. I have all the baggage that comes along with being a grown woman now. You could say that I'm damaged goods."

With a chuckle, I pulled her up. Having her standing in front of me, facing me, our bodies only inches apart, had my dick getting hard.

"I'm a doctor. I fix damaged people for a living. If you've got problems, I'm the perfect guy to help you get rid of them." Pulling her right hand to my mouth, I watched her lips quiver as I kissed her palm. "Give me a chance, Zandra."

There had always been a part of me that was mad at her for running away, for never telling me she was pregnant with my baby, and for giving him away. But the biggest part of me simply wanted her. I would get to the whys of that later on.

For now, I only wanted her again. In my arms, in my bed, in my life. And that meant in Fox's life too.

I would have to say her name some time, after all. She didn't know who he was, but he would know who she was right away, and he would definitely say something.

For now, I wanted to keep the cat in the bag. I knew next to nothing about Zandra's life, or her state of mind. I had no idea how she would take the news that I had our son and had had him since he was born.

How will she take that?

As I looked into her eyes, I saw a lot more strength there than I had seen eleven years earlier. She wasn't a girl anymore; she was a woman. A mature woman who'd been through a lot and had come out the other side of it a stronger person.

"I do not want to be fixed, Kane. I'm not willing to become your patient."

The idea of playing doctor with her began to fill my head, and it made my dick grow harder. "Oh, but I could make that a lot of fun, Zandra." I pulled her into my arms, brushing the hair off her face as I stared deeply into her eyes. "Come on, give me what I want. Say yes. You know I can talk you into it. Don't make me beg, baby."

Her body shook as I held her. My cock pulsed against her cunt, making her cheeks flush. "Kane, please," she moaned.

Moving my mouth closer to hers, I gave her my demand. "Give me what I want, and I'll let you go."

"I can't," she muttered. "Please."

"No." My lips grazed hers, teasing. "I still want you."

"Oh, God," she whispered, and then leaned in to meet me halfway.

The kiss sent me back in time to that one magical night when I'd had her underneath me. To when I'd been panting with such intense passion that I thought I might pass out. The sex had been off the charts that night. We'd fucked like wild animals after our first soft session when I'd introduced her to making love for the first time.

If I hadn't been expecting Fox to come back to the office at any moment, I would've put her ass on that desk and taken her nine ways to Sunday. But he was going to be back, and most likely soon.

He couldn't catch us like that. Pulling my mouth away from hers, I had to smile when I saw the raw desire on her beautiful face. "So, that date I want. Can I get it now?"

Her chest rose and fell against mine. "I really can't."

"Wrong answer, Zandra." Grabbing the back of her head, I grabbed a fistful of her silky hair, pulling it back, then kissing her again. Harder, more demanding this time. I wanted her to give into me the way she had when we were young.

I could feel her heart pounding in her chest. Her tongue danced with mine. Her hands gripped my arms. When I took my mouth off hers, I was panting too. "Tell me what I want to hear."

"He'll be coming back soon, Kane. You don't want your little boy to see us like this." She searched my eyes as she went on. "I can't go out with you. I'm sorry."

"I'm not the kind of man who takes no for an answer when I know damn good and well that you want exactly what I want too." My blood boiled as it raced through my veins. "Tell me that you don't want me, and I'll leave you alone."

Staring into her eyes, I defied her to lie to me. "You know I do. But I just can't get involved with you."

Letting her go, I walked away from her in frustration. I could've just spit it all out—let her know that I knew her secret. Let her in on the secret I was keeping from her, too.

You're the mother of my son!

It would be out in the open, and we could see where things would take us. I could tell her that I forgave her for never telling me the truth. And she could tell me what the hell had happened back then.

Why had she let her parents force her to put our son up for adoption? Had she wanted that too? And why in the hell had none of them seen fit to let my family know a thing about the baby she carried?

Instead, I took a deep breath to control myself as Fox came back into the office, holding up a brownie. "See, they did have something!"

Zandra ran her hands over her shirt to make sure it was straight, looking down as she did so. "Well, I guess I should be going. You've got work to do, Kane. It was nice to see you again after all these years. Being that we're both living in Charleston, I'm sure we'll run into each other now and then. It was a pleasure to meet you, Fox." She rattled on as she made her way to the door.

Fox took a seat on the sofa again, munching on his sweet treat, basically giving it all of his attention as he virtually ignored us. While he was distracted, I headed to the door, placing myself between it and her. "I'm not busy at all. Please stay a bit longer. Let's catch up."

One brow cocked as she gave me a sly smile. "Haven't we already done that?"

"Verbally," I whispered. "I don't want you to go yet."

"I know what you want." She winked. "Sorry, Kane. I can't."

"You can." I leaned back on the door. "And you will."

It had been a very long time since I'd craved anyone like this. But now that I had her, I felt a hunger for her that rivaled anything I'd ever felt. I would have her obstinate ass under me again if it was the last thing I did.

Fox got up to toss the napkin, now empty of brownie, into the trashcan. "What are you guys doing anyway?" He walked up to my side, looking at me with a confused expression. "It sounds like you two are fighting about something."

"We're not fighting," Zandra said as she looked down at him, running her hand over his head. The maternal action made me catch my breath, and I wondered if she had any idea that this was the boy she'd grown in her belly for nine months. "Your dad's just being silly, is all."

Fox looked at me, his tone surprised, "You're being silly?"

It wasn't like me to be silly, and Fox knew it. "No, I'm not being silly. I've just asked her on a date."

Now his eyes grew big. "A date?" He looked at Zandra. "You should say yes, 'cause my dad never goes on dates." Then he looked back at me. "You must really love her, Dad." He tried to whisper that little bit, but I was sure people on the other side of the hospital could have heard him.

Zandra choked a little as she backed up, holding her throat as she looked down at the floor. "I just can't. I really can't."

Patting my son on the top of his head, I said, "Grownups don't talk about love so soon, son. But I would like to take this nice young woman out for dinner and maybe some drinks and dancing, if she's not opposed to it, of course. Gentlemen never force themselves on a lady. You remember that, Fox."

Zandra suddenly found herself with the upper hand as she saw that I wasn't about to teach my son to bend a female to his will the way I'd been trying with her earlier—and fully planned on doing again. "Glad to hear you think that way, Kane. So you do understand that I just can't go out with you on any kind of a date. Sorry about that."

"Aw, man, Dad. She don't love you back." Fox shook his head. "Sorry, Dad. That's gotta hurt."

"Oh, it does." I held my hand over my heart. "Just one little date is all I'm asking for."

Fox turned to look at her. "Please, lady. I've never seen my dad like this. He's so, so—um—acting so weird, is what he is. It's just dinner, drinks, and dancing. Come on. Please." Then my son put on his most pitiful pleading face as he tried one last time. "Please. Can you do it for me?"

The way Zandra looked at him made my heart stop. Her eyes shimmered a bit, and I could tell she was holding back tears. Maybe she was thinking about the boy she had given away.

She had no idea she was looking at that same child.

"You two are making this very hard." She looked up at me. "Kane, if I thought it would be a good idea, I would say yes. I'm sure nearly every woman in this city would love to go on a date with you. I know that's how it was back when we were in high school."

"But I'm not asking any of them out—I'm asking you out." I crossed my arms over my chest and looked at her with a sexy grin. "Come on, just say yes already."

Fox walked over and put his hand on her arm. "Come on, please? Just tell him you'll go on at least one date with him. I've never seen him this way."

Reaching out with her left hand, the one with the bandage wrapped around it, she said, "I just can't, Fox."

He caught her by the wrist, looking at something on the inside of it. "Hey, you've got my birthday tattooed on you."

Holy hell!

CHAPTER 11

Zandra

REALLY? He even has the same birthday?

I didn't think life could by any crueler to me than it already had been when it came to my son, but apparently I'd been wrong. I could feel a pain in my chest that I didn't think would ever go away at the idea that Kane had been raising a son so similar to our own, while the one we'd created was somewhere being raised by strangers.

Kane's little boy looked me right in my eyes. "What's your name?"

I cut my eyes to Kane, trying to hide the pain I was sure was obvious in my own, and found him holding his hand over his mouth as his eyes bored into the back of his son's head. Each slow step he took led him to us. But he didn't say one word.

Looking back at Fox, I said, "My name is Zandra Larkin."

He let my wrist go as he took a few steps backward. His father caught him from behind, hugging him. "This is your mother, Fox." He said the words so softly, I was sure I must have misheard.

"I know," came the boy's choked reply. "Mom, it's you. It's really you." Tears began to flow from his little eyes before he turned to his father, putting his arms around him, hugging him tightly as he sobbed. "We found her, Dad! We finally found her!"

With no idea what to do or say, I felt my head going light, my vision starting to tunnel. "What the hell's going on?" I asked breathlessly, feeling as though all the air had been sucked out of my lungs.

Kane moved quickly, still holding his son as he came to steady me before I fell down. "Let's all sit down over here on the couch."

He helped us both sit down, and I felt the heat of tears burning the backs of my eyes. "Kane, I don't understand what's happening here. Please help me understand," I said, hearing the desperation in my voice, but I was beyond caring.

I'd never imagined in a million years that he knew about the pregnancy. I'd had no clue that he knew we had a son. And not an inkling that he had actually had our son all these years. My mind was ablaze with questions, but my mouth didn't seem to be working as I sat there, slack-jawed.

Kane helped fill in the blanks, taking a deep breath before telling me everything. "Your neighbor overheard your parents yelling one night, and she found me and told me that she'd heard that you were pregnant. She'd been at that party and had seen us go off together. She had a strong idea that I was the father, so she told me about what had happened."

I looked at him as Fox cried, still hugging him, his face buried in his father's shoulder. The sight was too much for me to bear, so I focused on Kane's eyes. "How did you know he was yours?"

"Come on, Zandra," he said with a smile. "I knew. And after the baby was born, we had a DNA test done to prove it, so we wouldn't have any issues should something come up in future."

"How'd you adopt him?" I knew I was still missing a lot of pieces to this puzzle. "You weren't even eighteen yet when he was born, were you?"

"My aunt and uncle adopted him. They tracked your family down. They found the adoption agency you registered with, and they made sure they were chosen to adopt the baby." Kane ran his hand over Fox's head. "But I've been his dad since day one."

Fox pulled his head off his dad's shoulder, wiped his eyes with the back of his hand, then turned to look at me. "Can I ask you something?"

I looked into his eyes—into the eyes of my son. My heart felt like it was trying to leap out of my throat. Nodding, I said, "Sure."

"Did you want me?" He sniffled as he looked at me with glazed eyes.

I could feel my heart breaking all over again, just as it had that day that the nurses took him from my arms. I held myself back from reaching out for him. I wanted to hold him so badly, it was an ache.

"More than I've ever wanted anything, Fox." Then the floodgates opened, and I spilled it all out for them. "My parents made me do it all. They took me away, took me out of school. They kept me locked up and took away my phone, so I couldn't contact anyone. They even watched over me when I did my online schoolwork, so I couldn't get on any social media to contact anyone. And I never told them your name, Kane. Never. I never wanted you to know what was going on. I was ashamed. Embarrassed. And so, so guilt-ridden. I knew it was my fault. I didn't want you to pay for my lie."

Kane reached over, stroking my hair. "We can talk about all that later. All Fox and I ever really wanted to know was if you wanted him or not."

"I did. I wanted him so bad. You have no idea." I wrung my hands in my lap. "I didn't want to let him go after I had him. He was the most beautiful thing I'd ever seen."

"It was my aunt who took him from you," Kane said, making me sit up and drop my jaw.

"That was her? I thought she was a nurse."

Kane nodded. "It was Aunt Nancy. She was there in the delivery room with you the whole time. She took him to meet Uncle James, and they kept him in the hospital for a couple of days. Had the DNA test done. And when the results proved he was mine, they brought him back to Charleston where we all cared for him. My parents, my aunt and uncle, and me."

"He's been loved all this time." I began to cry again, feeling a huge amount of relief, like a huge weight had just lifted from my shoulders. "I've always worried about that. I've always wondered if he was okay. Wondered if he was loved. And now, to know that he's been with his own blood this whole time—well, it's like it's too good to be true." I reached out for Fox, and he came into my arms. Finally. Smelling his scent, I took my son into my lungs for the second time in my life. "I've loved you all along, Fox. Even though I didn't know you, I've always loved you."

"I knew you did." He pulled his head off my shoulder to look at me shyly. "Can I call you Mom?"

The swelling in my heart felt so odd, I swore I could feel the hole filling back up. After all this time, the hole was going to be filled. "You certainly can call me that. I would be so happy if you did."

Fox looked at his father, who also had tear-filled eyes. "I've got a mom now."

"You sure do." Kane reached over, taking my hand. "Your family is complete, kiddo."

"Kane, I don't know a thing about being a parent." I blurted it out before I could stop myself. That probably wasn't a great thing to say in front of your kid—admitting you had no idea what you were doing.

Fox laughed as he climbed off my lap and went to get a box of tissues out of the desk. "Don't worry. Dad can teach you. He's pretty good at it. Most of the time he is, anyway."

"Most of the time?" Kane asked with a smirk. "I think I'm pretty good at it more often than that. Like all of the time, is more like it."

"Well, he does make me eat spinach," Fox went on as he pulled out a tissue then handed the box to me. "Here ya go. And he does make me go to bed too early, too. That seems like what parents are supposed to do."

All I could do was smile at Kane. "Sounds like he's an awesome father." After wiping my tears away and blowing my nose, I got up to toss the tissue in the trash.

"I like to think so." Kane took a tissue to wipe his own tears away, though his were unshed, unlike Fox's and mine. He came up behind me to throw his tissue away. "Sounds like life just got a hell of a lot more interesting for the three of us, doesn't it?"

"It sure does," Fox said brightly, coming over to hug us both. "I've got all my parents now! Wow, wait till Pax and Jake hear about this. They're gonna freak!"

Kane took my hand as he looked into my eyes. "So, about that date. The reason you turned me down wouldn't happen to have something to do with this little secret between us?"

Nodding, I confessed, "Yeah. But now that the cat's out of the bag, I suppose I could take you up on that offer."

"Oh, you suppose, do you?" He smiled at me then took my other hand too. Leaning his forehead against mine, he said quietly, "I'm glad to have you back in my life, Zandra. You have no idea how much I've thought about this."

Fox came up behind me, hugging me again. "We're gonna be a happy family, aren't we, you guys?"

"I hope so." I had no idea what the future would hold for us. No idea what it held for me and Kane.

Kane seemed sure. "It will be a happy future." It was as if he'd been able to read my mind.

He and I didn't know each other at all. Sure, we had a kid together, but we'd never really known each other. And with eleven years of separation between us, I wasn't as certain as he was about our future. At least, not when it came to the two of us.

No matter what, I knew that I wouldn't let my long-lost son go now that I'd gotten this second chance at having him in my life. Knowing Fox was mine made my heart swell, but seeing Kane again hadn't done anything other than make my panties wet and my pulse race. But then again, that's how it had always been.

I was in a room with two virtual strangers who had just become my family in a matter of second. Or at least kind of a family. Kane and I shared a son, a son he'd taken care of for ten years. Ten years of being a parent had changed him too, it seemed. Here he was, a responsible doctor who took great care of his kid. And that thought made me realize something else I didn't know about him. "Is Fox your only child, Kane?"

Fox laughed. "I told you that Dad doesn't go out on dates. And I know you guys didn't date either, but he's just my dad now so far."

Somehow, I doubted that Kane Price had been celibate since our night together, but that would be a discussion between Kane and me for another time, and in private. Though Fox seemed to know a lot about the ways of reproduction for a ten-year-old, I didn't think he needed any more lessons right now. "I see. So, it's just us now, huh?"

"It's just us," Kane said with a wicked smile. "Momma."

Momma?

"Wow, that's going to take some getting used to." I had to go back to the couch and sit down. They both came to take seats too. One on my left side, one on the other. I picked up one of each of their hands, holding them to my heart. "But I think I can get used to this fairly quickly."

Fox grinned, making his nose squinch up. "I hope so. Dad, can she come up to my school and meet my teachers and stuff like that?"

Panic rushed through me. *Everyone is going to know about the pregnancy!*

Kane cocked his head. "When she's ready for that, we can talk about it." He brushed the back of his hand across my cheek. "She's been forced to keep this a secret for a long time, you know. Let's give her a chance to take this all in, okay, champ?"

Once again, the man seemed to be able to read my mind.

With a nod, Fox agreed. "Oh, yeah. I already forgot 'bout that." He pulled his hand out of mine to put his arm around me and lay his head on my shoulder. "You'll get used to this soon. I hope then you can be my mom in every way. You can come to my baseball games and cheer for me—then everyone will know that I'm your kid. Man, that's gonna rock!"

"You play baseball?" I asked as I ran my hand over his silky hair. "Just like your dad, huh? An athlete."

"Yeah, I'm like him." He pulled his head up to look at me. "And what were you good at? I wonder how I'm like you."

"Um—I made okay grades." I had no idea what I'd been good at back then. In my opinion, I had never been much of a success at anything.

But then Kane spoke up, "You remember me telling you that your mother was really good at writing stories, don't you, Fox?"

"Oh, yeah!" Fox patted me on the back. "Dad said that the English teacher read his class a story that you'd written. It was a short story about fairies and dragons, and it was really good, he said."

I looked at Kane in surprise. I recalled writing the story, but I didn't remember anything about it being read to a class by the English teacher. "When did this happen?"

Kane smiled. "After you left. Mrs. Stubbing, like the rest of the staff and students, might I add, felt out of sorts when you just didn't show up to school again. The teachers said you'd registered and were just as surprised as the rest of us when you never came back. No one knew where you went. No one but that neighbor, at least, and she only ever told me about what had happened. And I only told my family."

For a moment I was puzzled. "So, who knows that I'm Fox's mother now?"

Kane and Fox looked at each other, then at me before Fox said, "Everyone."

Blinking, feeling like I might be about to pass out, I leaned back on the sofa and fanned myself with my hand. "My secret has been out all these years, and I've been hiding out in Chicago for no reason at all? God, my life is completely different than I thought it was."

Fox laughed. "Yeah, it is. So, maybe coming to my school and meeting my teachers and friends ain't such a bad idea after all, Mom."

Mom.

Man, that felt weird. But a good weird. Tousling Fox's hair, all I could do was smile. "Yeah, it ain't such a bad idea after all. I may as well get over myself. It was my parents' idea to run away from it all, and to try to prevent anyone from ever knowing the trouble I got myself into. I never cared as much about that as they did."

Kane's expression turned serious. "About that. How's your relationship with them, Zandra?" he asked.

"Strained." I shrugged. "Nearly non-existent." I ran my hand over Fox's cheek. "I mostly hate them for what they made me do."

His lips pulled up to one side. "Dad says that it's not good to hate anyone."

"It's not," I agreed. "But I do hate them just the same. It hurt when I had to give you away, Fox. And it was their fault that I had to do it." I couldn't stop staring at him, wanting to know him—my flesh and blood. He was just as beautiful as I'd always imagined he'd be.

"Yeah," he said with a nod. "But I was given to my aunt and uncle and dad, so it all turned out okay."

He was right. But that had been some big crazy fluke. There's no way my parents had known that it had all worked out that way, and I didn't even know if they would've allowed Fox to go to Kane and his family, had they known. "I'll work on it. But only for you, Fox."

"Good." He rested his head on my shoulder again. "'Cause one day I'd like to meet them too, Mom."

"Oh, I don't know about that." I looked at Kane, trying to tell him with my eyes that that was a terrible idea.

He and I would have to have a conversation about my parents and their archaic beliefs. In their opinion, our child was an abomination in the eyes of God. He represented a horrible sin that never should've happened. They would never be the doting grandparents I was sure Fox was used to.

Kane's hand ran up and down my arm. "That's something to talk about another day. Today, you've got your mom, Fox. Let's take a while to let that all sink in and to let you get to know her. And she'll get to know us too. We're all kind of new to each other, you know. We need to take the time to settle into this new family."

I had no idea how much time it would take to get comfortable with this new situation. With my son in my life now, I worried about my chosen career as a waitress. It didn't seem to be the most motherly thing to be doing. I had to make a lot of changes if I wanted to be the mother that the boy deserved.

His father was a doctor. I didn't want him to have to say his mom was a waitress at a nightclub.

Change had been in the air, and now it was thick with it. So thick, it made it hard to breathe.

CHAPTER 12

Kane

THE OVERWHELMING EMOTION of Fox and Zandra's reunion had helped ease my hard-on situation. With all the crying and heartfelt words, keeping a hard-on proved to be impossible.

The day had finally come. Zandra and Fox were together again.

I had to admit that I never saw it coming. I had never really thought that we would see her again.

My emotions had been mixed on that subject before seeing her again. Now, I knew I wanted her to be a part of Fox's life, and mine. But I had to admit that I didn't know the woman who now sat next to me.

I had to take things slow. For my son, I had to watch what I did and how much I let Zandra in. That same old lust that I'd always felt was still there, burning a hole in my pants. But I had a kid now. And that kid had to be my number one priority.

She'd accepted the date I'd offered her, so we would finally be getting to know each other on a level we'd had the chance to explore before. It was a great start, and one I hoped would end up with us being close enough to raise our son together.

And screw around, too.

My dick was hard for her. I knew that particular organ would get what it wanted eventually. But I didn't know about my heart. About what it wanted, or what it would be getting.

For all I knew, Zandra could have some pretty nasty habits that I could never deal with. I already knew that I wasn't thrilled about what she did for work. With that kind of career, she most likely drank and stayed out late into the night more often than I did. She did work at a bar, after all.

Her lifestyle would prove to get in our way, I knew that already. Were there any other things about our lives that would make us incompatible?

"So, Zandra, are you working at the bar while you're going to college or in some kind of a program?"

Shaking her head, she ran her hand over Fox's head as he laid it on her shoulder, looking comfy with her already. "No. I should be honest with you, Kane. I've never looked past waitressing. My life has been kind of ... empty since I had this one here and had to give him up."

So she hadn't been in a good place since she'd had the baby. That also might've had something to do with how much of a negative spin her parents had put on the pregnancy, or how they'd taken her away from everyone she'd ever known, then made her give up the child who'd been a part of her for nine months.

Those circumstances could send anyone into a downward spiral. It was no surprise she'd felt a bit stunted after that.

"You should get therapy." Reaching out, I ran my hand over her other shoulder, the one where Fox wasn't leaning. "What you've gone through isn't easy. I'll make sure you get help."

She blinked at me a few times. "I think I can handle it. And now that I've got Fox in my life again, I think I'll be okay from here on out."

So she wasn't great at accepting help. That wouldn't be easy for me to deal with, stubborn man that I was. "Okay. Well, let's just take things nice and slow. And if you do feel like some therapy will help you, then don't hesitate to ask me. I know lots of great therapists, and I don't mind paying them to take care of you. As a matter of fact, Fox sees one once a month to talk about you."

Her eyes narrowed at me. "You make him go to therapy?"

"Yup," Fox answered for me, perking up again. "And I like Doc Parsons. He's nice, and he and I talk about all kinds of things. I've known him pretty much my whole life."

With Fox's words, her narrowed eyes had opened back up and she went back to stroking him, running her hand over his back. I noticed that she couldn't seem to stop touching him, and that made me so happy to see.

"Well, as long as you like doing it, then that's good." She looked at me. "As you can imagine, I don't like it when parents make their kids do things against their will."

Yes, I could already see that Zandra had been damaged by what her parents had done. Hearing more about how they'd handled the situation, I could only imagine that nothing about her childhood had been easy. Yet she wasn't willing to get help to begin to mend things within her.

This may not be easy.

Fox laughed as he looked up at her. "Dad makes me do lots of things I don't want to do. I've got to make my own bed even though we have a maid who comes in twice a week. I've got to take out the trash, too. And I've got to make good grades, or I have to go to after-school tutoring until I bring the grade up. I could go on and on about the things he makes me do."

Thankfully, she laughed, then tousled his hair. "Yeah, I bet you could. But those sound like good dad things that he should definitely be making you do. I would have to agree with him about those kinds of things." She looked at the floor. "But he's the one you should be listening to, Fox, not me. I don't know if I'm even considered your mother still, legally."

Though I was thrilled that Fox had his mother in his life, I wasn't sure if I wanted to change anything legally just yet. "We'll see how things go, Zandra. I don't want to rush into anything. At least this is just between you and me. My aunt and uncle no longer have any paperwork tying him to them. He's mine and mine alone. Well, you know what I mean. On paper he's mine. Only mine." I spoke quietly, trying to keep this just between Zandra and me. Unfortunately, Fox had great ears.

But he surprised me by standing up and looking at me with defiance in his eyes. "Dad! She's my mom. I don't want to see how things go. I want you to make her my mom for real!"

My kid didn't get away with throwing tantrums, even if they were about important and valid topics. I stood up and pointed at the chair. "Over there, now."

"Dad, I'm serious," he said in a much quieter voice.

"So am I. Now, son." I pointed at the chair and looked at it.

Reluctantly, he went to sit down, and I caught Zandra chewing on her lower lip. "Kane, please don't be mad at him."

"I'm not mad, Zandra." Turning my attention to my son, I said, "Fox Colton Price, are you allowed to ever raise your voice in an ugly way to anyone?"

His arms crossed over his chest as he looked at the floor. "No, sir."

"Eyes on me." I made him look at me. "I understand that this is very important to you, and that you're very excited about meeting your mother. That said, I am your father, and I decide what's right for you. Do you understand me?"

His eyes grew big as he shook his head. "Not about her, I don't. That's my mom. And nothing you or anyone else does can change that."

"Oh, Kane." Zandra came up behind Fox, putting her arms around him as he sat in the chair. "I'm sure he didn't mean to get so loud with you. Tell him you're sorry, Fox. Tell him you won't yell at him again."

"Sorry, Dad." He looked back at Zandra. "I'm sorry I yelled, but not sorry for what I said. No one can take you away from me. No one. Not even Dad."

His words chilled my soul. I had no plans on keeping him from his mother, but that boy had always been mine. Just mine. Sure, my parents and aunt and uncle had helped raise him, but it'd always just been me and him. In name, he'd been mine alone since my aunt and uncle had turned over custody to me.

This didn't feel good at all.

Fox had his mom now. A woman neither of us knew, really. And what I did know wasn't exactly great, so far.

But I could see now that I would have to watch what I said in front of my son. And I'd seen a side of him I'd never seen before—a side that must've come from his mother, because my side of the family didn't act that way.

Her parents had been real hard-asses after all. Could my son be capable of fighting just as hard as they had to keep him a secret?

The future had seemed so bright only minutes before, but now I was getting a glimpse of just how challenging it could be.

Zandra's eyes met mine. "Kane, we've got a lot to take in. Maybe we should part ways now to let things sink in. I could use a drink, anyway."

And there it was. She wanted to leave her son already to go have a drink. And it was only five in the evening, at that.

Well, I guessed five was about when most happy hours started, so I guessed the average person thought it was okay to partake in the cocktails at that time. But I couldn't help feeling a little judgmental— she wasn't just an average person; she was my son's mother, and I'd do anything to protect him.

"Yeah, I guess you probably do need one." I could concede that she'd had a harder day than normal, though.

"I bet you do too," she teased as she made her way to the door.

"Nah." I followed after her. "Hey, we need to exchange phone numbers. Give me your cell."

"Oh, yeah." She reached into her back pocket, taking it out then handing it to me.

Fox came up, wrapping himself around her again. "Don't go. Please. I just got you. Please."

She looked a little bewildered as she said, "Um, Fox, I can't sit here in this office all night. I've got to get home."

"How come?" he asked her, a pitiful look on his face.

Handing her phone back to her, I tried to make him understand things. "Because she probably has things at home that she needs to take care of." Then I thought about something else I might want to have. "How about you give me your address, Zandra?"

"Oh, sure." She went to the desk, found a blank piece of paper, and wrote it down. "Here you go." Patting Fox on the back, she said, "I'm off tomorrow. If it's okay with your dad, I can see you then."

"I've got to go to school," Fox said with a frown. He looked at me with a smile. "Can she take me to school, Dad?"

"Oh, I don't know." I looked at her. "Is that something you want to do, Zandra?"

"Um ... I ... don't—" She had that deer-in-the-headlights look about her again.

"I think we've caught her a little off guard." I chuckled and shook my head at my son. "I think we've got to give her time to get her bearings before something like that. Heck, we don't even know if she's got a car to take you to school in."

"Of course I have a car, Kane." She looked a little miffed. "I'm actually doing pretty well financially, now that I work at Mynt. I can take him. What time do I need to pick you up, Fox? And from what address?"

It occurred to me suddenly that the school had rules about who could pick up the kids and drop them off. "I forgot, Fox. She's not on the list. We'll have to get her on the list first."

"Can you do it tomorrow?" he asked as he looked at me with droopy eyes. "I really want her to take me sometimes, and even pick me up sometimes too."

How could I tell my kid that I had no idea if his mother was in any way capable of taking on such a big responsibility yet? How could I let him know that I had no idea about her moral character, or if she would even be fit to do things like pick him up or take him to school?

And how could I do it with her standing right there?

"Tell you what, Fox. Let me hammer out all these details with the school this evening, and I'll call your mom to work things out with her too."

That should work for now.

"Okay, thanks, Dad." He wiggled his finger at Zandra. "Can I have a kiss on the cheek before you go, Mom?"

She laughed then leaned down to kiss his cheek. "You'll make a mother out of me yet, won't you?"

"I will." He beamed at her, looking so proud of himself as he opened the door for her. "I'll walk with you out to your car. I don't want anything to happen to you, Mom."

"I'll join you two." I came up on the other side of her as Fox took her hand. "It seems he's taken a shine to you, Zandra," I whispered over his head.

I had to admit to myself that my son's behavior was a little bothersome to me. Could I really be feeling jealous that he'd taken so well to his mom?

I shook the feeling off. We would work out all the kinks in this new thing we'd all fallen into. I had to keep in mind that Zandra had been completely caught off guard, much more so than either Fox or me.

Hell, she'd had no clue that I had the boy or that I even knew he existed. This had to be knocking her out of the water. It would've done the same to me if the shoe were on the other foot.

As we went outside, she pointed at a shiny red Mustang. "That's me over there."

"The sports car?" Fox asked. When she nodded, he added, "So cool! My mom's gonna be one of those cool moms." He pumped his fist in the air. "Yes!"

As a doctor, that wasn't exactly the kind of mother I wanted for my son. I wanted her to be one of the respectable moms—one of the responsible ones. A cool mom wasn't something I had ever dreamt of for him.

Her long legs bent gracefully as she sat in the low-profile car.

"Thank you, boys, for walking me out." She put on a pair of Ray-Bans, making her look even more beautiful, and yes, I could admit, cooler too. "I look forward to hearing from you later on tonight, Kane."

"I'll call you when I've got my ducks in a row. It'll be after nine, after I've put Fox to bed." I closed the door for her, and she gave us a little wave.

Fox looked up at me as he knocked on her darkly tinted window. "Hey, wait."

"What are you doing now?" I asked him as I put my hand on his shoulder.

"You'll see." He looked at his mother as she rolled the window down.

"Yes?" she asked him.

"Why don't you just come over to our house and Dad can cook for us out on the grill?" He looked up at me. "She could stay the night, and we can all go to school together, and you can get her put on the list first thing in the morning. Please, Dad."

"Um ... I—" He'd put me in one hell of a hard place with that.

She looked at me too, but the dark sunglasses hid her expression from me. I had no idea where she stood on this.

But I knew, as a responsible father, that you didn't go bringing strangers into your home. And you didn't let them spend the night. And that was that.

"Dad, why are you taking so long to answer me?" Fox pushed further. "Just say yes already. Please."

"I've got to say no on this one, buddy. Zandra has a lot to take in, after all. Let's give her some space. Sorry." The way he looked at me crushed me. Well, almost crushed me. I was a dad, and dads didn't crush all that easily.

One day he would be a dad, and then he would understand. But until then he was just a little boy who'd finally gotten a mom, and he wasn't happy with my decision.

"Fine!" He stalked back into the hospital.

"Whoa," Zandra said. "Well. I'll talk to you later then."

She backed up at what I thought was too fast a speed. Her tires spun a bit as she left the parking lot, and I both adored her as a man and didn't much like her as a father.

What the hell have I gotten into here?

CHAPTER 13

Zandra

THE STEERING WHEEL felt odd in my hands as I pulled away from Kane after our son stalked off, angry at his father. My mind was numb from all the new information.

I've got my son back!

In a matter of a few minutes, I'd become a mother to a ten-year-old boy. It defied the imagination. And the odds, too.

The odds of Kane's aunt and uncle finding where my parents had relocated us hadn't been good. The odds of them finding the adoption agency my parents had signed me up with were just as slim. The odds of Kane turning out to be a good father weren't all that good either.

But even with all that going against this situation, somehow it all had worked out in our favor. It didn't make sense to me. Mostly because I wasn't used to good things happening to me, I guessed.

My life had shown me that, more often than not, bad things happened to me. Like being a virgin and getting pregnant after having sex one time—and at barely sixteen. Like being born to parents who'd made me give up the baby I had loved so much. While working as a waitress had helped me gain my freedom from my parent and make ends meet, it wasn't easy, and I'd had a lot of difficult nights and found myself in more than one shitty situation.

It definitely wasn't a job that a shy girl like I'd been would've ever thought of doing. Well, not until push came to shove and I'd had no other choice.

Pulling into the apartment complex, I spotted Taylor's BMW parked in front of our apartment. Glad to have someone to talk to, I hoped she was awake. With so much on my mind, I figured talking to her would help.

As I went into the apartment, I smelled burnt toast. "I'm home," I called out.

"Good." She rounded the corner from her bedroom to the living room. "I tried to make some toast in the oven then forgot about it. I wanted to go out to get something to eat, but I didn't want to go alone." She picked up her purse as she looked at my hand. "Did they give you stitches at the hospital?"

"No." I pulled the bandage off my left hand. "I got butterfly bandages. Well, that, and a son." I waited for her to catch on to what I'd said, watching her face for her reaction.

She stopped, put her hand on her hip, and looked me in the eyes. "Give me that last part again, will ya?"

"I found my son, Taylor. The one my parents made me give away. The baby I told you about. I found him." My heart pounded as I said it out loud for the first time. "I've got him back, Taylor." The dam burst, tears pouring down my cheeks and a few sobs slipping through.

Taylor had me in her arms in no time, hugging me as she cried too. "Oh, Zandy! This is amazing. You've got to sit down and tell me everything. I want to know all the details, girl."

"Wine. I need wine," I gasped.

After helping me take a seat on the sofa, she left me to go to the kitchen to get what I'd requested. "Screw wine. I'm making us some mimosas. This is champagne kind of news. And since I don't like it on its own, I'm mixing it with orange juice."

I tried to gather myself and stop the waterworks. "Thanks, Taylor. This is something to celebrate." Going to the half bath off the living room, I grabbed some toilet paper to blow my nose and some more to dry my tears.

Staring into the mirror, I looked at my red-rimmed eyes and saw something else there that hadn't been there before. I couldn't pinpoint it exactly, but I would say it had to be something akin to joy.

It was hard to tell. I hadn't ever experienced so much joy in my life. But something was definitely different with me.

"Come on, Zandy," Taylor called out. "I've got the drinks, and I'm dying to hear about your day."

Heading back out, I took the champagne glass she'd set on the coffee table and took one long drink, hoping to steady my nerves. "Okay, the guy who got me pregnant is now a doctor. Dr. Kane Price, to be exact. And you've met him."

"I knew it!" She pointed at me. "You lied to me. It was that guy from last night. You bitch!"

"I know." Another swallow of the drink helped me steady myself to go on. "I'm sorry. I have no idea why, but I didn't want you to know that he was the one. None of that matters anymore. The whole town knows that I had a baby. The whole town knows that Kane is the father."

Perplexed, she asked, "And how is that?"

"He told me that one of my neighbors overheard my family when that whole thing went down. My parents screamed at me a lot, so I can't say I'm surprised by that. She went to school when it started up again and told Kane about what had happened. She was pretty sure he was the guy, since she'd seen us together at that party." I took another drink, finding my glass empty. "Well, hell."

"I made a whole gallon of it." Taylor jerked her head toward the kitchen. "On the counter."

I got up to go refill my glass. "Great thinking. This news is a bit overwhelming."

"I bet it is." She put her glass down, watching me. "Okay, so somehow this guy was able to track you down, without you knowing, and he was able to get the baby you'd been forced to put up for adoption?"

"Well, technically he didn't do it—at least not alone. He said his aunt and uncle did the research and were the ones to officially adopt the baby. His aunt was even in the delivery room when Fox was born. She took him shortly after the delivery was over." I filled my glass up then looked at it. "I bet most moms don't drink as much as I do."

"Who knows," Taylor said, then laughed. "Maybe they drink even more than we do. I mean, dealing with kids doesn't seem like a picnic."

She was right. The exchanges between Kane and Fox didn't exactly look easy. "Yeah, I bet it's not a picnic at all."

"So, this kid's name is Fox?" She nodded, as if she approved of the name. "Pretty cool name."

"Fox Colton Price," I murmured. "My son's name is Fox Colton Price. I'm a mom." *Now that just feels weird.* "Am I ever going to get used to this, Taylor?"

"How the hell should I know?" She leaned forward as I passed by her, holding out her glass. I clanked mine against hers. "Congratulations, Zandra Larkin, on becoming a real mother today. So, what's the plan now?"

I took my seat again, pondering her question. "I'm not really sure. Kane wants me. I know that much. Fox wants me around—I know that too. What I don't know is if Kane actually wants me around all that much."

One of her brows arched in confusion. "Wait. Kane wants you. The kid wants you. But you didn't feel like Kane wanted you around? I don't get it."

"Me neither." It was true. I didn't understand everything yet. "Fox asked if I could take him to school in the morning. Kane shot that down."

"Be thankful." She nodded. "That school traffic is a nightmare. Not that I've ever been in it, but I've seen it."

"Yeah, I suppose so," I agreed. "But there was something about the way Kane looked when Fox asked that. Like he didn't think it was a good idea. And just before I left, Fox asked me to go over to their home for dinner and to stay the night. Kane shut that down too, and quickly. And I don't know why he did that."

"I thought you said he wanted you," Taylor said, taking another sip of her drink as she contemplated my words. "Did you mean sexually, he wanted you?"

"He did. Before he told me that Fox was my son, the two of us were alone in his office for a little while, and Kane was all over me. He asked me out on a date then, too." My body got warm as I recalled the way it felt to have that man's hands on me again. "At first I said no way. You know, because of the whole secret baby thingy. But once I found out everything and he asked me again, I said yes. So, we've got a date sometime."

Taylor seemed to be deep in thought. "So, he wants to see you. But he doesn't want you to be at his home with him and your kid. That's odd. Don't you think that's odd?"

"Kinda." I thought about it a bit. "But then again, it's not. You know?"

"No," she said, shaking her head. "No, I don't know what the hell you're talking about. He wants you, but he doesn't want to share you with your son?"

"I think he's just being cautious." I put the glass down then looked at the tattoo on my wrist. "He's always been out of my league, Taylor. He still is. He's a doctor, and I'm just a cocktail waitress with no aspirations. He asked me if I was waitressing while going to college. I had to tell him that I wasn't doing anything, and I saw the disappointment in his gorgeous green eyes."

"Those eyes are like emeralds," she mused, her lips curling into a dreamy smile.

"Hey!" I made her look at me. "I know he's not mine, technically. But he's mine. So no thinking about which gem his eyes most resemble. And by the way, our son has his eyes, too. He's such a handsome little guy."

"I bet." She chewed her lower lip. "That man is built, too. Oh, Zandy, am I jealous."

"Stop it." I gave her my take-no-shit expression. "I don't like the look you've got on your face right now."

With a laugh, she changed her expression. "Sorry. I would be mad too if you went on about some guy I'd been with."

"Good. So, we understand each other then." Picking up the glass, I took a dainty sip. "I've got so much to learn about being a mother. If Kane allows that, I guess."

"Do you honestly think he won't let you be a mom to your own kid?" Her eyes narrowed as she looked at me. "Is there something you can do about that if he does try to keep you out of the boy's life?"

"I don't think there would be anything for me to do about it. I signed away my rights when they made me give him up." The thought hit me like a punch to the gut. "What if Kane thinks I won't be a good influence on Fox? What if Kane has a problem with my job or something, or the way I live my life? What if he just wants to screw me now and then, but won't let me be anything more than an occasional lay?"

Taylor shook her head adamantly. "No. You can't let him treat you that way. You're going to have to up your game, girl. We need to mother you up. We'll get you some mom clothes to wear around the kid—things that are less sexy and more casual or something. Maybe trade that Mustang for a minivan. Is the kid into sports of any kind?"

"Yeah, baseball. He's an athlete, just like his dad." The thought of a minivan made my stomach clench. "But I don't want a minivan. That's going too far, Taylor. But maybe something kind of sporty, but more like something a mom would drive."

She tapped her chin with her index finger. "My Beemer is kind of like that."

"Yeah!" I agreed with enthusiasm. "Something along those lines. I like the way you're thinking." But then I thought about the fact I would need to keep my current job to make that kind of a payment. "Or maybe something a bit cheaper. I'll have to look around, and maybe look around for a more suitable job, too."

Clucking her tongue, Taylor went on, "You know what the bills are here, Zandy. Not every job will pay well enough to keep the lights on."

She was right about that. There weren't many jobs that paid as much as I made at the club. Not for people with nothing more than a high school diploma, anyway.

Running my hand through my hair, I felt a bit of a headache coming on. "I should really think about expanding my horizons if I want Kane to see me as a woman who's fit to be the mother of his son."

"He's not only his son, Zandy," she reminded me. "He's yours too."

"Not on paper," I reminded her. "Fox is his alone and has been all this time. I wonder how Kane is going to feel about sharing him now."

"Oh, hell," she whispered. "I didn't even think about that. You said it's been ten years. That's a long time for it to have been just the two of them. I bet they've got their whole routine established. And where the hell will you fit into that?"

"I know." I took a long drink as I thought about what the future would hold for me. "This may only end up bringing more pain to my life, and not the joy I was thinking."

With a sad nod, she agreed. "Yep." She finished her drink then got up to refill it. "I hate to say this, but I'm not feeling as great about this anymore, Zandy."

Looking at the beverage in my hand, I thought about dumping it out. When my bouts of depression hit me, alcohol only made them worse. And I didn't want to fall into a pit of despair right when I'd just found my son and reunited with the only man who'd ever been able to push my sexual buttons.

CHAPTER 14

Kane

NOT USED to my son being angry with me, the quiet ride home wasn't comfortable at all. "So, what do you want for dinner, buddy?"

"I wanted you to cook out on the grill." He looked out the window, but I could still see the glare in his eyes. "I wanted my mom, the person you know I've wanted to see my whole life, to come over and eat with us. Now, I don't care what we have for dinner. It can be a bowl of cereal for all I care."

"Okay, Fox, I'm going to be very honest with you. That woman is your mother, yes. But we don't know her. All we know for sure is that she just moved back here from Chicago, and that she has worked in bars her whole adult life, and currently works in one." I thought about how to word my misapprehension when he looked at me like he didn't have a clue what I was talking about. "Okay, let me clarify. A lot of the time, the people who work in bars tend to live a wilder life-style than you and I are used to living."

"Wild?" he asked with a confused expression. "Like a wild animal?"

"Like a wild person. Drinking alcohol. Getting drunk. Staying up late." I stopped myself before I went too far and said something that might make him think badly about his mother. "Lots of things. And I have no idea if she does any of those things or not. I need to get to know her first before we figure out how involved she's going to be in your life."

"That's not fair!" he wailed. "Why do you get to do that and not me?"

"Because I'm a grownup who knows a thing or two about life and people and you're a little kid, Fox." The dull throb of a headache began, and I knew this wasn't going to end anytime soon.

"She's my mom!" he shouted.

"Fox, control your voice when you're talking to me. I'm not yelling, and you're not allowed to either." I had to keep our rules in place. This was the first situation where he'd really bucked me. But I couldn't let things get out of hand. "Now, let me tell you more about what I'm thinking. Maybe then you can understand where I'm coming from."

"Doubt it." He sulked as he sat in the middle of the backseat.

"Well, I'm going to try anyway." I paused, heaving a heavy sigh. *Man, this shit sucks ass.* "Since we don't know her yet, we have no idea if she's a good driver. And you wanted her to take you to school. What if she drives dangerously? I'll have you know she sped out of the parking lot back at the hospital. What if she's had a lot of wrecks?"

His eyes darted up to meet mine in the rearview mirror. "She's alive, isn't she?"

I had no idea what he was getting at. "And what does that mean?"

He gave me a stoic look. "It means that she's alive. She hasn't killed herself in a car wreck or something."

Sometimes this kid was too smart for his own good. I could already see that he was going to have an answer for everything. My job would be hard, but I had to do it. "Okay, so she's alive. But we have no idea if she's been in accidents in the past that have hurt her. Heck, we have no idea if she was involved in an accident that killed someone. That's how much we don't know."

"Drama." After all I'd said, that one word was his only reply.

Another sigh came out of me as my head began to throb. Rubbing my temples, I had never been so glad to see our home coming up. "It's not drama, Fox. It's being a responsible parent. And no matter how dramatic you think I'm being, I will do what I think is best to keep you safe."

After we stopped inside the garage, he took his seatbelt off and we both got out of the car. Stomping away from me, he muttered, "And what you think is best is that you get to know her better right now and I don't. Real fair, Dad."

"Life isn't fair, son." I gritted my teeth as the age-old saying came out of my mouth. But there was no other way to put it.

Life wasn't fair. People weren't always good. Children sometimes didn't understand why things were the way they were. It didn't make a difference. A parent had to do what a parent had to do.

Pounding the security code into the pad, Fox disabled the alarm system then slammed into the house. Now he was in trouble, and he had to have known that.

I came in right behind him. "Fox, you walk back out that door and come back in it the right way."

Ignoring me, he just kept on walking away. In ten years, I had never seen this side of my son.

Catching up to him, I tried my best to remain calm even though my head was pounding like a herd of elephants was disco dancing up there. One hand on his shoulder was enough to stop him, but I didn't expect what happened next.

Turning to face me, my little boy's face was glowing beet red. "Let me go."

I had never met Zandra's parents, though I'd heard a few things about them through the years, like how strict they were. And I knew they must've been pretty damn opinionated and obstinate as hell to make their daughter give up her baby. But I had a feeling that I didn't know the half of it. I could only assume this new side of Fox came from them.

"I'm going to schedule a meeting with Dr. Parsons tomorrow." I didn't let go of his shoulder, but I did ease up on the grip I had on him. "I know you don't understand or even agree with me about this, but you will respect me and my decisions. Now, do what I told you to. Go back out that door, come back in, and do not slam it this time. If you don't, then you can go on to your bedroom, take a bath, and go to bed for the night without dinner."

Shrugging my hand off his narrow shoulder, he didn't say a word as he went back to the door and did as I'd asked him to. I stood there, watching him, his face never lightening up at all. Instead, it stayed red and angry.

No longer stomping, he walked by me.

"Dinner will be in an hour."

"I don't want any," he told me as he kept on walking. "I'm going to take a bath then go to bed. I'm not hungry."

Stunned, I stood there, just watching him walk away from me. In the space of an hour, he'd found out he would have his mother in his life, and that seemed to mean that he didn't care about me anymore.

After a long moment of standing there in shock, I started walking to my den. A bottle of Scotch sat on the small bar. Pouring myself a drink, I tried to wrap my head around what had just happened.

Lying back in my recliner, I turned on the heat and massager to try to relax and think rationally about everything that happened that day.

Is he right for being so angry with me? Should I have been more careful about letting him learn who Zandra was?

Should I have, at the very least, let his mother come over for dinner, the way he'd wanted?

Should I have let her stay the night, the way he'd asked?

Closing my eyes, I saw Zandra in my mind. Her long dark tresses, adorned with deep blue streaks, flowed over her naked back as she walked away from me. The two dimples at the tops of both ass cheeks held my attention as I looked down her body.

Then she turned, beckoning me to join her as she wiggled one long, slender finger at me. "I'm not a girl anymore, Kane."

My cock stiffened. "No, you're not. And I'm not a teenage boy anymore, Zandra Larkin."

"I know." Her red lips parted, showing her pearly white, perfectly straight teeth. "Come show me what you can do to me now that we're all grown up, Kane Price."

"Dad?" my son's voice startled me.

Looking down at my crotch, I found some pretty good wood there, standing at attention. Luckily, he'd come up behind me and couldn't see that.

Grabbing yesterday's newspaper off the table next to me, I put it on my lap to make it look like I'd been about to read it. "Yes, son?"

"I want to say that I'm sorry." He walked around in front of me.

He had no idea how good that made me feel. "Thank you. It takes a strong person to apologize, Fox. I respect you for doing that."

"Good." Getting down on his knees in front of my chair, it looked as if he was about to beg me, and I could see he already looked on the verge of tears. "Dad, I know you want to do what's best for me. Please don't let too much time pass by before you let Mom be around me."

He hadn't had his real mom his entire life. He'd waited ten years for her, and I could see that he was ready to have her in his life, now that we'd found her. "I'll do my best. I promise you that."

"I know she's not like you. But that doesn't make her bad." He tried to prove his point.

"I know that." Taking a sip of the Scotch, I took a second to think about what to tell my son. *Our son.* "Let me just get the basics out of the way. I'll talk to her tonight. I'll ask her all the right questions. Tomorrow, if she'll meet with me, I'll talk more with her in person. We've got to see what she wants from us too, Fox." I knew he hadn't thought about this at all. "She may not want to be a mom. It's not an easy thing to be."

"She can do it, Dad. She wants to, I know it. She just needs us to help her. Tell me that you'll help her, Dad." He placed his hand on my knee. "Please." His voice cracked on that plea, breaking my heart a little.

"I promise I'll do my best to help her become a mom for you." How could I say anything else?

"Thanks, Dad." The smile on his face would be enough to see me through what I knew would be a difficult path ahead of us.

"So, about dinner," I said, thinking that his appetite would be back now that he'd gotten at least part of what he wanted. "How about we order a pizza?"

"Really?" he asked as he jumped up. "We hardly ever have that. Can I have pepperoni?"

"As long as you eat a salad too," I said as I took my cell phone out of my pocket. "And drink a glass of milk with it, too."

"Deal." And just like that, our fight was over.

In no time, we sat at the bar in the kitchen, eating the pizza the delivery boy had brought for us. Fox munched on a piece of pepperoni pizza while I ate my salad. "Don't forget the deal, Fox. You've got to eat your salad too. Not just the pizza."

Putting down the slice, he took a bite of his salad as promised. "Dad, we've got a big house here. Five bedrooms in all."

I already knew what he was getting at. Along with that, I knew I had to watch what I said, or we'd end up arguing again. "Yes, we do."

He took a drink of milk before adding, "If you don't like Mom being a waitress in a bar then why don't you invite her to live here, so she doesn't have to work?"

And here we were, on the cusp of what I hoped wouldn't be another argument. "You know, Fox, I think that's something I can talk to her about." *That should be good enough for him.*

"'K." He smiled, then stabbed his fork into the salad. "Make her want to come here, Dad."

I didn't even know if I wanted her to come live in our home yet, if ever, but I wasn't about to push my kid's buttons. "I'll see what I can do."

As if a light bulb had gone on in his head, his entire face brightened up. "You know what you should do?"

Go to my bedroom and hide from you.

Knowing I couldn't do that, I asked, "What should I do?"

"Ask her to marry you," came his tremendous answer.

I nearly choked on the water I'd just sipped. "Fox! She and I don't know each other well enough for that."

His eyes immediately drooped. "Yeah. I thought you might say that." He looked up at me with a weak smile. "I had to try though. I just want her around, like, all the time."

My heart began to ache for him. "Of course, you do." I ran my hand through his dark hair. Hair that would look just like his mother's if she hadn't dyed it. "That's understandable. And I'll do all that I can to make sure you get as much time with her as possible. She has a life too, though. You've got to understand that. She never saw this coming."

"I know." He looked sad as he stared at his food. "Why does life have to be so hard?"

"I wish I knew." But then I thought about how good we had it. "But you should be thankful for all the good you've got in your life. You've got a family who loves and adores you. You've got a nice home, plenty of food to eat, a great private school to go to."

He nodded then took a bite of the pizza. "And a great dad too. And now I've got my mom. My real mom. I thought that one day you might meet someone and get married and I might have a stepmom."

"You know, that still might happen," I had to let him know.

Looking at me with sheer determination in his eyes, he said, "I don't want a stepmom. I want my mom."

"I know, buddy." It didn't feel like the right time for any more mentions of marriage or other women. "We'll just see how things go. 'K?"

"'K." He went back to eating. "I like this pizza and salad. Thanks for getting it."

"You're welcome." I messed up his hair. "How about tomorrow you and I go get a haircut after school? You're getting shaggy, and I should try to look my best for your mom."

"Now you're talking, Dad." His smile went from one ear to the other. "Reel her in for us!"

I had no idea when my ten-year-old kid had learned anything

about reeling in a lady, but it made me laugh just the same. With no idea if I would even want to try to catch Zandra Larkin, much less reel her in, I prayed I wouldn't disappoint my son. Or make him angry with me again, because that argument had left me with an awful feeling.

CHAPTER 15

Zandra

Lying on my bed, I stared out the window at the rising full moon. Trying to be smart and responsible for once, I'd only had two of the mimosas Taylor made. I figured it was time for me to start acting more like a mother. And the only mother I had to pattern myself after was my own. She never drank at all. And she didn't cuss. She also didn't have any empathy, a trait of hers I was going to be sure to steer clear of.

My cell rang, pulling me out of my numb moongazing to look at the phone on the bed beside me. An unknown number flashed on the screen. I noticed the time was ten minutes to nine.

"Oh, well. Let's see who the mystery caller is." I mused to myself before answering the call. "Hello?"

"Is this Zandra?" came a little boy's voice.

I knew who it was right away. "Yes, it is. Is this Fox?"

"Yes, it is." He sighed, and I could tell he was happy that I recognized his voice. "Mom, I just wanted to call you tonight, and every night at this time, if that's okay, to tell you goodnight."

The swelling in my heart actually made my chest ache. "Fox,

that's the sweetest thing anyone has ever wanted to do for me." And then I thought about my work week. "And on Sundays and Mondays, you can call me. The rest of the days, let me call you. Most days I'll be at work at this time, but I'll make sure to take a quick break to call you every night before nine."

"Thanks, Mom," he said with what sounded like relief. "Can you save this number? It's our home phone."

"I sure will." I cradled the phone in a way I'd never done before, like I was somehow reaching through it to hold him. "How did things go between you and your dad?"

"Bad," he said then paused. "But then good."

Relief flowed through me, hearing that they'd worked things out. It had been clear to me earlier that the two had a few differing opinions about how they wanted things to proceed. "Good. Fox, please don't argue with your dad about anything to do with me. I would really hate to come between you two."

"You won't. And I'll try not to. It's just that I get real mad when it comes to you. Weird, huh?" he asked me.

My mind went to my parents, and the way they could get real mad too when it came to me. I guess I just had that effect on people. How charming.

"Well, you should work on controlling that, because being angry a lot isn't any fun. Your father is a good man. He'll do what's right, I know he will." At least I hoped he would.

"Yeah, I think your right." There was silence on the other end for a long moment before he switched gears, shocking me with his questions when it came. "Do you have anything that you've done that I should know about?"

I had no idea what kind of things he was talking about. "Like what?"

"Like wrecking a car, or like, killing people ..."

I stopped him right there. "No. I can see where you're headed, Fox. Your dad must've said something about my driving, didn't he? So here it is. I've had two tickets in my life, both for speeding. I tended to have a heavy foot back then. But I've got that under control now. I know I spun my tires a little when I pulled out of the parking lot, so your dad might be thinking I'm a reckless driver, but I'm not. That car has a V-8 engine, so sometimes I spinout on occasion without meaning to."

"Okay, good." I could hear tapping and thought it sounded like a pencil tapping on paper. Maybe he'd written a list of things to ask me. The idea made me smile.

My son wanted to get to know me, and I thought that was the sweetest thing in the world. "To let you know more about me, I've never been arrested. I've never been in a fist fight. I've never kicked a dog." I laughed. "Overall, I'm a pretty good person. But I've got to admit one thing to you, Fox."

He sounded a little worried. "What?"

"It's been a long time since I've had anyone in my life that I truly cared about. I don't know how good I'm going to be at being a mom." My chest deflated as the truth set in. I had no clue how to be a good mother. And I hoped to God I wouldn't become anything like my own mother.

"But you're gonna try, right?" he asked, sounding shy for once.

I had never dared to even dream that my son would come back into my life. But now that he was in it, I didn't want to let him go ever again. "I'm going to try very hard, Fox. I'm going to try harder than I've tried at anything else in my life."

"Good. You can do it, Mom. I know you can." His faith in me was also an unfamiliar thing in my life. No one had ever had any faith in me, least of all my parents.

"It's nine now. You better get to sleep." I heard the sound of a door opening.

Then Kane's voice traveled through from the background. "It's nine, sport. Time to get off the phone and into bed."

"'K. I just called Mom to tell her goodnight," Fox told him.

There was a moment of silence. "How'd you get her number?" Kane asked.

"Off your phone," he answered. "I've gotta go, Mom. Goodnight. I hope you have nice dreams."

No one had ever wished for me to have nice dreams. It felt so insanely great that I thought I must be kind of weirdo to feel such elation over these simple words of kindness from the son I thought I'd lost a long time ago. "Goodnight, Fox. I hope you do too."

"I love you," he said quickly, like he was blurting it out before he lost his nerve. As I caught my breath, feeling my heart swell again, he asked tentatively, "Is that okay?"

I didn't know what to say. The truth was that no one had ever spoken those words to me before. And here it was, my son once again being the first person to say such a thing to me. "Fox, of course that is okay. It's more than okay. I love you too." The words slipped right off my tongue, as if I'd said them thousands of times.

"I love you too, Mom. Goodnight." And then he hung up the phone.

I sat there, still cradling the phone in my hand, not ready to fully let go of the connection to my son. I finally put it down and closed my eyes. Everything was changing, and so quickly.

A part of me had a nagging notion that this would all end badly, as most things in my life had. The biggest part of me hoped like hell that this wouldn't end at all. I hoped this would grow and take my entire life in a whole new direction.

Only a short while later, my cell rang again. This time Kane's name came up on the screen. My heart raced as I looked at it. "Hi there," I answered.

"Hi. How're you doing?" he asked. I could hear clinking in the background, like ice cubes in a glass.

"Very good." I didn't want to admit to him that Fox had just said so many important things to me that I'd never heard from anyone else before. But that seemed rather pathetic to me.

A twenty-six-year-old woman who'd never been told those three little words, *I love you,* seemed like a tragedy. I didn't want Kane to see me as a tragedy.

"So, Fox tells me that you two will have your first ritual, the goodnight call." He chuckled. "I think that's nice. But how're you going to make that call when you're working nights at the bar, Zandra?"

I knew he was just protecting his son and making sure I didn't make any promises that I couldn't keep. "You're a great father, Kane Price. I had no idea, back then, that you were capable of being such a great dad." I paused for minute, not knowing if I should go on. But I couldn't keep all these thoughts to myself anymore. "If I'd realized that all those years ago, I might've just run away from my parents and gone straight to you."

He got really quiet then finally said, "Let's not talk about the past, Zandra. It's not like we can change any of it. And thank you for the compliment."

He was right. Why dwell on something neither of us could change? "You're welcome. So, I bet you've got a boatload of questions for me. You may as well start asking."

"Honestly, I do have some questions for you. Fox filled me in on your driving record, so I've got that one answered." He laughed again and I heard him taking a drink of something before he went on. "How about this one—have you missed me?"

My body froze, going completely stiff. My fingers gripped the phone and I couldn't think of what the hell to say to him.

Have I missed him?

He and I hadn't had enough time together to make any kind of a real connection, or so I'd told myself over the years. But I had thought of him a lot. Was that the same thing as missing him?

"Kane, you and I didn't know each other well enough for me to say that I missed you. I did think of you often, though." I thought about letting him in on the truth, and after a brief moment of hesitation, decided to go for it. "And I have to admit this to you. Even though you were my first sexual experience, you were also by far that best."

He let out a sigh. "You were mine too, Zandra."

I couldn't believe him. "No way. I don't want you saying anything just to get into my panties again, Kane."

"I'm not just saying it." His voice dropped an octave, sounding even sultrier than his normal tone. "You and I connected more that night than I've ever connected with anyone. I don't know what that says about me, but I know it's the truth."

If it was confession time, I decided I may as well lay it all on the line. "Kane, I did feel something special when I was with you. And I've compared you to every man I've ever had sex with, and you've won every single time. I've never connected with anyone either, other than that brief time with you. I guess that says something about us. Don't you think so?"

"I do." He took another drink and exhaled slowly. "But we've got to take things slow. Very slow."

He had no idea how badly I wanted to not take things slow. I wanted to dive right into life with him and Fox and never come out. But I understood him. "Being the excellent parent that you are, I will go along with you on this."

"Good. Follow my lead, Zandra, and I'm sure things will work out." His sexy laugh sent chills through me. "That said, I'm talking about being in Fox's life. When it comes to my life, to my bed, those rules don't apply. Tell me what you're wearing, baby."

"Kane!" I guess I should've expected it, considering the way he'd come onto me in his office, but I couldn't help my squeak of surprise at his one-eighty. "You're so bad." I laughed seductively, unable to help myself. He'd turned me into a hot mess—and in record time, too.

"I am. And I want to be bad with you. I've missed you, baby. I've missed the way your body feels when its pinned underneath mine. I've missed the way your tight pussy clenched around my cock. How your lips tasted and your tongue moved. How your tits felt when they were squished against my chest."

"Damn," I said, biting my lip and running my hand down between my legs. My pussy pulsed against my palm.

"You in your bedroom, baby?"

"Uh huh," came my whispered reply. How did he do this me? Get me to do anything he wanted, even when I knew I shouldn't?

"You naked?"

I wasn't, but I quickly shucked my panties then pulled off the nightgown I'd been wearing. "Uh huh."

A deep groan met my ear. "Good. Trail your fingers over your big tits. Pretend it's me touching you."

My nipples pebbled as I moved my hand over my boobs, pinching the nipples the way he'd done all those years ago. I could still recall every last detail of what we'd done that night. "'K."

"Do you remember when I kissed your pussy?" he asked me, sending heat coursing through my veins.

"Uh huh." I could barely breathe I was so turned on.

"My lips were the first to touch you there," he whispered. "I want them to touch you there again. I want my mouth to be the one you pretend is on your sweet, hot cunt every time you touch yourself."

"It already is." I pushed one finger into myself and saw Kane's face in my mind. "When I masturbate, it's always you in my fantasies."

"I want to fuck you for real, baby. I want to bend your ass over and fuck you until you're begging me to stop, but I won't stop until I feel your pussy pounding and pulsing as you scream my name and come all over my hard cock." He groaned, and I was sure he was jacking off.

Looking in the drawer next to my bed, I got out my vibrator and lube. If he was going for it, so was I. Turning it on, I let him hear the noise it made. "I'm about to put your hard cock deep into my pussy, Kane."

"Yes," he whispered. "Put me inside of you, Zandra. I want to be inside of you so damn bad, it's making me crazy."

Pushing the vibrator into me, I moaned with desire. The man himself would've been even better, but I didn't have access to him yet. At least he was on the other end of the line. Much closer than he'd been in years.

"Your cock is filling me up, Kane Price. You're inside of me, fucking me the way you did so many years ago." I moaned with plea-sure, imagining that his hard body was on top of mine. Arching up, I pushed the vibrator as deep as I could into me.

My legs shook, a thin sheen of sweat covering me as I pushed and pulled the instrument, all the while thinking of the time we'd been together. "Let me fuck you, Zandra. Let me take you to a place you've never been, baby."

"Yes," I moaned. "Take me, Kane. Make me yours."

"Oh, baby. My cock's about to blow. Get ready," he said through clenched teeth, then let out one long, deep growl. "Yes, baby. Yes!"

It didn't seem possible, but my body was going right along with his. My orgasm tore through me, my juices pouring from me as I had to let go of the vibrator and grab onto the mattress as I arched my back and screamed. "Kane! Yes!"

After a few moments with no sound but both of our labored breathing, he finally spoke. Softly, he said, "Goodnight, baby. I'll see you tomorrow."

Tomorrow!

CHAPTER 16

Kane

"Rocco, are you at the restaurant yet?" I asked my best buddy at ten minutes after ten the next morning.

"I am. What ya got, Kane?" he asked.

"I've got a problem." I turned the car in his direction, heading that way. "You see, I've found Zandra Larkin."

"You're shittin' me!"

Laughing at his response, I went on. "No, I'm not. And you'll never believe this."

"Believe what?" he asked.

"That waitress at Mynt on Saturday night was her." I stopped at a light and tapped in a text to Zandra, asking her to please meet me at Rocco's restaurant, The Lights of Italy.

"No way!" came his quick response. "So, what's the problem?"

Looking at my cock, which had swollen with just the knowledge that I would be seeing her in person soon, I answered, "I've still got it bad for her."

"And what's wrong with that, might I ask?" A logical question, unless you were the father of an impressionable young son.

"I don't know much about her, except that she's a waitress at a bar. That's the problem. I have to take things slow with her, for Fox's sake. Get to know her. I never really knew her, you know what I mean?" I asked him as the light changed to green and I took off. "And I want to meet her somewhere where I have a little support. Yesterday I had a difficult time keeping my hands off her. If Fox hadn't been about to come back into the office, I would've taken her right on top of my desk." I thought about the night before and decided to add, "And last night we had phone sex."

Surprise rang in his deep voice, "Goddamn, you guys just don't know how to wait, do you?"

"Apparently not." I knew that wouldn't be an issue if it weren't for our son. "But I've got to rein in my libido this time, and I'll probably need your help to do that, Rocco. Let me meet her at your restaurant this morning before you guys open for lunch. That way we'll have some privacy, but not enough to haul ass to the bathroom and do the thing that will surely make me lose all of my paternal instincts and forget all about my obligations to my son."

"Ah, I see it more clearly now." He laughed. "Yeah, come on down. That'll be fine. And I'll try to keep an eye on you two."

"Thanks." I turned onto the road that the restaurant was on. "I'm almost there. See ya soon."

After ending the call, I saw that Zandra had texted back that she would be there shortly. My cock grew a little more, and I gave it a dirty look. "You'll just have to wait this time, until after I get to know the girl. You know that Fox is worth it, you headstrong idiot."

Talking to my cock wasn't part of my usual routine, but that woman had scrambled my brains, and suddenly I was doing all kinds of things I never did. Or didn't do much anymore. The last time I'd had phone sex was in my first year of college.

Maybe it was her soft voice that had done it to me. I didn't know. I did know that I hadn't made that call with that in mind. I had other things I'd wanted to talk to her about. Instead, I'd gotten all hot and bothered with her.

She brought the bad boy out of me, no matter that I'd successfully stuffed that part of me away somewhere for the past few years. I didn't know what to do about it, either.

In my son's younger years, years when he wasn't aware of his father's promiscuous behavior, it had never mattered to me to be anyone other than who I was. And who I was then was a guy who liked a little variety, trying new flavors on a regular basis.

After Fox's third birthday, things changed. At the end of the party we'd had for him, my date for the evening had shown up. Fox seemed to be overjoyed that I had a woman next to me. And when he asked if she was his momma, I knew I had to be very careful who I brought around him.

That very night, I'd had some wild sex with the woman and then pledged that it would be the last time I did anything like that.

Of course, it didn't work out exactly that easily. I scored, but never dated. And none of the women I was with ever did much for me. It's not that I was thinking about Zandra all the time, either, but none of those other women ever hit me in the right place. My heart.

Pulling into the parking lot, I found myself getting excited about seeing Zandra again. "Calm down."

Rocco met me at the front entrance, unlocking the door and pushing it open. "Good morning, Romeo."

"It is a good morning," I agreed as I walked inside. "And help me put the Romeo away, please. I've got to admit that I've got a damn hard-on just from knowing I'm about to see her."

A loud laugh came out of him as he shook his head. "Damn, dude!"

Gesturing to the empty dining hall, I asked, "So, can I take a table anywhere?"

"Take that one in the back. It's the nearest one to the kitchen, and I'll be able to keep an eye on you better." He led me to the back of the large room. "How about I make the two of you something delicious for brunch?"

"I think that sounds great." I took a seat then wondered about having wine so early in the day. *What the hell.* "And how about a nice bottle of wine?"

"Of course." He went into the kitchen and I stared at the door, waiting for her to walk through it.

I hadn't intended for this to be so much like a date, but it definitely began to look and feel like one. When Zandra came into the restaurant, pulling her Ray-Bans off her gorgeous face and tossing her dark hair back over her shoulder before waving at me, I knew it was a date.

I got up, meeting her halfway, taking her hands in mine as I looked at her. "Damn, you're pretty." I kissed her on the cheek, even though my lips yearned to touch hers. My tongue wanted to tangle with hers too. But I kept myself in check. "This way, please."

She let me hold her hand as I led her to the table. "Isn't this the restaurant your friend's family owns?"

"It is." I pulled out a chair for her. "And he's here, making us some brunch."

As she took her seat, she gave me a dazzling, heart-melting smile. "How nice."

I took my seat. "Yeah, he's a pretty great guy." Looking at her as she sat just across the table from me, within touching distance, I couldn't help myself from teasing her a little. "Last night was pretty fun."

Her cheeks went pink, and she ducked her head. "It was."

That shyness was still there, just beneath the surface. "You've gotten over a lot of your shyness, but not completely I see." I didn't want her to be embarrassed, so I let her know what I thought about that. "I think it's adorable."

She lifted her head to look at me with a surprised expression. "You do?"

With a nod, I said, "I do." Then I moved my hand over the table, barely touching the tips of her fingers. "I think you're adorable."

On cue, the door to the kitchen opened and Rocco came out. "Nice to see you again, Zandra."

She smiled at him. "You too, Rocco. Kane tells me you're making us brunch. That's such a nice thing to do. Thank you."

He put two wine glasses on the table in front of us then filled them. "You're very welcome. I've got cannelloni in the oven as we speak. A cream cheese filling, a savory meat sauce on top, covered with ricotta and mozzarella cheeses. To start you guys off, I've braised some mushrooms in a red wine reduction and paired them with some fresh green beans that I'll spoon over a fresh bed of mixed greens. I'll be right back." He gave me a wink. "Right back, Kane." Then he looked at where my hand was on the table.

I moved it, knowing he was only trying to do what I'd asked him to. "Thanks."

He left us alone, and I noticed Zandra taking a drink of the wine. "Yum."

"I know it's early to be drinking," I said as I watched her lick the red wine off her pink lips.

She looked a little confused. "Then why did you order it?"

With a shrug, I answered honestly, "I'm not quite sure. Maybe to help ease the tension between us."

"You feel tense?" she asked as she put the glass down.

"Yeah." I picked up my glass and took a drink.

"I make you feel tense?" she asked, seeming genuinely confused.

"Yeah." Putting the glass down after taking a small drink, I clarified, "Sexually, you make me very tense."

The little smile that curled her lips only made me want her more. "I see. And you would rather not be so attracted to me, because of our son. Is that right?"

"Kinda." I didn't know she would see right through me the way she had.

"Funny how our son's the reason we have to take things slowly, isn't it?" She ran her hand through her hair and the overhead lights glistened off her shining silky strands. "Kinda seems like it's too little too late on that front," she said with a sexy, deep-throated chuckle.

I wanted to run my fingers through her hair. "I wish I could find it funny. Instead, I find it frustrating. But it is necessary."

I could see by the way her blue eyes glistened that she liked the effect she had on me. "I'm sure you're right." She leaned forward, her breasts resting on the table. "So, how are we going to do this then, Kane?"

"I wish I knew." I looked at Rocco as he came back out with the salads.

Sitting back, Zandra smiled at Rocco. "Those look good, Rocco."

"Thank you," he said as he put them in front of us. He looked at me. "I'll be back soon."

With a nod, I let him know that I knew he was watching us. "Thanks."

We ate in silence for a few minutes while I tried to think about how things could be done. Finally, I said, "I want to get to know you, Zandra."

"Good." She wiped her mouth with the white linen napkin. "I'd like to get to know you, too."

While we both were on the same page, which was great, I still didn't know exactly what page that was. "Okay. So, let me start by asking you about your living arrangement."

"I've got a roommate. Taylor and I work together at the club. You've met her. She's the blonde with rainbow spikes in her hair." Her eyes clouded just a bit. "And for the record, I know she came onto you. And if she ever does again, I would really like it if you told me about it, as I've asked her not to do that anymore."

I could see the jealous spark in her eyes, and it made me happier than it should. "I see. Is that because you see me as yours, Zandra?"

Shaking her head, that pink blush stained her cheeks once more. "I know you're not mine, Kane. But you are the father of my child, and I don't want any friend of mine messing with you."

"I think I can agree with that." I pushed my empty bowl to one side. "I don't want any friend of mine messing with you either."

Her eyes caught mine. "So, we agree again, then. Maybe all of this will work out just fine, Kane."

I hope so.

I couldn't stop looking at her lips. So plump, so juicy, and so completely kissable. "Yeah, it might."

"I'm an open book, Kane. Ask me anything." She moved the

empty bowl away from her just as Rocco came back out, making her turn her attention to him. "That was the best salad I've ever had, Rocco. You're a genius with food."

"So I've been told." He put the plates down then picked up the empty bowls. "I'll be back to refill your glasses shortly. Enjoy."

"I'm sure we will," she said.

All I could do was gaze at her. I wasn't a gazer. But with her, I was different.

As soon as Rocco was out of spying distance, I reached over, taking her hand as I looked into her eyes. "I'm going to need your help, Zandra."

"With what?" she asked innocently.

"With not going too far, too fast." Pulling her hand to my lips, I kissed the top of it. "You do something to me that no one else has ever done. I don't know if it's purely biological, or if it's because we already have a child together. But if it weren't for our son and the fact that I know we have to handle this whole situation carefully then I would take your hot ass to the bathroom, push you up against the wall, rip those panties off you, then thrust my cock into you so hard you'd feel me for days. I'm already hard as a rock for you."

Instead of blushing, she licked her lips. "So why don't you do just that then?"

My cock thumped, begging me to do it. She wanted it. I wanted it. Why not just go for it already?

Slowly but surely, sanity pushed its way into my sex-addled brain. "Because we've got to be Fox's parents first, together, before we can become anything else."

"Oh." Her eyes went to the table. "Okay, then." She pulled her hand away from mine. "Can you tell me how to do that? Because I only have my mother as a role model and I sure as hell don't want to be like her."

A thought came to me. "How about I introduce you to my aunt and uncle? Aunt Nancy is a great mother. She can teach you every-thing she knows."

Stunned, she asked, "You want me to meet your family?"

"Well, of course I do. Zandra, you're Fox's mother. You'll be in our lives from now on. If that's what you want. My family comes along with us." I sat back as I watched her think.

"My family wasn't normal, Kane. And it's been such a long time since I was even a part of them. I've been a loner." She looked at me for answers that I didn't have.

"You've always been that way, Zandra," I reminded her. "But that doesn't mean you'll always have to be like that. Fox wants you as his mother."

Her dark brows furrowed. "And what do you want me as, Kane?"

That answer didn't come so easily to me. "I don't know the exact answer to that just yet, and I don't want to lie to you. I want you. I want your smoking hot body. I also want you to be Fox's mom, and I won't feel one hundred percent comfortable with that until I know the real you. I guess you can say that what I want is for you to let me in. And in turn, I'll let you in. That's not a thing I've ever done for any woman."

I was ready to do that for her. But I couldn't ignore the burning fear that I might not like what I would find if she let me in.

CHAPTER 17

Zandra

Wiping down the bar, I waited for the new bartender, Ashley, to make my drink order. At ten on a Friday night, the club was busy, taking most of my attention. After the way things had been going, I felt very grateful for that.

Four days had passed since my brunch with Kane. Agreeing to take things nice and slow, we'd parted ways without even a kiss good-bye. I supposed both of us knew where that kiss would lead, so we'd avoided it.

I'd already called Fox for our nightly goodnight ritual. He asked me if I thought I could make time for him on Sunday, since he knew I would have the day off. I told him I was free but that it would be up to his father if we could spend time together or not.

I had the distinct impression that Kane wasn't sure about me at all, other than the fact that he knew he wanted my body. And how could I blame him?

A whole week went by without my finding another job that paid as well as my position at Mynt. On top of that, I hadn't found the time to see about trading my Mustang for something more suitable for a mother.

I knew Kane wasn't pleased with the lack of change. And I knew that because he and I talked every day on his lunch break. He would ask me how the job search was going. I would tell him it wasn't going well. He would ask me if I'd gotten down to any car dealerships to see about trading my car in, and I had to tell him that I hadn't. He would ask when I thought I might find time to do those things and I would tell him I didn't know. Then he'd sigh and wish me luck and we'd end the call. The same old conversation each day.

I knew it had only been a week, but that afternoon call was already becoming a thing I didn't look forward to. Not because I didn't love to hear his deep, smooth voice that had just the slightest hint of a southern accent, but because I could hear the disappointment in that sexy voice each time he asked a question and I had nothing positive to report.

Hell, I hadn't even gone shopping to buy myself some appropriate "mom" clothes. I hadn't done anything, other than sleep, eat, and go to work.

Working nights meant sleeping most of the day away. Generally, I worked until two in the morning. When I got off, I would usually go somewhere to eat with coworkers. That would take an hour or so. I would head home then and would need an hour or so to wind down before I'd finally be able to go to sleep. That meant it was usually around five in the morning when I finally made it to sleep.

My day would start around one in the afternoon, when Kane called me, waking me up. And that was another thing he didn't seem to understand. Of course I sounded groggy from being woken up. He would ask if I'd been asleep, and I would say yes. Then he would sigh and ask me what time I had gone to bed.

Being a doctor, Kane had to let me know that staying up that late and sleeping all day wasn't healthy. Fox deserved a mother who tried her best to stay healthy, he'd remind me. And I had to agree with him about that, but I didn't have much choice in that, with the job I had.

Not if I wanted to continue living where I was. The apartment was nice, and it did cost more than most of the apartments around town.

So, I faced the dilemma of whether I would stay where I was—job, apartment, and all—or move into something cheaper and get a job that paid less.

I seriously had no idea how single mothers did it. And I had no idea how I was going to do it, either.

"Handsome stranger at two o'clock, Zee," Ashley said as her eyes looked over my shoulder.

Turning around, I saw that Kane had come to pay me a surprise visit. I couldn't say I was exactly thrilled by that. "Hey," I said as he came up to the bar, taking the tall stool next to me.

"Hey." He took my hand, pulling me to him and kissing my cheek. "It's Friday. I don't have work tomorrow, so I thought I'd come out and spend some time with you."

Despite my initial lack of enthusiasm about his visit, I couldn't help how my body reacted to him. Wet heat pooled between my thighs and my head went light. "How sweet of you." I kissed his cheek but wanted so much more than that. Some motherly instinct crept up inside of me. "And who's with Fox?"

"Aunt Nancy came over to stay with him while I'm out. He was already asleep when I left." He smiled at me, making my heart flip. "And I'm happy to hear you ask about him."

And then I got a little mad about that. "I care about him, Kane."

"I know." He let my hand go and looked at Ashley, who seemed to be hanging onto our every word. "Can I have a rum and Coke, please?"

"Sure thing," she said before her eyes shifted to mine. "Your drink order is ready, Zee." Putting the tray on the bar, she winked at me. "He's a cute little secret, isn't he?"

My cheeks warmed as a blush covered them. "I suppose so."

A look of disappointment came over his handsome face. "You haven't told the people you work with about me? About us?"

Shaking my head, I picked up the tray. "No. Only Taylor knows.

I've got to get these drinks out. Don't think I'm ignoring you, Kane. It's just a busy night, and I've got to keep working."

"You go work. Just come back and say hi from time to time." He smacked my ass as I walked away. "Be good."

Although I wasn't in the market for a boyfriend—I never really had been at any point in my life—the fact that Kane sometimes treated me like I belonged to him kind of made me angry. He hadn't made anything official between us, after all. Yet there he was, watching me, touching me, telling me to be good. I didn't understand him at all.

"Here're your drinks, ladies." I placed the cocktails in front of the women at my table who were out hoping to have a great night.

When I turned to go to my next table, I caught Taylor talking to Kane out of the corner of my eye. Jealousy shot right through me. But I didn't have time for that, as I had to get the next table's order.

"What can I get you guys?" I asked the three men who'd just sat down.

"Beers," came one's reply. "Anything you got on tap. And cheap, too. I lost a bet, and I'm buying the rounds tonight."

"Got ya." I left them and went to the next table, as that order would be easy to remember. "Hi, you two, what can I get for you this evening?" I asked the couple who'd sat down while I was at the bar.

"A gin and tonic for me," the man said as he wrapped his arm around the woman at his side. "And she'll have a martini, a dirty one, please."

"Okie dokie," I said before heading back to the bar.

Taylor, still chatting with Kane, spotted me and waited for me to get to them. "I hope you don't mind. I wanted to properly introduce myself to Kane. The baby-daddy."

Kane's frown at that name let me know that he probably wasn't a fan of hers so far. "I don't think I like that title, Taylor."

Giving her a stoic stare, I added, "Me neither." Ashley came to get my order. "Three drafts, whatever's the cheapest, a dirty martini, and a gin and tonic."

Ashley nodded. "By the way, Rob came up and told me to let you girls know that he wants you to step it up. Do a little dancing on the bar, get some guys doing body-shots. Ramp up the atmosphere." Then she set to work on the drinks.

Taylor winked at me. "Oh, goody! You get to show off your sexy moves, Zee."

I did not want to show off any sexy moves with Kane watching me. "I'll sit this one out."

"The hell you will," I heard Rob say from behind me. His gray eyes flashed to Kane. "Is this your boyfriend, Zee?"

Kane stood up, extending his hand. "Hello, I'm Dr. Kane Price. Zandra and I have a son together."

"Is that so?" Rob asked as he shook Kane's hand. "Well, she and I have a boss/employee relationship, and as her boss, I'm asking her to get on top of this bar and dance, and then allow men to drink shots out of her bellybutton. Are you opposed to that? Wait—I don't care whether you are or not. This is her job, and she'll do as I say or she can go find another one."

Not liking the aggression in my boss's voice, I interjected. "Rob, he's not saying I can't do it. I just don't want to." I looked him in the eyes. "Not right now."

"You don't want to because he's here," he said. And he was right about that.

But I didn't want Kane to think that. "No. I just don't feel like it right now."

Kane took his seat, sipping on the drink he'd ordered, letting me fight my own battle. I liked that about him, but then again, it would've been nice of him to say something maybe.

I saw an opportunity for Kane to be my hero, my knight in shining armor. He could've told Rob that he would take care of me and that I could quit the damn job and go live with him and our son and we would have our happily ever after. Only he didn't do that. He sat there, sipping on his drink, waiting to see what I would do for myself.

"Well, I said do it, Zee," came Rob's reply.

Knowing Kane was watching me to see how I would handle this

situation, probably analyzing my every word to see how I would handle similar things when it came to Fox, I squared my shoulders and prepared to do battle with my boss. "I said no. Now move, so I can take these orders to my customers."

I didn't know if there was a fire in my eyes, or what the hell had happened, but Rob stepped to one side. "Fine."

I won!

Or had I?

Rob's expression was hard. I had a sinking feeling he wasn't exactly letting me win. But for now, it looked that way. Being in front of Kane, I didn't let it get to me too much.

Taking the tray, I went to serve the drinks, feeling the weight of Rob's stare on my back. "Fucking asshole," I muttered underneath my breath.

For the next hour, I worked my ass off, barely getting the chance to say a single word to Kane, who still sat at the bar nursing the one drink. Everything was going well until a rowdy group of college boys came into the club, sitting at one of my tables. I quickly became the center of their attention.

"What can I get you guys?" I asked the group. There were eight of them in total. They were all pretty big, and the testosterone filled the air around them.

One burly guy got up, picked me up without a word, and sat me on the table. "Body-shots. On your sexy little body, baby."

To my horror, another waitress, Jerrie, came up to the table with a bottle of Captain Morgan in her hand. "I've got ya, Zee."

"But I don't—" that's all I got out before the big guy pushed me back on the table and Jerrie filled up my bellybutton with the first shot.

She smiled as she poured the cool liquid. "Loosen up, Zee. Have some fun."

Any other time, I could've totally let go and gone with the flow. But this time Kane was there. Watching me. Judging me. Finding me guilty of not being the kind of mother he wanted for our son.

I tried not to worry as the guys took turns doing their shots. In the end, the big guy helped me up then placed a hundred in my hand. "Thanks, baby."

Shame filled me for the first time in a very long time as I placed that bill into my bra. "Yeah." Ducking my head, I had to go back to my locker to put some of my tips away before they overflowed.

Making sure to take the long way around to avoid Kane, I went into the back. I tried my hardest to sneak past Rob's office, but he heard me. "Come in here."

"Fuck!" I pushed the door the rest of the way open. "Look, Rob, I can't do this right now. I'm a fucking mess. I know you don't get it or even care to, but I'm a wreck right now."

"Yeah, I know that." he pointed at the chair. "Take a seat."

I didn't want to take a seat. What I really wanted to do was just grab the rest of my tips, head out the back door, and run away from everyone—Kane included. But his stern look had me sitting down. "'K."

"You need to tell that man not to come back here," he said. "He's affecting your work."

"I can't tell him not to come here, Rob." I looked at him with pleading eyes. "I'm trying to be a part of our son's life. I'm trying to become what I need to be for my son."

"And I'm trying to run a fun and profitable nightclub. So what you're trying to do and what I'm trying to do isn't meshing. Tell him to leave and not to come back or I will. End of discussion." He pointed at the door. "That's all. Get back to work."

Getting up, I had no idea what to do. I couldn't tell Kane to go away. I went to my locker, put the cash away, and then headed back out. Kane was no longer at the bar, and I didn't know if I felt relief or panic.

Ashley came up to me. "He left."

"Did he ask you to tell me anything?" I asked, hoping he would've at least told her to tell me goodbye or something.

She shook her head. "He didn't say a thing. He put a twenty on the bar then left." She pulled the money out of her pocket. "I assume he wanted you to have it."

Shaking my head, I said, "You keep it. I don't want it." I had to see if he'd gotten out of the club yet. "I'm taking a few minutes, Ash."

"'K," she said, looking like she understood.

I headed to the exit to see if I could catch him, though I highly doubted I would. And even if I did, I didn't know what I would even say to him.

This will never work.

CHAPTER 18

Kane

I COULDN'T DO IT. I could not sit there and watch Zandra let those men treat her like—touch her like that. It made me sick. Literally.

That night, I barely got any sleep. The next day, I had trouble concentrating on anything. Playing some mindless video games with Fox was about all I could muster. Then Sunday came around, and my son decided to nag me until I was ready to scream and leave the house just to get away from him.

"Dad, please! I just want Mom to come over and eat dinner with us. Please!" he said the last word louder than the rest.

Cocking one brow as I looked at him, I cautioned him, "Do not start yelling, Fox. That will only get you into trouble. And I've already told you that I don't think it's a good time to start that yet. She's got some growing up to do before she's ready to become a mother."

No one was more disappointed by that fact than I was. I had an itch that I knew only she could scratch. But my son came first, and that was that.

Putting down the controller, he got up off the sofa to look me in the eyes as he stood right in front of me. He took my controller right out of my hands. "Dad, we need to talk."

The way he was acting almost made me want to laugh. *Almost.* "Son, there's nothing to talk about. I've already told you that I'll be making the decisions where she's concerned. And you'll just have to accept that fact. I'm not doing it to hurt anyone. I'm only doing it for your wellbeing."

He put his hands on my legs as he leaned forward, as if it would help if he got closer to my face. "Dad, what if being around me helps her grow up? What if being around me will help her become a better mom? How can she learn to be one if she doesn't have no kid to be one to?"

Valid point.

I sat there, with my son in my face, thinking about what he'd said. "But what if she and you get close and she runs off or something?"

"I don't think she will," came his childish answer.

Of course, I hadn't told Fox what Zandra had done at the club that night. He didn't need to know that about his mother. But I thought about how much easier things would be if he was older, more mature, and could understand things like that.

"Well, I don't share your optimism." Taking him by the shoulders, I moved him away from me then got up to go see about making something for lunch. "I'm going to make lunch. You want a ham and cheese sandwich?"

"No. I want my mom to come over, and I want us to cook outside and have a nice family day together. That's what I want." He crossed his arms over his chest. "I'm not gonna give up, Dad."

"Your mother probably isn't even up yet, Fox. So let's eat some lunch, and maybe you'll feel better once you get some food in you." I almost wanted to give the kid a sedative, he was getting on my nerves so much. Not that I would ever do that, but damn!

"How do you know she's not up?" he asked as he trailed along behind me as I went to the kitchen.

"Because she works late." I thought about what she'd told me before. "She goes to sleep around five in the morning."

"Isn't that the time you usually get up to go to work, Dad?" he asked, seeming a little bit interested in what I had to say for once.

"Yes, it is." I pushed one hand through my hair, shoving it back before washing my hands in the kitchen sink. "And she told me she usually gets up around two. So, what you want couldn't even happen for about three more hours. Maybe more. She would have to get up, have a shower, and put on some makeup and clothes. That all takes time, Fox. Then she would have to come over here, and it would most likely be around five or so before she got here."

"Okay, I can deal with that." He took a seat at the table. "Can I have some chips instead of vegetables with the sandwich this time?"

"I don't even buy chips." I looked at him and wondered what the hell was going on inside of his brain. "You know that."

"I do." He nodded with a frown. "And you don't buy snack cakes, candy, soda pops, or ice cream. You don't buy cow's milk, American cheese, or cake. You don't let me stay up late, not even one night. You don't let me ..."

I stopped him, as I could see he was having himself a pity party. "Fox, just stop. I'm a doctor. I know what that crap does to a person. None of those things are good for grown people, much less children who need nutrients to grow big and strong. One day you'll thank me, I promise."

"Well, it won't be today. Today I want potato chips with my sandwich. And I'd like the ham and cheese on white bread, instead of wheat bread for once too." He seemed to be on a roll. "And I would like an ice-cold soda with that, instead of unsweetened almond milk. Things need to change, Dad."

"Well, they're not going to." I set to work on making the sandwiches, cutting up the carrots and broccoli for the sides and then pouring us a couple of glasses of almond milk. "I'll have you know that most children would love to have a father who made sure they ate healthy, son. And after lunch, you and I will take a walk to the park and back."

With a huff, he picked up his sandwich and took a bite, looking at his plate as if it had dog crap on it, instead of homemade food. "Fine."

Lately, ever since his mother had come into the picture, my son didn't seem much like my son anymore. He'd never questioned the way we lived or the food we ate or drank, before meeting her.

As we ate in silence, sitting across the small table from each other, I began to think that Zandra coming into his life had been a very bad thing. A chain reaction had begun, and I didn't like it at all.

And even as I thought that, my cock thumped in my shorts. Yes, that thing still wanted her. But my brain was thinking better of it.

Zandra had a ways to go before I would be giving into my body. And it had to start with her getting a new job. But the woman had to make more changes than that.

Zandra's lifestyle might have been working just fine for her before Fox and I came back into her life, but it didn't work for a woman with responsibilities, a woman who needed to be a role model. But things had changed now, and Zandra needed to act in a way that Fox could look up to.

A whole week had passed and so far she'd done nothing to change how she lived now that she had the chance to be a mother to the son she'd been forced to give away.

I found that to be a bad sign. A sign of things to come.

Part of me wondered if having sex with her would help her see fit to make those changes. Maybe it would give her an added incentive to start sorting things out, so we could all move forward. But then I thought that would just be manipulating her. I didn't want to make her do what I wanted. I just wanted her to do what was right, and I wanted her to do that all on her own. But then I began to wonder if she could.

At first, when her boss had told her to dance on the bar and do the body shots, she'd stood her ground. I'd admired her in that moment, watching her stand up for herself. And then she'd gone and let those guys touch her in ways I couldn't even think about, and a bit of that respect had vanished in a flash.

Plus, it had made me jealous as hell. It had taken everything in me not to go throw those assholes as far away from her as I could. But

I didn't want to be a Neanderthal, and I didn't want to be with a woman who would bring that out in me.

In short, my body wanted one thing, and my brain wanted another.

And I couldn't understand why Zandra wouldn't step up to the plate and be the woman I expected her to be. She was the mother of my child. I guess a part of me had just assumed that she would instinctively know what I expected of her. Yet, she didn't seem to know at all. And I didn't want to explain it to her.

What I did want was to take her like I owned her. Keep her tucked away in my bedroom like my favorite toy. And I knew that was wrong of me, especially with everything else so up in the air.

With so many complex, mixed emotions where that woman was concerned, I had no idea where things would lead. All I knew was that she had some changes to make, and until she made them, things wouldn't be moving forward with Fox or me.

"Done," Fox announced when his plate and glass were empty. "Can we take that walk now?"

I downed the last of my almond milk then nodded. "Yep. Let's go, sport."

The food did seem to calm him down, and that made me a hell of a lot happier. We set off for our walk, which turned into a run before we got to the park. "Can I play on the swings for a few minutes, Dad?" he asked once we'd gotten to the park.

"Sure. I'll just be here, sitting under this tree while you do that." I watched him take off to play with the other kids and took a seat under the shade of an old oak tree.

Pulling out my phone, I went to check my social media apps to see what was up in the world. I saw that Zandra had made friend requests on all of them, so I quickly added and checked out her profiles, looking to see who her other friends were.

All I found was picture after picture of her partying and hanging out in bars. None of it made me feel better about our future. It seemed Zandra still lived her life like a girl in her early twenties, instead of a woman approaching the later years of her twenties. She was only one year younger than me, but looking at her pictures made me feel ancient in comparison.

The one thing that did stand out to me was the fact that I saw guys commenting on her pictures, flirting with her, with no flirty responses back from her. But then again, that was probably because of her loner mentality.

Zandra didn't let people in. She never had. Who was I to think she would do that for me?

I supposed I was hoping for something she wasn't capable of. How could she be someone she'd never been? And how could I expect so much from a person who'd grown up the way she had? Her parents had done a number on her, and I knew that. But knowing who to blame didn't help me much.

Fox was the center of my world. He deserved more from his mother. But could I get her to understand that all on her own, without me telling her what I wanted?

Was it even fair of me?

Staring up at the many branches of the old tree, I wondered what the hell I should be doing.

Should I ask her to come over? Should I ask her to stay the night? Should I take her under my wing and show her how I want her to be? How I dreamed our family should be?

Shaking my head, I tried to rid myself of those thoughts. It wasn't up to me to mold her into the person I thought she should be in order to be a mother to my son.

And then it hit me that I kept on calling him my son, thinking about him as my son only. He was hers too, and I kept putting that in the back, rather than in the front.

Should I let Fox and his mother make their own relationship? Should I stay the hell out of it and let them find their own thing? Can I even make myself do that?

I'd never considered myself to be controlling before. I thought of myself as a responsible man who put his child first in every situation. But could I have been hiding some things from myself?

Fox ran up, bringing me out of my thoughts. "Hey, Dad. Can you call her now and see if she's up? I bet if you call her and tell her that she can come over, she'll hurry up. I bet she'll be so excited, and then she'll get up right away."

And there he was, bugging me about the very same topic that had taken up my whole morning. "No. I might call her later. I've got to think about it, buddy."

His green eyes narrowed at me. "Fine!" he shouted, then took off running toward home.

I had no choice but to get up and go home with him, knowing he was mad at me and knowing the tension between us would once again fill our home when we got there.

Not wanting to catch up to him, I let him run as fast as he could while I stayed back a few feet. He beat me home and ran straight into the house, then into his bedroom.

I felt I should give him his space, so I went to take a shower and change clothes. My temper wasn't any better than his at the moment. If I tried to talk to him, I knew I would just make things worse.

After a nice shower, I felt refreshed and went out to the kitchen to get some juice. Passing by his bedroom, I knocked on the closed door. "Hey, buddy, do you want some juice?"

When no answer came, I opened the door. He wasn't in there. I went to look around the house, calling out his name as I went into each room. And I found each room empty.

Heading outside, I figured he was out in the back, maybe throwing the ball or something. But he wasn't out there either. "Fox!"

No reply came. I didn't want to panic, but it was beginning to bubble up inside me. I went back inside to check one more time, and then I called my aunt to see if he'd gone over there. "Hey, Aunt Nancy, is Fox over there by any chance?"

"No. Why do you ask? Is everything all right?"

Shit!

CHAPTER 19

Zandra

"So, I haven't heard from him at all since he came to the club Friday night," I told Taylor as I walked out of my room, my hair wrapped in a towel since I'd just gotten out of the shower. "But last night I talked to Fox, of course. You know, our goodnight phone call. He asked me what I would be doing today. He's been asking me that for a few days now. He really wants to spend some time with me."

She poured two cups of coffee for us. "And what do you want, Zandy?"

Pulling my robe tighter around me, I shrugged. "I want to spend time with him too. But his dad is in charge, and I respect that. The issue is that his dad hasn't called me to let me know when I can see him again."

Taylor put the cups of coffee on the table. "I'm making myself some pancakes. Do you want any?"

"Sure." I went to sit at the table, taking the warm cup in my hands.

She got the pancake mix out of the pantry. "So, what makes you think you can't call Kane and tell him what you want?"

"I just don't think I can, is all." I took a deep sniff of the steaming liquid, the pungent scent helping me wake up.

Shaking her head, she said, "Zandy, you're letting your shyness get in the way of your relationship with your son."

"I don't think it's that." I took a little sip of the hot coffee. "I think it's more like I don't trust myself where Fox is concerned. I trust Kane to handle things."

"And so far that way he's handled things has kept you from spending even one minute with your son." Mixing the batter, she gave me a stern look. "You're his mother, Zandy. You should start taking that seriously."

I knew she was right. "Well, with that said, you know I need to find another job. And that most likely means I won't be able to afford to live here, right?"

She bit her lower lip as she picked up the stainless-steel bowl full of batter, giving it a good whipping with the whisk she held in the other hand. "About that. I want you to know that I can afford all the bills on my own. I've done it before, and I can do it again. So you could get a lower paying job if you really want to. But do you really want to? Do you want to be broke all the damn time, just so Dr. Kane Price can say his son's mom is something other than a cocktail waitress in what he deems a rowdy bar?"

"I appreciate your offer, but I don't think that would be the right thing for me to do, Taylor. First of all, I don't want to live off you, which I would pretty much be doing if I went to work as, say, a waitress in a restaurant." I took another sip of the hot coffee before going on. "I've looked into waitressing positions in some of the local restaurants, even the more prestigious ones. I would be lucky to bring home a thousand dollars a month at those places."

Taylor nodded. "Yeah, I figured as much. But what about applying at one of the stores here as a cashier? My cousin works at In and Out Convenience Store, and she makes a little over twenty thousand a year. You could get by on that."

She forgot one thing. "I don't have any experience working in retail. What chance do I have of getting a job as a cashier?"

"Apply and find out, I suppose." She pulled a pan out from under the counter then put it on the stove. "But again, I ask you, do you really want to switch jobs just so you can impress the good doctor?"

"It's not just to impress Kane." I took another sip of the coffee, which had begun to get too cool. Getting up, I went to pour some more in my cup to warm it back up. "It's so that I can be a good mom. The kind Fox deserves. He's ten and in school. I don't want him to have to tell kids in his class that his mom is a waitress at Mynt. What will their families think? I want to be respectable for my son. I know Kane would take me either way if he didn't have Fox to think about. But he does. And he has his reputation as a doctor to think about too."

"That's exactly why I don't mess with men who think they're too wealthy or too important." Taylor poured some of the batter into the hot pan.

"Sure, that's why?" I said sarcastically.

She looked at me like she'd just been slapped in the face. "It is!"

Taking my steaming cup back to the table, I took my seat again. "Taylor, you're into guys with no future. That way you don't have to think about growing up yourself."

"Wow, Zandy." She nodded. "I think you're settling into your mom role just fine. Just listen to yourself. But you can't do this little psychoanalysis on me and not do one on yourself too. Why do you make the choices you do?"

Because I never look past tomorrow. But now I've got to.

I didn't say that, though. I merely shrugged and huffed. "I'm going to get dressed while you finish making the pancakes."

Getting up, I headed to my room, putting on shorts and a T-shirt and then pulling my hair into a ponytail. If Kane did call, I could put myself together a little better before I saw them. If not, then I wouldn't feel I'd gotten myself all made up for nothing, and there'd be no cause for disappointment.

But I was already disappointed that I hadn't heard from him. And I had to admit that I was disappointed in myself, too. I'd made a vow to get on my computer to look for other jobs that day, and the next day I would go out and scout the town for jobs that might not be posted online.

I had to start making changes, or Kane would think I was too immature and irresponsible. The last thing I wanted was for Kane to see me as someone who was going nowhere. Though I had to admit that was exactly how I'd seen myself up until I found my son.

Looking in the mirror, I told myself, "You can do it, Zandra Larkin. You can be what you need to be for Fox."

I even pulled my cell out of my pocket and found Kane's name on my contact list. My finger hovered over his number.

But then Taylor called out from the kitchen. "It's ready, Zandy."

"After breakfast," I told myself, and then shoved the phone back into my pocket. "For sure, I'll call him after I eat."

Taylor had already sat down with her stack of pancakes, pouring syrup all over them. "Yum, sugary." She looked at me as I walked by her to make my plate. "Hey, will you make me a big glass of chocolate milk, since you're up?"

"Yeah." I put a pancake on a plate for myself then made her some chocolate milk before going to sit down. My coffee still sat on the table. "Here you go."

I put some syrup on my pancake, noticing that she was looking at my plate. "I made us three each, Zandy. You can have the other two."

"I'm not really that hungry." Mostly I wasn't hungry for this sugar-laden food, but I didn't want to tell her that. She'd gone through the trouble of making it, so I didn't want to gripe or come off as ungrateful.

"Suit yourself." She munched away on her pile of pancakes. "So, if you don't do anything with Dr. Delicious today, then what are you gonna do with your day off?"

"Don't call him that." Jealousy shot through me so quickly that it surprised me. "And if he doesn't want to do anything with me then I'm going to get on my computer and stay there until I've found a job."

"I see." She looked toward the sliding glass doors that led out to a patio. "I think I'll have a day beside the pool, catching some sun and letting the guys ogle my bod. But you stay inside in front of a computer screen all day, Zandy."

Rolling my eyes, I said, "You do that, Barbie. I've got better things to do than that."

"You sure do." She winked at me. "You've got to turn yourself into Holly Homemaker so you can win the heart of the good doctor and his son."

"Our son," I corrected her. "And there are worse things to turn myself into."

She was just teasing me and I knew that. Taylor would never stand in my way of becoming what I wanted to be. She'd always been a good friend, but she was still a kid in many ways. She probably just didn't understand why I would even want to take on the role of mommy to a son I'd given away minutes after he was born.

Thinking about Kane and his disapproval the other night at the club, I wasn't sure why I wanted it either. Living up to Kane's standards might not suit me at all. But for some reason, I wanted to at least try. Besides, my becoming a mom wasn't about Kane, it was about Fox.

A knock on our door had us both looking up from out food. "Now who could that be?" I asked as I got up to answer it. Not that Taylor cared, but she was still in a short nighty that she'd worn to bed. I didn't think she was dressed appropriately to open the door. "I'll see who it is. You might want to get up and put on a robe, Taylor."

Stuffing another forkful of pancakes into her mouth, she asked, "Why would I do that?"

Shaking my head, I went to the door and looked through the peephole. "Oh, my God."

"Who is it?" she asked with a full mouth.

"My son." I opened the door, a huge smile on my face. "Hey, Fox."

His face was beet red, and sweat was making his dark hair cling to his face. "Hi, Mom. I came to see you."

Stepping back, my smile slowly faded as I realized something was a little off. "Come in," I said, looking out at the parking lot for his father, but seeing no one. "And where's your dad?"

"Home." He looked around at the living room. "Nice place."

"Thank you." I closed the door. "How did you get here? Your dad didn't just drop you off and leave, did he?"

"No." He looked at Taylor and the pancakes she was shoveling in her mouth. "Hi, I'm Fox."

She nodded then swallowed her food before saying, "I'm Taylor. Nice to meet you, Fox. I've heard a lot about you. You want some pancakes and chocolate milk?"

I headed toward the kitchen to make him a place, certain he would want some too. "I'll get you some. Take a seat, Fox."

"Uh." He stood still as he looked at Taylor's nearly empty plate. "I can't."

"Sure you can," Taylor said. "There's plenty."

Something inside of me clicked, and a little motherly instinct came out of my mouth, "So, if your dad wasn't the one who dropped you off, who was it, Fox?"

"I ran over here by myself," he informed me as he kept looking at Taylor's plate. Then he looked at me. "Hey, you're my mother. You can tell me I can have some pancakes, right?"

"Okay, hold on a minute." The idea that his father had let his ten-year-old son sprint across the city to my apartment, alone, didn't sit right in my brain. "Fox, does your father allow you to go places all by yourself?"

"Um, well, I'm allowed to walk to Aunt Nancy's and Uncle James', and I'm allowed to walk to the park with my friends sometimes." He glanced at the glass of chocolate milk in front of Taylor, which was still half full. "Hey, if you said it was fine, then I could have some of that milk too." He looked back at me. "Is it real cow's milk?"

"Hell, yeah, it is," Taylor said, then looked at me. "What's wrong with you, Mom? Get your kid something to eat, will ya?"

I had a strange feeling that there was a lot more going on than Fox was saying. "In a minute. Fox, does your father know where you are?"

"Um, he's probably figured it out by now." Jerking his head toward the kitchen, he said, "So, how about that milk and those pancakes now?"

As adorable as the kid was, I knew I had to make a phone call before I did anything else. "How about you take a seat on the sofa and I call your dad?"

His green eyes went to the floor, his small shoulders slumped. "Oh, man."

"I knew it! You left your house without telling him, didn't you, Fox?" I was horrified and knew Kane would be furious.

All Fox did was nod as he went to sit down. "I'm really hot from running all the way over here. It was like fifteen blocks or something like that. I looked up the address on my computer and found you."

I went to get him a bottle of cold water from the fridge and gave it to him before taking my phone out of my pocket and making a call I never expected I'd get to make. Even when all this started, I never imagined I'd be the one to call Kane to let him know that he'd been anything less than vigilant in watching and caring for our son.

Kane answered with the very first ring, "Please tell me Fox is with you!"

"He's here with me, yes." I could actually feel his fear coming through the phone.

I could tell his teeth were gritted as he growled, "Keep his ass right there, Zandra. I'll be right over."

"Kane, can't he stay with me a little while? I've missed him so much." I ran my hand over his little sweaty head. "And he must've missed me too. I know what he did was bad—"

"It was a terrible thing," he interrupted me. "Not just bad, Zandra!" he shouted at me.

"I know. I know he did, but Kane, he's here now. He's safe now. Please, just let us visit a little while before you come get him." I felt like I was begging, and I didn't like that I had to beg anyone to be able to see my own son for a little while, no matter what the circumstances were.

"Zandra, what he did was dangerous." He sighed heavily. "He had to cross two busy streets to get to you. He's got to be punished."

"I agree, but not right away. I'll talk to him about how dangerous that was and how he should never do it again, but for now, can he and I just visit?" My heart ached thinking about the trouble Fox had gotten himself into. I didn't even want to think about what kind of punishment Kane was going to give him. "He only did it because you haven't let us see each other, Kane."

"I know," came his soft reply. "I'll give you guys a few hours, and then I'm coming to get him."

"Okay."

I'd won this battle, but I had a feeling there were going to be more of them in the foreseeable future. I just hoped we wouldn't have a war.

CHAPTER 20

Kane

KNOWING that Fox was with Zandra did little to stop the anger and frustration that had built up inside of me over his little stunt.

Her apartment was a little over a mile away from our house. Busy streets with speeding cars weren't the only thing I worried about. Fox was just a little kid, no matter what he thought. He'd had no business walking over there, and he damn well knew that.

I had no idea exactly how I would address this behavior, but I sure as hell was going to try my damnedest to get my son back to the good kid he'd been before his mother came along.

Aunt Nancy and Uncle James came over once I told them Fox was safe with his mother. Aunt Nancy made chamomile tea to help calm us all down. She handed me a warm cup. "Here, sip on this and let's all just take some time to decompress. That boy sure did give us a scare, but at least we know he's safe now."

My hand shook as I took the cup she held out to me. "Well, for now he is. Once I get a hold of him, I'm not so sure about his safety."

Uncle James stood behind my chair, and he clapped his hand on my shoulder. "Now, Kane, don't be so hasty. Let's think about the right way to handle this. The boy wanted to see his mother very badly. Frankly, I don't understand why you haven't let him. She's all he's been talking about, and he told us how he talks to her each night before bedtime. And he was looking forward to spending Sunday with her all week long. Were you not going to let him do that? Is that why he ran away?"

He'd hit the nail on the head. "Well, I didn't say no. He just brought it up this morning and I told him to let me think about it. But he got all impatient and ran off on his own." I put the cup down on the coffee table in front of me. "I still can't believe he did that. I never would've expected something like this from him. Not my son."

Aunt Nancy laughed. "Oh, Kane, he'll do many things you'll never see coming. It's what kids do." She sat down on the loveseat across the table from me. "Now, let's talk logically here. What's stopping you from letting Fox see his mother? What is it that you've been spending so much time thinking about?"

"She works in a bar," I stated. "You guys know that already. But what I haven't told you guys is what kind of bar it is, and how she acts while she's there."

Uncle James took a seat next to Aunt Nancy. "I'm sure it's pretty crazy. Well, crazy to you, Kane. You grew up quickly. That's not your scene anymore. Maybe you're judging her a little harshly."

Taking a second to think about it, I had to admit, "Yeah, maybe I am. Maybe I'm expecting her to hurry up and grow up the way I did."

"But she didn't have the responsibility you had, dear," Aunt Nancy reminded me. "She had no reason at all to grow up. You can't very well expect her to do that overnight, especially if you won't let the two of them spend time together. How will she ever know what goes along with having a child if you never give her the opportunity to experience what it takes to look after one?"

She was right. I could admit that I'd been wrong. "But what if she does something to hurt him? I don't want him to be scarred, emotion- ally speaking, because I allowed her into his life too soon. What then?" I picked up the tea to take another sip. It did seem to be helping with my nerves.

"Don't you think we worried about the very same thing when we started letting Fox stay with you when you were just eighteen?" Aunt Nancy asked. "He was a baby back then. He couldn't tell you what he wanted or needed. But we took that chance. We let you keep him all by yourself sometimes, so you could bond with him and learn how to become the boy's father."

Uncle James added, "When we decided to give him to you, do you think we didn't have fears that we were putting too much on you? All the responsibility that came along with Fox rested squarely on your shoulders for the first time then. But you did it."

"But I came from a good home. And I had you guys and Mom and Dad to show me the way. Zandra had horrible parents. Even before they made her give Fox up, living with them had made her into a shy girl who hardly knew how to make friends. They turned her into someone who didn't have the wherewithal to get away from them when she was pregnant to let anyone know what they were doing to her and the baby she carried." I thought about how terrible that must've been for her. My heart ached with the thought. "I don't want her to instill that same thing into my son."

"He's hers too, Kane," my aunt reminded me.

"I know. I'm having a hard time adjusting my thoughts about that, though," I admitted. "For so long he's been mine and mine alone. I'm having a hard time adjusting to him having a mother."

"That's understandable," Uncle James said. "But you have to adjust, for Fox's sake, if not Zandra's."

I knew I would have to speed up my adjustment process. "So, the punishment. What should I do about that?"

Aunt Nancy came up with an idea, "How about you make him do the yardwork for a week?"

"Or you could take away his game system for a week," Uncle James said.

"Or both," I decided. "A little physical work along with the denial of his favorite thing sounds good. I just want my good kid back. I don't want to worry about him flying off the handle and doing things that might get him hurt, or worse."

"And you need to come up with a visitation plan for him and his mother, Kane," Aunt Nancy said. "Something he can count on. And you can't deny their visits as a form of punishment either."

"But—" I didn't know what else to say.

Aunt Nancy shook her head. "But nothing, Kane. It was your indecisiveness that caused Fox to run away. You have to make a decision and stick to it."

"I don't really want her alone with him at her apartment. She lives with another cocktail waitress with highly questionable morals." I thought about it some more. "And Zandra doesn't know any of my rules either."

Uncle James gave me a stern look. "Only because you haven't brought her around or spoken to her about how you want your son to be raised. Do yourself a favor—invite the girl over the way your son has asked you to a thousand times this last week. Then she can learn the ropes, and I'm sure she'll want to keep doing what's best for Fox."

"You're right," I had to admit that to them and myself. "I'll head that way and see if I can clean up some of the mess I've made."

On my way over to Zandra's apartment, I found myself calming down a lot. I would take her and Fox back home with me, and we would have the evening our son had wanted.

As I pulled up in front of her apartment, I noticed her red Mustang wasn't there. Little spines of worry began to pop up. Getting out of the car, I went to the door and rang the bell.

A few moments later the door opened and a bikini-clad Taylor opened the door. "Well, if it isn't Dr. Dad. I thought you told Zandy you would give her a few hours alone with the kid."

"Yeah, well, I've changed my mind." Looking behind her, I asked, "So, where are they?"

"She took him to buy him a bathing suit. He wants to take a swim in the pool. He saw it out the glass doors, just in back of our apartment." She opened the door wider, backing up. "Come in. You can wait for them."

"No, thank you." I was hot as hell over Zandra taking my son anywhere without asking me first. If she'd asked, I would've told her no, as I still had no confidence in her driving ability. "I'll be waiting in the car for them to get back, and then I'm taking my son home."

"Your son?" she asked with a hint of sarcasm. "Isn't he Zandy's too?"

I wasn't about to get into it with her. "I'll be in the car."

Sitting in my car, I gripped the steering wheel in my hands and tried not to bang my head against it. I couldn't remember a time I'd been so mad. And when the little red Mustang pulled up next to me, I nearly flew out of my car.

Fox looked at me with his mouth hanging open when he got out of the car. "Dad, I thought you said I could stay for a few hours."

Zandra got out too, looking at me with a stunned expression. "Kane, what's wrong? Your face is as red as a beet."

"Get in the car, Fox," I said with a low, threatening tone. "Now."

"But, Dad—" he whined.

"Do as I say. And do it right now." My hands fisted at my sides as the anger rose up in me. I was about to let her have it, and I didn't want my son to hear me berating his mother.

"Kane, stop it," Zandra said. "We can talk about this. I have no idea why you're so mad."

"You didn't ask my permission to take him anywhere." I tried to keep my voice below a roar. "You've got no idea what it takes to be a parent, Zandra. I always make sure I know and trust a person before I allow my son to ride with them." I looked at Fox again. "Get in the car. I'm not going to say it again."

Zandra turned to look at him. "Go on inside and put on your swimming trunks. We're going to swim just like I promised you."

The air went out of me as my son walked away from me and went into the apartment. "No."

Zandra came up to me, looking me in the eyes with a determination I'd yet to see in her. "You and I need to talk, Kane. Would you like to do it inside where my neighbors won't be listening, or out here?"

"You can't ..."

"I can," she said. "And I will."

"I'm not going in there. So say your piece out here and then I'll happily call the police if you won't let me son come with me," I let her know.

"Have it your way." She stepped back, crossing her arms over her chest. "This is your fault. You've kept stringing him along. He's only human, Kane Price. And I know I had to give that boy up, and I'm damn glad it was you who got him, but he's mine, too. He wants to have a relationship with me, and by God, he will."

"That's not up to you two," I reminded her.

"The hell it's not!" She leaned her ass against the hood of my car. "If you didn't want me in his life, then you never should've told him I was his mother! Do you think you can control that boy for the rest of his life?"

Do I?

"I'm not trying to control him." I held my hands up in the air, having no idea what I was supposed to do in this situation.

Have I lost control of everything?

"Kane, I know that you don't know me well. But the fact is that eating one meal together or coming into my work for one night isn't going to be enough to know me, either. If you think I'm not fit to be a mother to Fox because of the way I acted that night at work, then you need to know that that's not even who I am. When I'm at work, it's all an act, and that's all it is."

My heart began to ache as my mind filled with the sight of those men's lips touching her stomach. "You sure are a great actress, Zandra."

"I've had to be." Pulling her sunglasses off, she wiped a tear from her eye. "I had to get away from my parents. And I couldn't do that without making enough money to provide for myself. So, I became a waitress at a nightclub where an older woman taught me how to flirt and how to tease, how to be comfortable doing what was needed in order to make big tips. You know how shy I was. You have to know that when I'm at work, that's all an act."

I had to be honest with her. "I don't like it. I don't like you working there. I don't like it for a lot of reasons, Zandra."

"I'm looking for another job, Kane. I know it doesn't seem like it, but I am. As a matter of fact, that was how I'd been planning on spending my day today if you never called me. But now that I've got Fox around, I want to spend time with him. Tomorrow I'll start looking a lot harder than I have been." She stood up and looked at the door to her apartment. "It's hot as hell out here."

"Yeah, it is." I walked up to her, taking her by the hands as I looked into her eyes. "I don't want to tell you how you should be, Zandra. I want you to just know how to be. Does that make sense to you?"

She nodded. "It does. And I know you've got high expectations, Kane. But things take time. I've only got a high school education, and waitressing is the only job I've ever had. I can't make something out of myself overnight."

"You're right. You can't." My heart had started beating faster as soon as I felt her hands in mine. It was distracting me from all other topics of conversation. "I kind of hate what you do to me, Zandra."

Her pink lips barely parted as she whispered, "What do I do to you, Kane?"

"You take me back to who I was a long, long time ago. The man I've become disappears, and the kid comes out in me again. That's not what I want at all." Even as I said those words, my body leaned in.

"You can't always be in control of everything." She licked her plump lips. "Why are you always trying so hard to keep things just the way they are, the way they've always been? What's so bad about change?"

"Because I don't know any other way." It felt good to finally get the truth out, and I knew without a doubt that there were other things that would feel even better when they came out of me and went into her.

"I think you should let things play out however they're going to."
She leaned in, getting her sweet lips closer to mine.

"I think you're going to ruin me." It was the truth, and I was sure
we both knew that.

Her mouth came so close her lips grazed mine as she whispered,
"Ruin? No. Change? Yes."

Oh, Lord, have mercy!

CHAPTER 21

Zandra

THE INSTANT OUR LIPS TOUCHED, a fire ripped through me. I knew it then, without a shadow of a doubt, that my body had been claimed by this man from the first moment he'd touched my skin all those years ago. No one could do to me what Kane did.

Now all we had to get past was the fact that we shared a child.

His arms went around me as he pushed me back against the side of his car. One hand fisted in my hair, pulling it in a way that had my panties soaked instantly. His body pinned mine to the car, his cock thumped against my sex, and I knew that if we weren't in public, he would've taken me right then—and I would've loved it.

But we were in public, a fact Dr. Price knew too. His mouth left mine. We were both breathing in short pants as we stared at each other. "Come home with me, Zandra."

"'K." I ran my fingertips over his clean-shaven face. "I think we can work things out, Kane."

"I think I need you in my bed, Zandra." His lips touched mine for only a second. "And then we can go from there."

In his bed!

"'K." Butterflies filled my tummy as he took my hand, leading me up to my apartment.

"Pack a bag, baby. You're staying the night." He stopped outside the door, and then turned to face me. "Let's keep this under wraps when we're in front of Fox, though. There's no need to further complicate things with him."

I understood that we couldn't be all over each other in front of the kid, but I kind of felt like he wanted to keep me a secret. "For now."

With a nod, he let my hand go then opened the door. Fox sat on the sofa with a glass of chocolate milk in his hand. "Fox, what the hell is that?" Kane asked him.

"Chocolate milk, Dad. Taylor made it for me." Fox looked over his shoulder at Taylor, who still hanging around in her itty-bitty bikini.

Kane looked at me. "I don't let him have sugar, chocolate, or cow's milk, Zandra."

I couldn't believe what he'd said. "Are you serious?"

He nodded, then looked back at Fox. "And you know I don't let you have any of those things. Go pour it out, wash that glass, and put it away." Kane looked at me. "Go pack."

"Aw, man. I didn't even get one sip of it," Fox whined as he got up to do what his father had told him to.

I headed to my bedroom to pack. "Should I bring anything special? Like, what's the plan for today?"

"I'm going to cook us dinner out on the grill," he told me. "Just like Fox has wanted since a week ago today."

Fox shouted, "Yeah! And you told her to pack a bag. Does that mean she's staying the night with us?"

"Yes, it does. I think she needs to be around us so she can learn our rules, son." Kane's tone turned stern. "That way you won't be able to take advantage of her for not knowing what's allowed and what's not."

Fox looked very guilty all of a sudden. "You're right. Sorry, Dad."

I left the room to pack and couldn't help the thrill that ran through me.

Kane's taking me home!

When I finished packing and the three of us headed out the door, I went to get into my car. "Did you leave something in there?" Kane asked me.

"No." I turned to look at him. "I thought I would drive my car over. You know, so you don't have to bother with me in the morning when you take Fox to school and go to work."

Kane shook his head. "It's no bother at all. Besides, I want to take you to the school and get you signed up to drop him off and pick him up. If we're going to do this, then we're going to do it right. So come on and get in my car; you're riding with us."

I had no idea what had suddenly gotten into Kane. He'd spent all of last week keeping me and Fox from spending time together. Now he was including me in everything.

I wasn't about to complain, though.

He opened the passenger door for me as Fox got into the backseat. "Thank you." I sat down, taking in the decadent, creamy leather seats in his Mercedes. "This is a very nice car, Kane."

"Thanks." He closed my door then went around, getting in the driver's seat.

Fox buckled his seat belt, sitting in the middle seat. "Okay, Mom, lesson number one, I always sit in the middle seat in the back. It's the safest place in the vehicle." His father smiled, looking proud of Fox for letting me in on the rules. Then Fox added, "Now, if you guys have another baby, then the baby will go here, and I'll take one of the other seats in the back. And that way I can help with the baby, too. You know, give him a bottle or his binky. That's what my friend Josh does with his baby sister. His mom calls him her little helper."

Kane looked at me and I felt my cheeks heating. "Blushing, huh?" He snickered. "Get ready to be doing that a lot. Kids don't really have much of a filter. At least, ours doesn't."

Ours!

Everything felt surreal. Our little family was taking our first drive together. And we were heading to the home that I thought we might share one day, if everything worked out.

I knew I was getting ahead of myself, but I just couldn't help it.

Fox piped up, "Yeah, Mom, when I think it, it comes out of my mouth."

"Good to know." A smile took up residence on my face, and it stayed there during the entire ride to their home.

Their home that was located in the Charleston Country Club community. Their home that was more like a mansion than any home I'd ever seen.

"Here we are," Fox called out as Kane pulled into a horseshoe driveway and then into one of the stalls of his six-car garage.

"You've done extremely well for yourself, Kane, even for a doctor." I got out of the car and looked at the other stalls. One had a tall, four-wheel-drive truck in it. One had a Chevy Suburban in it. There was a motorcycle in another one, and the rest of the spaces were empty. "You've got a lot of vehicles in here."

Fox hopped out of the car, coming up behind me. "Yeah, Dad's got lots of cars and stuff. The boat's in the shop, getting ready for the summer. And the yacht stays at the marina."

"Damn." I caught my slip up. "I mean, dang."

Kane went to the door then stopped abruptly. "Come here, Zandra. I need to show you how to use the alarm system."

"Oh, I don't know." I didn't think I would need to be in their home without them in it. "Why would I need to know that?"

"Just in case," he said as he waved his arm, gesturing for me to go to him.

Which I did. "Okay, I guess so."

He pointed at the pad. "Okay, I want you to do it. Punch in twelve fifteen, then hit the green button."

The number hit me like a brick in the chest. "Twelve fifteen?"

"Yes." His smile grew. "Does that number mean anything to you?"

"It's the time my baby was born." I looked at Fox. "It was the time you were born."

"Yeah, I know. Dad uses that number for everything. He says it was the instant that his life changed," Fox let me know.

"It was for me, too." My heart skipped a beat.

Kane had to be the best father in the entire world. Our son was lucky he had him. And I hoped I might get lucky enough to have him too, one day. And hopefully that day wouldn't be too far away in the future. But for the time being, I was happy just getting to spend time with the two of them.

We walked into an enormous kitchen with gadgets that I didn't even know existed. "Oh my gosh! Do you have a cook who knows how to run all this stuff?"

Kane laughed. "No. I know how to run all this stuff, Zandra. And I can teach you if you want."

I was in over my head and knew it. "You're a lot smarter than I realized you were, Kane Price. I mean, a doctor, and apparently some kind of a financial genius as well, and now I find out you're a master chef, too. All I can say is ... wow."

"Yep. Dad's got it all, Mom. And he knows how to work on cars and motorcycles too." Fox beamed at his father, pride radiating through him. It was clear his dad was his hero—and I couldn't fault him for that. I was started to think Kane might be my hero too.

Kane finally looked the slightest bit sheepish. "Well, I know a little bit. I still let my mechanic handle the majority of those kinds of things." He took my hand. "Come on, I'll show you the rest of the place."

As we passed through one room after another, I realized there was at least one more thing to add to the list of things he'd mastered. The man knew how to decorate a home. "I can't believe you did all this, Kane."

"All what?" he asked as we stopped in front of a painting that was clearly meant to be the focal point in the foyer.

I held my arms out then spun around. "All this decorating."

"Oh, Dad didn't do that. Aunt Nancy did," Fox informed me. "Dad, can I take her upstairs and show her my bedroom now?"

"Yeah. I'll let you show her around up there while I get the pit going. I've got some pecan wood I want to use, and it'll need time to burn down and get all smoky." Kane left us, giving me a wink. "Be good, Momma."

I had no idea how he did it, but with just a couple of words, Kane had me going weak in the knees again.

Fox grabbed me by the hand, taking my attention away from the sight of Kane's backside as he retreated. "Come on, Mom."

"Your dad sure has changed his way of thinking, hasn't he?" I asked as we went to a staircase made out of shiny oak.

"Probably 'cause Aunt Nancy and Uncle James talked to him." He led me up the stairs, tugging my hand as we ascended to the second floor. "Those guys always help me out the most when it comes to Dad. He listens to 'em."

"That's good to hear. When do you think I'll get to meet them?" I went into his bedroom with him, finding it decorated with sailboats and ships. "Pretty nice, Fox. I like the nautical theme."

"Yeah, me too. I really like it when we go out on our boats. I like the ocean a lot. But I like lakes too. I guess I just like water." He walked over to a large model of a ship. "You'll probably get to meet them soon. Me and Dad worked on this for a whole month last year. Do you like it?"

"It's great." I ran my hand over one of the flat pieces of the ship. "Do you know what kind of a ship it is?"

"It's an aircraft carrier." He pointed to the name on the side of it. "It's the U.S.S. Lexington. Me and Dad went to Corpus Christi, Texas, last summer and we saw it in person. It's ginormous!"

"It sounds like you two had a great time." I looked around the bright room and thought how lucky he was to get to live the way he did. Not in a million years had I pictured the baby boy I'd had to give up living such a tremendous life.

"We did. We always have a good time. Most of the time Dad and me get along pretty good, even if he is stricter than any of my friends' parents." He walked toward the door. "Come on, I'll show you the rest of upstairs. There's a media room and a room just for playing around, with all kinds of fun toys. And four rooms for guests. But the only guests we've ever had stay over are Grammy and Gramps. And now you." He opened the door across the hall from his. "This is Dad's bedroom."

My heart sped up. "It is?" I peered in, and then Fox turned on the overhead light. "It's nice." Done in dark brown and teal, it also had the slightest hint of a nautical theme, but more like a ship's captain's quarters.

"Yeah, I think it's pretty good too." Fox closed the door, and we went on to the next room.

One door after another, he showed me the entire second floor. And then we went down to join his father in the backyard. We found Kane at a large stone patio, where he was building a fire in his big barbeque pit. "There they are. Did you get the grand tour, Zandra?"

"I did. Fox is an excellent tour guide. And I saw the ship model you two built. It's impressive." I took the glass of iced tea he handed me, our fingers touching slightly as it changed hands. Even just that little contact had my tummy getting tight.

"Glad you liked it." The way his green eyes sparkled as he looked into mine made that tight tummy do a flip. "Did you see my bedroom?"

I looked away to see where Fox was. He was getting something out of a storage room, out of hearing distance for now. Then I looked back at Kane. "I did."

"I'm putting you in the room right next to mine. Maybe you'll see fit to sneak into mine later tonight." He made a low growl. "If you can be quiet enough that Fox won't hear us."

Now I was wet too. "Kane Price, you're terrible." I hit him lightly on the shoulder as I smiled coyly at him.

"You think?" He looked to see if Fox was watching, and when he saw that he wasn't looking at us at all, he swatted my ass. "I think you've been bad. Maybe you need a little spanking."

My body flushed with heat. "Kane, you've got to stop. You're killing me." I took a long drink of the iced tea to cool myself down.

He smiled cockily, pleased with himself for the state he'd put me in. "Why don't you take a seat right there at that table while I go grab the meat to put on the pit?" He walked away from me, and I had to fan myself.

"You hot?" Fox asked as he came up right behind me.

Startled, I asked, "What?"

"Hot? Are you hot, Mom?" he asked again. "I can turn on the sprinkler if you are. It helps cool things off."

"Oh." I pulled my head out of my ass. "No, that's not necessary."

Holding up a baseball, he asked, "Wanna throw the ball with me?"

I couldn't help but smile. "I sure do."

The two of them were making me feel right at home. I had never imagined being a part of any home, never mind this beautiful one with my son and his father.

It was like a dream come true, a dream I hadn't even dared to imagine. Life was changing in ways I'd had no idea were even possible.

CHAPTER 22

Kane

THE WOMAN HAD me running on an overload of libido. Sure, it had been a while since I'd had sex, but with Zandra around, everything was that much harder—and one thing in particular was very hard. My mind sprinted forward to the night ahead of us. Her in my arms, her body glistening with our combined sweat as I pumped into her.

Stop it!

I had to slow my ass way the hell down. What was I thinking?

The main goal here was to figure out how to incorporate her into Fox's life. And here I was thinking more about all the ways I was going to fuck the hell out of her, and not thinking about what she was actually there for.

Aunt Nancy came out the patio door. "Knock, knock."

Zandra looked at me with panicked eyes. I smiled at her, hoping to convey that everything was fine. "I invited Aunt Nancy and Uncle James over to meet you."

She fanned herself. "Oh, heck."

My aunt went straight to her. "Do you remember me, Zandra?"

"You haven't changed a bit." Zandra met my aunt halfway, then Aunt Nancy took her into her arms for a big hug.

"That was so long ago. I was afraid you would've forgotten me." Aunt Nancy let her go. "It's good to see you, Zandra."

"You too." She looked a little overwhelmed, and I stepped up beside her, putting my arm around her to steady her.

Uncle James came out the door. "Hey there." He held up a twelve pack of beer. "I brought the suds. Let the party begin."

"And what did you bring for me, Uncle James?" Fox shouted.

Uncle James held up a brown paper bag. "Some boxes of apple juice. You know I never forget about my little man."

"Thanks," Fox said with a smile.

After he put the drinks in the minifridge in the outdoor kitchen, Uncle James joined us and I introduced Zandra to him. "Now, you two have never met. Uncle James, this is Zandra."

He held out his arms. "Well, can I have a hug too?"

She walked to him, letting him hug her. "It's nice to meet you."

"You too, Zandra." He let her go, and we all took seats around the large glass patio table.

With Aunt Nancy and Uncle James around, the flirting would have to stop for now, but I thought that might be a good thing. I don't know how the girl did it, but she tied my ass in knots.

Zandra had taken the chair next to mine. "You want a cold beer, Zandra?"

She hopped up. "I'll get you one, but I'm good." She looked at the others. "Can I grab you guys one?"

I got up, stopping her. "No. I'll get them. You take a seat. You're not working today."

She kept heading to the fridge anyway. "Sit down, Kane. I'll get them. It's fine."

"No." I grabbed her by the waist, picking her up then putting her back in the chair. "I'll get them."

"Fine." She laughed. "But can you get me an apple juice?" She looked at Fox, who stood near us tossing the baseball into the air and catching it. "If Fox will share with me, that is."

"Yeah, sure." He stopped throwing the ball and looked right at me. "See, Dad, she's not an alcoholic just 'cause she works at a bar."

I froze then looked at Zandra, who thankfully wore a smirk. "I told you he has no filter."

She shook her head as Aunt Nancy put her palm over her face in embarrassment. "For the record, I'm not an alcoholic, or drug addict, nor am I promiscuous, or any of the other things you've probably been thinking about me, Kane Price," she stated for all of us to hear.

"What's promiscuous mean?" Fox blurted.

"Never mind," I grumbled, then looked at Zandra. "And I'm sorry for even saying those things out loud. In my defense, I didn't know he was eavesdropping on my private conversations with other people."

"Yeah, Dad." He tossed the ball up really high then looked at me. "I'm pretty much always listening."

"Good to know," I said, then got the drinks.

Zandra looked back and forth at my aunt and uncle. "So you two tracked down my family, found the adoption agency I registered at, and even managed to get my son in the end. That's just plain amazing to me. How'd you do it?"

My uncle laughed. "I was in Special Ops in the Navy."

"And I was a secretary for a private investigator," Aunt Nancy added. "Together, we were an unbeatable team. Kane's parents called us in as soon as Kane told them the news. We all wanted to make sure the baby got to stay in the family."

Uncle James went on, "We took him home a couple of days after he was born. We were going to keep Fox whether he was really Kane's or not. But we didn't want to introduce Kane to the baby until we knew for certain whether he was his or not."

"So we waited for the DNA test to come back," Aunt Nancy said as she popped the top on her beer. "A week later we knew Fox was indeed Kane's, and we brought him home to Charleston to meet his father and grandparents."

Zandra looked a little misty-eyed. "And he's always lived in a home with a loving family. You have no idea how many nights I lay awake, worrying about him, wondering if he was okay. And to find out that he was more than okay … it means everything to me." A tear fell down her cheek, and I leaned over, wiping it away.

"I know now that I should've tried to contact you once you turned eighteen." I put my arm around her shoulders, giving her a little squeeze. "I knew your parents must've had a lot to do with you giving the baby up, from the story your neighbor told me. But a part of me thought that you would've found some way to keep him if you'd really wanted to. I had no idea the extent they would go to keep you from talking to anyone. I'm so sorry for that, Zandra."

The way she leaned her head on my shoulder made my heart race. "I don't blame you, Kane. Don't be sorry for anything. I'm just so glad you've been such a great father to him. You have no idea how grateful I am to you and your whole family."

Fox had to chime in, "And I'm grateful for you, Mom." He came up behind her and put his arms around her neck. "I love you so much." Then he kissed her cheek, making the tears really pour from her pretty blue eyes.

I laughed and got up to grab some napkins for her. "I've got ya."

"I'm sorry for being so emotional." She took the napkins I handed her, drying her tears. "I'm not usually like this."

Aunt Nancy reached over, patting her on the leg. "It's understandable, honey. Tell me, have you ever gotten any help after the trauma you've been through?"

I knew that was a touchy subject, so I tried to change the topic of conversation. "So, who wants to help me in the kitchen for a few minutes? Zandra?"

"Oh, yeah, I can help." She got up, sniffling still, and came with me.

"We'll hang out here with Fox," Uncle James called out to us.

Zandra leaned in close to whisper, "Thank you."

"No problem." I led her into the kitchen and went to get the meat from the fridge. "I didn't really need any help. I just thought you needed saving."

"I figured." She leaned back against the counter then blew her nose. "Where's the trash can?"

I pointed at the door behind her. "Behind that door."

She walked away and I watched her go. Her ass looked so enticing in the shorts she wore, which fit her just right. "Those blue jean shorts and that white T-shirt look good on you, Zandra."

When she came back out, she had a grin on her face. "You think so?"

My cock sprang to attention as she walked toward me. Her tits bounced just the slightest bit under her shirt. Her dark hair cascaded around her shoulders. Then she was right there, within reach. But my hands were filled with a tray of meat.

"I do think so. And I think they're gonna look even better when they're spread all over my bedroom floor. After I take each piece off of that smoking hot body, one at a time." I leaned over the tray and pecked her on the cheek.

With a little giggle, she turned away from me. "Kane Price, the things you do to my body are unreal."

Following right behind her, I watched her sweet ass sway with each step. "What I'm going to do to you later will be very real, baby. Very real."

"I can't wait." She held the door open for me and I moved passed her, stealing a little kiss before we headed out where everyone could see us.

"Neither can I." I loved the way her eyes barely opened after the kiss, as if my lips had a drugging effect on her.

She blinked a few times. "Oh boy, I'm in trouble."

"Yes, you are." Jerking my head toward the patio, I added, "Come help me with this meat."

I looked over at her, finding her biting her bottom lip. "How do you do this to me, Kane?" I saw goosebumps rise along her arm and found that unexpectedly erotic.

She wasn't lying. My words really did have a physical effect on her, and I liked that. I liked that very much.

Aunt Nancy had her phone in her hand, holding it up to her face, clearly talking over video chat. "Oh, here she is, Linda."

"My mom," I told her. "Go say hello."

Zandra looked a little shy. "Oh, Lord. How do I look?" She ran her hands through her hair.

"Beautiful, as always." I grinned at her.

Aunt Nancy turned the phone around, and there was my mother's face as she called out, "Come here, Zandra. Let me say hello to the woman who gave me that perfect grandbaby."

Waving, Zandra said, "Hello, Mrs. Price. It's nice to meet you."

Mom was quick to correct her. "Mrs. Price was my long-gone mother-in-law. I'm Linda. How do you like life with the boys so far?"

"Um, it's good. Today's the first day I've gotten to spend much time with them though, so it's still new to me." Zandra took a seat after Aunt Nancy handed her the phone. "I have to say that you've raised one heck of a son, Linda. I feel like I'm constantly being surprised by all of Kane's accomplishments. And he's the best father I've ever met. At least, so far he is." She looked at me then winked.

"And I'll continue to be." I placed the steaks on the hot grill, making smoke rise up. "Oh, if you could smell this, Momma, you'd be in heaven. When can you make it down to meet this little lady in person?"

"Not too far from now, I think." Mom looked at me now, as Zandra had turned the phone toward me while I spoke. "Your father has a doctor's appointment for his gout next week. I've got a dentist appointment the week after that. The dog has to get his rabies shot on Friday, and the bird will have to be sent to stay with the neighbors, who won't be back from Hawaii until the end of the month."

"So, next month, maybe?" I asked, as she'd pretty much used up what was left of this one.

"Probably. We'll have to see. You know how it goes with us. Maybe you guys could come here. I bet it would be much easier that way," Mom said.

I looked at Zandra. "What do you think? Do you want to go to California to meet my parents?"

"Um. Uh ..." Zandra looked like I'd put her on the spot. "I'll have to see. I've got to get a new job, and getting time off might be hard at a new place."

"We'll see what happens, Mom." I let her off the hook.

"Turn me back to you, Zandra," Mom told her.

Zandra turned the phone back around. "Hi, it's me again."

"I just want you to know that you've got a place in this family, girl. You're the mother of my favorite grandson," Mom said.

"I'm your only grandkid, Grammy," Fox called out.

"Speaking of my grandson, let me see that boy, honey."

Zandra turned the phone around so Mom could see Fox. He waved at the phone. "Hi, Grammy."

"Hi, handsome. I hope you come see me soon." She jerked her head as if gesturing to Zandra, who held the phone. "Talk your momma into coming to meet me. I can't wait to get to know her."

"Me too," he said. "You're gonna love her just like I do."

"I bet I will." Mom's eyes searched me out as I walked into frame. "Treat her right, Kane."

I looked at Zandra. "I will."

The blush on her cheeks made my heart race. That girl did things to me that I couldn't comprehend.

At that moment, I knew I wasn't going to make the same mistake I'd made with her all those years ago. I wasn't going to treat her like a piece of ass that I just had to have. And it hit me suddenly that I'd pretty much been doing just that so far. Well, that would have to change.

The rest of the afternoon and evening went great. Fox had Zandra read him a book when he went to bed, and I met her in the hallway once she was finished. "Hey."

She smiled coyly. "Hey."

"Is he asleep?" I leaned back against my bedroom door, putting one foot up behind me.

"Yes, he is." Zandra's eyes went to the floor, her hand moving through her hair a little nervously. "He's really a great kid, Kane. You've done such a great job with him. I mean it."

I crossed the hall to take her hand, leading her down the hall to the bedroom next to mine. "Thank you."

She watched me push the door open. "So, I guess this is good-night then."

"Uh huh." I ran my thumb up and down her palm. "It is. And I'm locking my bedroom door tonight. And I want you to lock yours too. Wanna know why that is, baby?"

Her eyes dropped a bit. "Because you don't want me." Her head fell.

"No." I took her chin, lifting her face up so she had to look at me again. "I want you more than I can put into words. But I don't want it to be like last time. I want you to know that I care about you the next time we make love."

"You do?" she asked breathlessly.

"I do." And then I kissed her. Softly, with compassion and caring. It was different than any other kiss I'd given her before.

When our lips parted, I saw the shimmer in her eyes. "That felt different."

"I thought so too. A good different. Not quite so lustful."

She nodded. "Goodnight, then."

"Goodnight."

CHAPTER 23

Zandra

MOVING each dress one at a time, I searched for a dress that looked right for a mother. Pulling a nice blue one off the rack, I held it up. "How about this one, Taylor. Does this scream "mom" to you?"

She made a face that told me she hated it. "No, that one screams grandma." She held up a very short, hot pink dress with spaghetti straps. "I like this one. You should go try it on."

"That's not a mom dress at all, Taylor." I shook my head. "You're really no help. Maybe I should ask a saleslady for some help instead."

Taylor looked around. "Good luck with that. This place is one step below Target."

A woman, who looked to be in her thirties and who had two little kids sitting in her shopping cart, came up behind me. "Sorry to interrupt, but did I hear you say you were looking for something that looked a little more motherly?"

I turned around and smiled at her, checking out her outfit. "I am. Am I in the wrong department or something?" I asked.

"No, but this place just might not have what you're looking for. I can see that you've got some fashion sense, but your style is a little young." She tapped her chin as she looked me up and down, taking in my short skirt, tight button-down shirt, and thigh-high boots. "I suggest you go down the Savanah Highway and look for a place called Jordan and Jane. They've got a great selection, and it's a good mix of fashionable yet sophisticated. I know a lot of young moms who shop there."

"Thank you." I looked at Taylor. "I'm going to head that way, and you're not coming with me."

"Party pooper," Taylor said, then stuck out her tongue. "Have it your way."

"I've got to try harder to be the mom Fox deserves, Taylor." I put the dress I'd been holding back on the rack.

The woman who'd made the suggestion perked up a little at what I'd said. "Do you mean Fox Price?"

I looked at her again. "Yes. Do you know him?"

"He and my son, Jake, go to school together. He's been telling everyone about how he found his mom." She clapped her hands. "And here you are. Isn't this exciting?"

"Sure." To be honest, I found it a bit more nerve-wracking than exciting. I thought I'd have a bit more time to settle in as Fox's mom before having to meet the other parents from his school.

"I'm on the parent-teacher board. It's kind of like the PTA, but since the school is private, we call it that." She put her hand on my shoulder, as if we were old friends. "I would love to see you at the next meeting. Dr. Price always goes. He's an avid supporter. I can't wait to see you around the campus."

"Um, thanks. I'm Zandra Larkin, and you are?" I asked, as she'd yet to tell me her name and I didn't want to go to some meeting at the school without knowing the name of at least one other mom.

"Oh, how silly of me." She extended her hand and I shook it. "I'm Christina Flanders."

"Okay, well, thanks for the fashion advice. I look forward to seeing you at the meetings, I guess." I grabbed my purse out of the empty basket I'd been pushing around.

But Mrs. Flanders had one more thing to ask, "So, how is he?"

I wasn't sure what she was asking me. "How is who?"

"Dr. Price." She fanned herself. "That man is something else. I'm assuming since you're back in his life, you must be back in his bed. Who could resist?"

"Um, I'm not really comfortable answering that." I started to walk away, feeling my body heat with anger and shock at her forwardness.

Who the hell does she think she is?

"So, you're not with him?" she called out after me.

"Not officially, she's not," I heard Taylor say. "But she sure does have a thing for him, I can tell ya that."

People would talk. I should've known that. But I hadn't realized how much it would bother me.

As I walked out the door a couple of young girls, who looked like they were still in high school, looked me over. "Cute outfit," one of them said.

I couldn't even say thank you. I knew I must've looked like one of them, and not like the mother of a ten-year-old. Maybe that was why that Flanders woman thought she could ask me such a thing. I looked like I was in junior high, like I was the kind of immature young woman who would love nothing more than to gossip about boys.

Getting into my car, I looked in the mirror on the back of the sun visor, checking myself out. My makeup was thick, over the top. I was wearing false eyelashes, and I'd plumped up my lips using the most expensive plumper I could afford. My hair was curled in a way that accentuated the blue streaks. This was not a look I would associate with a responsible mother.

"You are the mother of Fox Price. You have got to get yourself together for that boy." I looked in that mirror and swore I would never again see such a childish face looking back at me.

Glancing around the shopping center, I found a hair salon and drove straight to it. Marching inside, I spotted a flamboyant male hairdresser. He spotted me too, and he stood there, looking at me with his hand on his hip. "Oh, honey, please tell me you're here to let me make you over."

I put my hands on my hips. "I'm the mother of a ten-year-old boy. I need you to make me look like it."

"You don't happen to have any pictures of you with your natural hair color, do you?" he asked me as he pushed his hand through his own thick head of dark hair.

Pulling out my cell, I wiggled it at him. "I do."

Two hours later, I emerged with a bare face and a head full of the same brown hair that I'd had in high school. The hairdresser had even added in caramel highlights that looked exactly like the ones I'd had naturally back then. The cut was still long, but fell in gentle waves.

Now all I needed were the right clothes, and I'd finally feel like a mom.

I got back in my car and drove down the highway until I spotted the sign that led me to Jordan and Jane. The price tags were a bit on the scary side, but the quality and style were worth it. Finally, this was exactly what I'd been looking for.

I left the store with a bag full of outfits that would make any kid proud to call me Mom. Sensible shoes, pants that fit just right, though not too tight, and shirts that covered me up respectably.

Once I got home, I put on some makeup, though I used it sparingly, toning it way down from the way I'd been wearing it for the past eight or so years. Emerging from my bedroom after putting on a pair of pale green slacks with a light gray, silky top and flats to match, I made Taylor's jaw drop when she first spotted me.

"Who the hell are you and what have you done with Zandy?"

"You like?" I asked as I spun around, running my hands through my hair.

"Um, well, let's see," she held her chin as she looked me over. "I hardly recognize you. So there's that. You're very pretty. Gorgeous, even. But you're not you."

"I know!" I shouted with excitement. "Isn't it great?" I skipped across the room and went to get a glass of wine. "I feel so ... I guess the word is classy."

"Yeah, you look classy." Taylor frowned at me. "You don't look like a cocktail waitress, Zandy."

"I know." I took a drink of the red wine then smiled. "It feels so cool."

"Yeah, sure." She seemed skeptical. "Um, how much do you think you'll make in tips looking like that?"

Shrugging, I didn't really care much about that. "You know I'm looking for another job, Taylor."

"As what?" She eyed me then took my glass from my hand, stealing a drink. "A schoolmarm?"

I took my drink back. "Come on, Taylor. I don't look that prudish. I just look better. More mature. Sophisticated, even." I looked at myself in the mirror behind the table. "I like it. Do you think Kane will, too?"

"Sure." She got her own glass and filled it to the brim with wine. "I would guess that he likes women who look like you. Old."

"Old?" I gave my reflection another look. "I don't look old. I don't have any wrinkles or blotchy skin." I ran my hands over my boobs. "No sagging tits. You don't know what you're talking about."

She flopped down on the sofa. "Not, like, physically old. Like mentally old. You know?"

"Mature?" I asked as I went to take a seat too, making sure to sit like a lady. Legs crossed at the ankles, the way the queen grandmother taught her princess granddaughter in that movie.

"Yeah, mature," Taylor said as she gave me an eyeroll. "Boring."

"Hm." I looked at her then took another sip of my wine. "Now I can see why parents find the eyeroll so annoying."

"Funny how you were rolling your eyes at me just yesterday," she mused, "and now that you're dressed like a nun, you're condemning them."

I didn't care what she said. I wasn't going to let her get to me. I sat there, sipping my wine with great satisfaction, knowing I would stun both Fox and Kane.

"What's Rob gonna say, I wonder?" Taylor pondered.

I hadn't thought about him even once during my whole makeover. "Do you think he'll fire me?"

"If you do your makeup closer to what you usually do and then pull your hair into a messy pony, you might fit in. The uniform would not look right on you if you kept up this subdued look that you've got going on right now." She sat up, looking me over. "Yeah, just cake on makeup and mess that hair up and you'll keep your job."

But I didn't want to go back to that look. I wanted to stay the way I was. I felt more comfortable than I'd ever felt before. "I can't. I'll have to let Rob know that I'm looking for a new job. But I won't cake on the makeup or do my hair any differently."

"Bye, then," she said with a snarky tone.

Taking a long drink, I wondered if I'd just made a big mistake. Had I jumped into something before I was ready?

I knew I was ready to make this change in my life—I wanted to make it more than anything. And that included changing my job. But I didn't have a new one yet, and it wouldn't be good to lose it before I found something else. Maybe I'd moved too fast.

When my cell rang, I checked the screen and saw that it was Kane. "Oh, I'll take this in my room."

"Why, you two gonna have phone sex and you don't want me to hear?" she joked.

"No. He's decided to treat me like a lady, I'll have you know." I closed the door behind me then answered the call. "Hi there."

"Hi, baby. How was the rest of your day?" he asked me with that smooth, deep voice.

"Good." We'd had a wonderful breakfast together at his place, Fox, Kane, and I. "You make a mean ham and cheese omelet. Thanks for making breakfast. If you ever let me sleepover again—"

"Which I will," he interrupted.

I felt my body heat up. "Well, then I'll make breakfast next time. I've been watching cooking shows on *YouTube* all day long. And I even watched some videos about all those gadgets in your kitchen and found out how they work. So I just might surprise you guys next time."

"That sounds like a great idea." He paused then went on, "I know you've got work tomorrow night, but I was wondering if you could call in or something so that I can take you out on a real date. I really meant it when I said I want to show you that I care about you before we do anything sexual."

That was a great reason not to go into work the next day. And that would give me at least one more day to try to find another job so that I wouldn't have to worry about going back to Mynt. "That sounds nice, Kane. I would love to go out on a real date with you."

He sounded relieved, as if he'd thought I might've said no or something. "Good. So, I'll pick you up at seven?"

"That sounds good to me. Should I get all decked out, or just wear something nice and simple?" I asked, secretly pleased I'd done all that work on myself just in the nick of time.

"Um, well, let's see. This was supposed to be a surprise." He seemed to be stumbling around his words, which wasn't like him. "Well, I've made reservations at Circa 1886 for us. I'll be wearing a black suit and tie. So, can you dress accordingly?"

Now I was really glad that I'd had my hair done and bought some appropriate clothes. "I believe I can." I tried to picture what he'd look like in a suit and tie, and my blood rushed through my veins. "A suit and tie, huh? I can't wait to see that."

"I clean up all right," he said with a chuckle. "I can't wait to see what you come up with."

I could not wait to see his face when he saw me the next evening. "I just might surprise you, Dr. Price."

"I hope you don't take this the wrong way, but I hope you do."

I took a drink of the wine, trying my best not to get offended by what he'd said, but I had to admit that it did sting a bit. "I know I don't look the part, Kane."

"I don't want to tell you what to do, Zandra." He huffed. "I just want things to be as good as they can be for us. For all of us."

"And that means I need to have a respectable job, drive a respectable car, and look respectable too." I knew what I needed to be for him and for Fox.

"Image is kind of important in our world. At Fox's school and at my work," he said. "It may seem like an arrogant thing to say, but it's true, Zandra. If I had green hair and a Mohawk, how many patients would I have?"

He must've thought I was being sarcastic, but I wasn't. "I understand, Kane. I agree."

The sigh he let out told me more than his words had. He needed me to be more. He needed me to be mature, responsible, and he needed more than just my words to reassure him that I was on the same page. Most of all, he needed me to not be an embarrassment to him or our son.

And that was okay. I was ready.

CHAPTER 24

Kane

ZANDRA HAD BEEN one of those rare natural beauties back in high school. I remembered really seeing her for the first time. She was a sophomore, probably fourteen or fifteen. Her hair wasn't very long, just shoulder-length, a rich chestnut brown color with golden strands that would catch the sun now and then.

She'd been walking outside, along the sidewalk. Alone, with books in her arms covering a chest that hadn't blossomed yet, she kept her eyes on the ground in front of her.

I'd brushed my shoulder against hers as we'd passed each other, and she didn't even blink an eye or look my way at all. She'd merely whispered a timid, "Sorry," as if it was her fault.

Stopping in my tracks, I'd turned around to watch her walk away and had wondered what the hell was up with her. Was she stuck-up? Or was it just insecurity that made her so shy?

Of course, later I'd figured out it was insecurity. And I thought she still had a strain of it running through her now. That had to be the reason behind all the makeup and the dyed hair. The skimpy wardrobe, I assumed, was so she could fit in with her younger co-workers at the club.

The way she presented herself now was so different than how she'd been in high school, and I didn't truly believe that either version was her real self. While she used to hide from people by looking at the ground and trying to fade in the background, now she was using her clothes and style to hide the true Zandra from others.

I really did believe that, with my help—and Fox's too—Zandra would be able to grow into the woman she was truly meant to be. I knew she'd settle into adulthood and become the kind of mother Fox needed; she just needed someone to go on that journey with her.

Step one was taking her to a nice place where her too-young style wouldn't fit in. And I hoped that she would transform accordingly into the gorgeous butterfly I knew was ready to break out. I couldn't wait to see the woman I knew was buried inside all the makeup, dye, and skimpy clothes.

Some people might call me manipulative and controlling, and I would have to say that there might be some aspects of my plan that would fit those descriptions. But in the end, my mission was only to help her become the confident and mature woman I knew she could be. Once she felt comfortable and stable in this new life, I'd step back and let her do whatever she saw fit.

The truth was that I could see Zandra in a light that she, herself, couldn't see. *Yet.* She couldn't see that woman who waited to come out, *yet.* But she would. And I just wanted that to happen sooner rather than later. For Fox, and for myself.

Sure, I could leave her just as she is. But then what?

Zandra would be a large part of Fox's life. We both hoped she would be at school functions, joining in and becoming a part of it the same way we had. We hoped she would come to his afterschool practices and his baseball games on the weekends. And neither Fox nor I wanted her to be ridiculed by anyone.

The cold hard truth was that if she didn't change her appearance, then the other moms and dads wouldn't see her the way we did. They wouldn't see the hardworking woman she'd become, who'd survived a difficult childhood that had only grown worse after I'd taken her virginity and left her with a baby growing inside of her. They'd never know how much that baby had changed her life, and all that she'd had to go through to get to where she was.

If I'd just been able to leave her alone all those years ago, she would've graduated from high school and most likely gone to college. Her parents seemed to care a lot about appearances too, after all. I was sure they would've made her go to college, like the rest of her graduating class.

But Zandra had missed all that because they'd kept her hidden at her home, which they'd made more like a prison. At least that's the way it sounded when she'd talked to me about it on the phone the week before.

I'd gotten to know a lot about her over our phone calls. And I had to admit that I had been wrong to judge her. I'd thought her weak. I'd thought she'd taken the easy road, leaving the harder one for someone else to take.

As easy as that road seemed to be, that road had a dead end, and it wouldn't be too many more years before she reached that ending. I'd never seen any thirty-year-old waitresses working at nightclubs in all my earlier years of partying. She wouldn't be able to work the types of clubs she was used to forever. And then what would she do?

I figured I might as well give her a little push, some incentive to move forward now, instead of waiting for the rug to be pulled out from under her later. And she might as well do it with Fox and me at the front of her mind, giving her a reason to strive for something more than she'd had before us.

Circa 1886 was the kind of restaurant where men wore suits and ties, and women wore gorgeous evening gowns. If she didn't know the place by reputation, I knew she'd be able to get an idea of the dress code from looking it up online. She would see exactly what she would have to wear in order to fit into this kind of place.

And I just had to wait a few minutes longer to see if she was able to meet this one challenge out of the many more she'd likely have to face in the coming months.

I'd texted her right when I left my house, telling her I was on my way. She'd texted me back, telling me to wait outside in my car, that she would come out to me. So I did as she'd asked, and I sat waiting. Five minutes later, she came out the door.

At first, I thought I had to be seeing things. Maybe it wasn't her at all coming out of her apartment and walking toward me. But then again, it had to be. There was that same chestnut brown hair she'd had back in high school, the evening sunlight making a few blonde strands glisten. She was still wearing a bit of makeup, but only enough to enhance her natural beauty. No fake lashes, no overly plump lips. Just her lovely features shining through.

I got out of the car, obviously stunned. "Zandra. My God."

She smiled brilliantly as she spun around slowly. The chocolate brown dress she wore went below her knees, the bottom billowing out, flowing in the breeze as she turned around. "You like the new me, Kane?"

The boatneck top covered her breasts, not allowing any cleavage to show, but accentuating their round curves. A thin blue belt showed off her narrow waist, and it matched her two-inch heels. Creamy pearl earrings matched the necklace that hung around her long neck, which was beautifully on display thanks to her hair being pinned up.

She stopped turning to look at me. "Kane?"

"Uh ... umm." I was speechless.

She laughed lightly as she walked toward the passenger door. "I know. I look very different. Older."

Her movement pulled me out of my daze. "Older? No." I hurried to get to the door before she did, opening it for her. "I would use many words to describe you—gorgeous, sexy, and naturally beautiful —but old would never cross my mind, Zandra Larkin. I'm very proud to have you at my side this evening."

"Ah." She ran one finger along my jawline. "He approves. I've done good then."

"You've done better than good." I pressed my lips to her cheek. "You've taken my breath away. That's never happened to me before."

Her dark blue eyes peered into mine. "Really?"

All I could do was nod as I stared back into those eyes, getting lost in them. The same ones I'd looked into so long ago. No thick black mascara surrounded them. No eyeliner either. Just the slightest bit of brown mascara and neutral eyeshadows that blended in so well, they looked like they were hardly there at all.

She sat in the car with a sweet smile on her pink lips. I closed the door and went around to get in, taking a deep breath to try to shake off this star-struck feeling.

She'd thrown me for a loop, and I had to get back on track.

With step one completed, I knew the next few ones were up to me. And I was feeling very optimistic about them.

It took me a little while to come back around to being myself as we drove to the restaurant. But when I reached over, taking her hand in mine, her touch, and the connection that always sprang between us, helped me. "How did your boss take you calling in tonight?"

"Not well." She sighed. "And I know he's going to bitch me out for this change in my look."

"Fuck him." I stopped at a red light and looked at her. "You look amazing."

The smile that curved her lips made my heart race. "Thank you, Kane. Taylor wasn't on board with my new look, either. She said it makes me look old."

"You look mature," I told her. "And it suits you. Please tell me you won't go back to the old look."

With a nod, she said, "I promised myself that very thing yesterday. I won't be going back, only forward from now on."

Relief spread through me. "That's so good to hear, baby. So good. Forward is the best way to go. Unless you're a girl and you're dancing, then backward is okay. But only then."

She laughed and I chuckled with her, and it felt amazing.

The atmosphere of the restaurant did much to make the night special for us both. She ran her hand over the white linen tablecloth after we'd sat down. "Don't laugh at me please, Kane." She looked at me with a shy grin. "I've never been in a place like this before. It's kind of surreal. I just want to touch everything, to make sure I'm not dreaming."

Reaching across the table, I took her hand in mine. "You're not dreaming. And I think it's adorable that you feel that way. To be honest, I feel that way too."

Her chest heaved as she sighed and looked around. "I'll remember this forever."

"Good. So will I." I let her hand go to take a look at the menu. "I think we should start with the chilled oysters Rockefeller." I put it back down, taking her hand again. "Does that sound good to you?"

"It does. It sounds very good to me." She leaned in close, then whispered, "But aren't those considered an aphrodisiac, Dr. Price?"

Winking, I answered, "Yep."

"If it helps you make any plans for later tonight, then I want you to know that you're making me feel very special and cared for." Her smile turned sexy. "If you know what I mean."

My cock was hard in an instant, and I was glad for the cover of the table. "I do." I could've jumped her gorgeous bones right then. But I wanted things to progress a little further than they had so far.

The waiter came back with our white wine and two glasses. "Have you made a decision on the appetizer?" He poured a little bit of the wine in one of the glasses then handed it to me.

"We have," I told him then tasted the wine. "And this is perfect."

He filled a glass, placing it in front of Zandra, and then filled mine the rest of the way, leaving the bottle on the table. "And what can I bring you first?"

"The oysters to start," I let him know.

"I'll get to that and be right back to take the rest of your order." He left us, and I saw Zandra watching him.

"I've never served food before. I wonder if I would be any good at it. It seems kind of complicated," she pondered.

I didn't want her to limit herself to just serving, but I didn't want to interfere with every decision she made, either. "I'm sure you could be great at it if you put your mind to it, Zandra." I took her hand again, letting our clasped hands rest on the table. "Whatever you put your mind to, I'm sure you can do. Don't let anything stop you."

With a nod, she pulled her hand out of mine to pick up the menu. "I suppose I should have a look at this so I can make a decision before he gets back."

I opened mine too. "The Piedmontese beef looks good to me."

"I'm torn between the catfish and the scallops," she said, then looked up at me. "The sides are throwing me off, though. I've got no idea what any of them are. But I know I like scallops, and I know I like catfish. Do you think you can take a look at them and tell me which one you would pick?"

I took a look at the sides and read that a grilled zucchini dish with a fancy Italian name was served with the scallops. She had liked the ones I'd made when we had our little Sunday dinner. "I think you'd like the scallops."

Putting the menu down, she picked up the wine and took a drink, looking happy as a clam. "I bet I will, Kane. Thank you."

Finishing the decadent meal with a dessert called Island Bombe, we left the restaurant and headed back to take her home. Even though all I really wanted to do was take her back to my bedroom and kiss her all over.

Resting her head on the back of the seat, she ran her hand over her flat stomach. "Oh my gosh, that was the best meal I've ever eaten. Thank you so much for taking me, Kane."

"If you'll accept more dates with me, then I'll take you to a ton more places you've never been." I took her hand, holding it between us on the console. "So, do you think I'll get a second date?"

Turning her head, she looked at me, blinking slowly. "A second, third, fourth—you name it, you've got it. I had more fun with you tonight, and on Sunday too, than I've ever had with anyone."

"If the weather is good, we could take the yacht out this coming weekend." I knew I was getting ahead of myself, but I couldn't seem to stop.

"If I'm off, then I would love to join you." She turned her head to look out the window. "Hopefully, I'll have a different job by then. I won't know my schedule until that happens."

I pulled up in front of her apartment. "Here we are." Her hand in mine felt good, comfortable—right.

She looked back at me. "Yep." She moved her fingers a little. "I guess this is goodnight, then."

With a nod, I said, "I guess so."

"Okay, then. Thanks again. I had the best night of my life." She tried to pull her hand out of mine.

I held it tight. "Me too."

She looked at our hands. "Are you going to let me go, Kane?"

"Do I have to?" I wanted her. I wanted her more than I ever had.

She smiled. "Did those oysters get to you?"

Shaking my head, I admitted, "You got to me."

"I bet they helped," she said with a smile. "Would you like to come inside?"

"I would. But I'm warning you, I'm going to pull you into my arms and kiss those sweet lips, and I'm not going to want to stop." I pulled our hands up to my lips then kissed hers.

"I won't want you to stop." She leaned in. "Let's go inside, Kane."

"You know what that means." I looked into her eyes. "I really do care for you, Zandra Larkin. More than I've ever cared about any woman."

"Good." She kissed my lips just once with a soft kiss. "So let's go inside and I can show you how much I care about you, too."

Lord, have mercy!

CHAPTER 25

Zandra

THANKFULLY, Taylor was working that night. And that meant we had the place to ourselves for at least four hours. Probably even more than that, if she went out to eat with the other employees we worked with.

My body already tingled at the thought that I'd get to feel Kane's hands all over me again. Many times throughout the years I'd ached to feel the man's touch again. No one had ever even come close to comparing to Kane. Even though he'd been just a seventeen-year-old teen when we'd had our one night of sinful pleasure, he'd known his way around my body. I couldn't wait to see what he'd learned in the last decade.

Kane held out his hand, palm up. "Give me your keys, and I'll open the door."

Placing them in his hand, I purposely let my fingertip graze his palm as I licked my lips. I was sure what I wanted to do to the man was considered criminal in some states, and I was going to do everything that I'd ever dreamed of doing to him. "Here ya go."

Not moving for a beat, he eyed my finger as it moved over his palm. "Oh, baby, you're not gonna hold anything back from me, are you?"

All I did was shake my head. Seeing that, he hurried to unlock the door and then grabbed my hand, pulling me inside. I kicked the door closed then he pushed me up against it, forcing a heavy breath out of my lungs. His mouth came to mine, inhaling the breath I'd exhaled.

I felt his hand behind me, locking the door.

Always the responsible adult.

At least he'd had the wherewithal to think about that. I hadn't thought about anything but him and how badly I wanted to be naked with him ASAP.

Our tongues fought for control as his kiss went deep and sensual. I had no choice but to give in to his demands. Pulling his lips from mine, he whispered, "Take me to your bedroom?"

Taking his hand, I led him through the dark apartment to my bedroom where he promptly closed the door behind us, locking that one too. Waiting for him to tell me what he wanted me to do, I stood there in silence. It took me back to that night when I hadn't a clue what sex was about, and how he'd taught me so much in the few hours we'd had together.

Pushing me back a bit, he ran his hands over my shoulders then turned me around to unzip my dress, letting it fall in a heap around my feet. Next to go was the pearl necklace, then the matching earrings. He walked away from me, putting them neatly on the dresser, then he stood there in the dim light.

I looked over my shoulder to see what he was looking at, as I could feel his eyes on my body. In only a bra and panties, I felt on display for him, and I liked the way it felt. I ran my hands down my sides, leaving them on my thighs.

"Step out of the shoes and go to the bed, Zandra." His eyes stayed on my body as I did what he said.

I didn't take a seat, as he hadn't told me to. I did remember that Kane liked to be in control. He'd loved orchestrating every little detail and aspect of what we'd done that night so long ago, and I figured he still liked things that way.

It seemed like forever before he began undressing himself. Again, I was taken back to that night. He'd stood in front of me, taking his clothes off slowly. I was so shy back then that I'd ducked my head. That had made him stop, pull my head up by my chin, and tell me to look at him. I'd done as he'd wanted me to back then, and I was ready to do the same now.

Reveling in each inch of his tanned skin that was revealed, my body pulsed with excitement, want, and need. Once he was completely naked, I gasped at his cock, which was somehow even larger than I'd remembered. "Kane!" I yelped, unable to take my eyes away.

With a wink, he moved toward me. "Yeah, I kept growing in a couple places even after high school, baby." His hands made quick work of my bra before he ripped my panties off me, making me gasp again.

My thighs shook as the material cut into them for only a second before breaking free. I reached out, clutching his muscular biceps to steady myself. His hands finally ran up my body, gliding along both sides before he took me by the waist, lifting me up then laying me back on the bed. Pulling my ass back to the edge of the bed, he grinned at me before going to his knees.

I couldn't breathe as his lips pressed against my throbbing pussy. He took each leg behind the knee, lifting them both up then placing my heels on the bed. Totally spread and open for him, he went to work.

Grabbing two handfuls of the bedspread underneath me, I held on tightly as Kane kissed, licked, and sucked me into a state of arousal that seemed as close to heaven as I'd ever been.

He'd been good at oral sex back then, but now, he was excellent. I didn't want to think about who he'd practiced on but had to admit that I was pleased that he'd gotten even better.

One long lick up, then he went back down through the folds with his pointed tongue before pushing it into me. He used it to fuck me into a mindless state that left me screaming as an orgasm moved through me, starting at the top of my head, ending in my toes.

Satisfied with my reaction, Kane got up. He walked back to the pile of his clothing and leaned down, taking something out of one of the pockets. The light from the window, the only light in the room, caught the shiny foil packets.

I leaned up on my elbows, looking at what he had. "I'm on the Pill, Kane. You don't have to use those. And this time you can trust me. Take a look at the package of birth control pills on my dresser."

He did take a quick glance at the pills on the dresser, but he kept coming toward me with the strand of condoms still in hand. "Good. I'm glad you've decided to take care of the birth control thing." Pulling one of them open, he slipped it over his hard dick.

"So why are you still putting one on then?" I wanted to feel the real him inside of me. Skin to skin.

"Diseases," he said nonchalantly, as if that wasn't insensitive or insulting in the least.

"I don't have any diseases, Kane." I moved my body up on the bed then pulled the blanket down so I could get on the sheet underneath it.

I couldn't believe the lopsided grin he had on his face. "And how do you know if you have any or not? Did you get checked out after your last sexual encounter?"

He'd struck a nerve. I hadn't gotten checked out in the last six months. I'd only had sex a few times though. And with guys who didn't seem like they had any diseases.

When I didn't answer, he climbed onto the bed, giving me that knowing look he had. "So, let me just take precautions this time, baby. I'll personally give you an exam tomorrow at my office so we can be sure you're clean."

I had to be honest with him. "All this talk of diseases has put a bit of damper on things."

With a kiss to the tip of my nose, his knee moved between my legs, spreading them open again. "Sorry about that, baby. It's a necessary evil. And you can imagine how much both of our spirits would be dampened if I came up with an STD. Let me take care of things. I'm pretty damn good at it." He pushed his fat, long, hard-as-a-rock cock into me and everything I'd been thinking vanished in an instant. "Better?"

I moaned, low and slow. "Better."

Rocking back and forth, his body was tight to mine. The mound of flesh above his cock moved rhythmically over my clit as he moved deep inside of me. Unimaginable desire coursed through my veins as his lips pressed against mine.

My nails dug into his back as he took me higher and higher until a wave of intense pleasure shook me to my core. But he wasn't about to stop there. Just like before, first came the slow and easy, then came the rough and rowdy.

"On your knees, Zandra." Kane's eyes were ablaze with passion as he issued his command.

Squirming to get to that position, I held my breath, waiting for the first slap. A sharp sound pierced the air as he hit my ass, making it sting in the best way ever. Not many men knew just how to deliver a well-placed slap that would make a girl go wet all over.

Barbaric as it may seem, having my ass smacked by Kane sent me into a deep state of arousal that nothing else could. His hand connected with my ass over and over before he thrust his cock back into me.

Fucking me from behind, he stopped slapping my butt to put his pinky into my ass, making me squeal. My body was so overwhelmed by sensation, I could hardly control the sounds that were coming out of my mouth.

"We're gonna start spreading this out so I can take you here too, baby. I want to take you every way imaginable."

My inner thighs quivered as I thought about his fat, long cock plunging deep into my asshole. "Yes," I groaned with a raspy sound.

I felt him switch to a larger finger, which he pumped it into me at the same speed he pumped his cock. "Looks like you like the idea too. Your ass is really pulsing, baby. You want me to fuck your asshole, don't you?"

"I do," I growled. I did want that, so badly it wasn't right.

"Kissing your asshole, licking it, sucking it, biting the soft edges then slamming my hard cock into it, making you scream in the best pain imaginable before pumping it into you until my cum bursts inside of you."

He groaned then as his cock jerked inside of me. I didn't get to feel the hot fluid filling me; the condom caught all that. But I could feel the intense jerking and the way he moaned with every pulse sent me into another climax that made my head feel like it was floating.

Slumping over my back, he kissed me between my shoulder blades. "One down, only ten or eleven more to go." He pulled out of me, and I fell on the bed, face-first.

Panting, I tried to catch my breath before saying, "Fuck, that was good!"

"I need water." He walked to the bathroom attached to my bedroom, coming back out with a washcloth.

I rolled over to find his cock glistening where he'd wiped it clean, the condom gone. Wiggling my finger at him, I beckoned him to come to me. "There are a few bottles of water in my top drawer. I keep them there so I don't have to walk all the way to the kitchen if I get thirsty when I'm sleeping. You can drink one while you let me play with your sweet cock."

He went to get the water then came back to me. Opening the bottle, he said, "Get to it, baby." Then he held up one finger to stop me. "Wait. First, I want to get things straight between us. You're mine. I don't want to share you."

As if I'd ever want anyone else.

"Is that so?" I moved to the edge of the bed on my hands and knees then sat on my ass, my face level with his cock, which was already growing with arousal at the thought of me sucking him off.

"That's a fact, Zandra Larkin." He moved one hand through my hair, pulling out what was left of the pins that had held it up. My hair hung freely around my shoulders. "You're mine, and I'm yours. If you want me."

For a brief moment, I wasn't sure exactly what he meant. So I asked, "Does this mean that you and I are a couple?"

He nodded then took a drink. "It does."

I needed more clarification than that, though. "Even in front of Fox?"

Now he froze. His eyes went up as if he had to think about that, and I wasn't a fan of that at all. I started moving back on the bed but was stopped when he tightened the hand he had in my hair, wrapping his fist around the strands and preventing me from retreating from him any further. "Don't do that. We'll have to take things slow in front of him. But eventually, we'll let him know we're a couple. I just don't want to get his hopes up too early on."

"Can we hold hands and kiss each other on the cheek in front of him?" If he said no, then I wasn't going to go any further.

My body language may have told him that as he smiled at me before answering, "Yeah, we can do those things."

"Good. Then we can keep doing this thing, Dr. Price." Moving back into position, I stretched open my mouth, ready to show him what I'd learned during our years apart.

I hoped he would be pleased too.

CHAPTER 26

Zandra

ONE GLORIOUS MONTH passed with Kane and I sneaking in as much alone time as humanly possible. One steamy night, we'd even gone so far as to exchange our first "I love yous." Moving forward at what he considered a traditional speed, we hadn't been completely upfront with our son.

I did have the sneaking suspicion that Fox was getting wise to us though. He would stare at our clasped hands anytime he found us holding hands, a big grin on his face. He would pay attention when we gave each other modest kisses on the cheeks when we parted ways. But he never asked anything about any of it.

I assumed he just liked the time we all got to spend together, especially when we were doing all the things he'd wanted me to do with them. Going to his practices, games, parent-teacher meetings—doing the things that families would do together. All of those had our son on cloud nine.

When you added in spending every Sunday together, doing various fun things as a family, our son seemed very happy with the way life was going. And I had to admit that I was too. And Kane told me he was happy all the time.

The only bump in our perfect road was my job. Without any real education other than a high school diploma, my job search was severely limited. I'd applied for other jobs, but they all paid minimum wage. I couldn't live on that, so I was still working at Mynt as a waitress.

To say that Kane wasn't pleased with that was a huge understatement. "I don't understand, Zandra," were his exact words when I told him day after day that I hadn't found anything yet.

I had tried to explain to him the reasons I was having trouble finding a new job that would be more acceptable for the girlfriend of Dr. Price, not to mention the mother of his child. "Kane, you don't understand. I really only have Mondays free to go to interviews. Every other weekday I spend most of the day sleeping, catching up on my rest."

His expression would always become grim then. "Yes, I know that. But what you're failing to understand is that if you go ahead and get up an hour or two earlier, then you might have time to do an interview each day."

He had no idea that there just weren't that many jobs that I was qualified for, that I would even get an interview for. And I didn't know how to explain it to him without feeling pathetic as hell.

So, there I sat at the café we were to meet at for lunch, as I'd gotten up earlier than usual on a Friday to start trying harder, the way he wanted me to.

The waitress came to refill my coffee. Her dark hair had thick strands of gray in it. "More coffee, doll?"

Nodding, I asked, "Do you mind if I ask you how long you've been a waitress?"

She looked all of sixty to me, but I wasn't about to ask her actual age. "I've been a waitress since I was sixteen years old. I got knocked up by a loser in high school. Putting a roof over a kid's head wasn't easy when I was a damn kid myself, and all alone, too. All's I could do was work at the donut shop down the street from my parents' house. They would watch the baby for me most of the time."

Her story piqued my interest, since it was somewhat similar to mine. "So, your parents allowed you to keep the baby then?"

"Allowed me?" Her thinly drawn eyebrows rose on forehead. "Like they had a choice. I was having my baby. I didn't care if Clyde Barker was with me or not. I wanted my baby. And my parents had helped my older sister with hers too, so they were pretty used to it."

"That's good of them." I thought about why my parents couldn't have done the same for me. And when I thought about all that Kane's family had done, and the fact that they would've helped me then, no matter what, then I felt really miffed. "I wish more parents thought the way yours did."

"Yeah, they were pretty good to Brittany and me." She pulled out her cell then showed me a picture of her grown daughter. "That's her now. She's a dancer down in Florida. My only child. Some mothers might not be proud of the path she's taken, but I am very proud of her."

"Of course, you are," I said with an air of concern. "Why wouldn't you be? She's doing her best, after all."

"She is." She put the cell back in her apron pocket. "It ain't her fault that my parents were killed in a car wreck when she was only two, and we were on our own then. It was right after my high school graduation. They were in a head-on collision with a drunk driver, and our world turned upside down in a matter of a few hours."

I could not speak. She'd floored me. There I'd been thinking that she'd had help and that things hadn't been too rough for her. Not nearly as rough as things had been on me, I'd thought. In one fell swoop, she'd changed it all up.

Shaking her head, she poured coffee into my cup. I finally found my voice again, "So, what did you two do then?"

The way her eyes glazed over made my heart hurt. "We went to live with my older sister. Her husband raped me one night. I grabbed my baby girl and hauled ass away from there as fast as I could. I ended up in a woman's shelter."

"I hope that asshole got what he deserved," I said with indignation threading through my voice.

She only shook her head, making the gray strands flash in the overhead lights. "I didn't tell a single soul what he'd done to me. I knew my sister wouldn't believe me. I knew he would say I was a liar. So, I left and knew that it'd just be me and Brittany alone in the world from then on. And I never trusted any man ever again."

"You never got help?" I felt terrible for her and reached out to touch the back of her hand as she held the glass coffee pot.

Shaking her head, she said, "How can you get help when you refuse to tell anyone what's happened to you?" Then she looked right at me. Her lips formed a straight line as her dark eyes narrowed. "As a matter of fact, I can't believe I've just told you that. I've only ever told a few of my closet friends." With a huff, she turned and sped away as if I'd done something to force her to tell me her deepest, darkest secret.

With no idea how I could make her feel any better, I thought about my own dilemma. At least I didn't have anything as dark and evil as that hiding in my past. Everything that'd happened to me was out in the open. At least now it was.

Everything was looking up for me, except the job situation. There could be far worse things in my life holding me back, and I knew that.

When Kane pulled up, he parked in the front right next to my Mustang, which I'd yet to trade for another, more kid-friendly car. Without a new job, how could I make such a change without knowing what my income would be?

Besides, Fox liked that car. He thought it was cool. Kane could get over it. At least for a little while, I thought.

Smiling at me as he entered the café, Kane ignored the gawking young women who stared at him with mouths agape. Women of all ages couldn't help but gawk at the man—and though it always piqued that jealous side of me, I really couldn't blame them. He was gorgeous.

He came straight to me, leaning over to kiss me right on the mouth. "Hey, gorgeous."

"Hey, yourself, handsome." I pushed a menu to his side of the table as he took a seat across from me in the booth. In the month that we'd spent as an item, I had gotten very comfortable with the man.

"Did you find anything for me to eat here, Zandra?" His eyes scanned the menu.

"I was thinking that grilled chicken salad might be up your alley. And there's a steak too, but I doubt it'll be up to your high standards, Dr. Price." I reached over, moving my fingers over the back of his hand seductively.

"I doubt that too." He put the menu down. "Grilled chicken salad it is, then." Taking my hand, he pulled it to his lips, leaving a kiss on it. "I know it's Friday, but I thought you might call in sick tonight. I've got this itch I need you to scratch, and it's getting really bad."

Heat filled me. "Another itch, babe? Man. That makes four this week."

Not an ounce of shame existed in him. He'd come over before I left to go to work each night that week. And now it seemed he wanted the whole night with me.

"My aunt and uncle are taking Fox on a weekend adventure, and it starts right after school today. That means I'll be home all alone. Home." He leveled his eyes at me. "In my bed. The bed I hope you'll share with me one day. The bed I'd like to finally get you into, if just for one night or two." He winked at me. "Better yet, call in sick Friday and Saturday. I've just come up with an excellent idea, and I'll need those extra hours."

Laughing, I knew how the man's mind worked, and knew his idea would be plenty interesting—and plenty arousing. "I can't, Kane. I wish I could, but I just can't. It's a new month, and there are new bills to pay. I've gotta work this weekend. Sorry, hon."

Lacing his fingers with mine, he looked into my eyes. "I've come up with an idea that I hope you'll love as much as I do."

"What is it?" I asked as I gazed at him.

He's just so damn cute!

"Let me pay for you to go to school. You can do anything you want. I'll help you with everything. Together, we'll get you an education, Zandra. And you won't have to work at all, because I want you to focus on school. Move in with Fox and me. Be his full-time mom. If you're going to school, you'll even be on the same schedule as him, going to school when he does."

His words set off a fire in my belly. It filled it up, entirely. And then it made my blood hot. And that hot blood flooded my veins like molten lava. "No!"

How can he think I want him to take care of me?

"Why not?" he asked. He held tight to my hands even as I tried to pull away.

"I don't want to become your charity case, Dr. Price. I can do this on my own." He let go of my hand, letting me pull away from him.

With a huff, he rolled his eyes. "Zandra, how can you say that? You haven't done anything so far. And I don't mean that in a bad way. I just mean that you've never had the support system to do anything other than you've been doing. I can give you that."

"I've done fine on my own all these years, Kane." I got up, throwing my napkin on the table. "I've been fine figuring things out alone."

With a blank stare, he asked, "And how's that been working for ya?"

I didn't like the tone of that question and figured storming out was the only thing I could do.

Right?

CHAPTER 27

Kane

STUNNED, I watched her leave, thinking the whole time that she would see reason and turn around. That she'd come back to me and even say sorry. But I'd been wrong. Zandra got into her red Mustang and peeled out of the parking lot like a bat out of hell.

"Now, how the hell did she get her panties in such a twist over me asking her to move in with me while I paid for her to go to college?" I asked myself

A woman's voice answered the question I'd thrown out to the universe. "She don't want no one to take care of her."

Turning around, I found the waitress had come up behind me. Her gray-streaked dark hair told me she was an older woman, probably early sixties. I guessed she was probably a smoker, which made her look much older around the mouth and eyes. I'd learned long ago not to judge a book by its cover. The difference was in the wrinkles and lines and where they were on a person's face.

"And you know that because?" I asked the waitress, who was also looking out the plate glass window through which I'd watched Zandra's grand exit.

"I know that because I know a thing or two about damaged women," she informed me. Her dark eyes moved to mine then quickly away again. "I don't suppose you still want to order anything."

"No, I don't." Pulling out my wallet, I asked, "What's the bill?"

"She only had a coffee." She pulled out the ticket. "Guess I get screwed on this one." She put the bill on the table, and I could see that the total was only a dollar and fifty cents.

I gathered that life must've dealt her a very poor hand and I decided to make her day just a bit brighter. I pulled two crisp hundreds out of my wallet, laying them underneath the bill. "Sorry about that. I hope you have a nice day, ma'am." I didn't bother to look back to see her reaction to the money. I didn't need to see it.

All I needed was to find Zandra and straighten things out. It was hard for me to wrap my mind around her actions though. She needed some type of help, after all.

After getting into my car, I called the clinic to let them know I was taking the rest of the day off. Either I would spend it with Zandra, or, if she still didn't want to see reason, I would stay home. I wouldn't be any help to any patients with my mind elsewhere.

Figuring she'd gone to her apartment, I tried there first. I knew I could've just called her, but I thought she might not answer me. I had never seen her so angry. And over such a crazy thing, too.

When I turned the corner onto her street, I found Zandra talking to a man who was leaning up against a black Dodge Charger. By the way her hands were flying through the air and the way she paced back and forth, I thought the two of them were likely arguing.

Parking where she wouldn't notice me, I opened my passenger side window to see if I could hear anything. I could hear her yelling, but had no idea what she was saying.

The guy, who wore sunglasses, didn't seem to give a flying fuck if she was mad or not. He nodded, then walked around to get into his car. He left her standing there, glaring after him as he left the parking lot.

I pulled in, knowing something was wrong. She took one look at my car and turned to go into her apartment. But I parked and got out so fast that she wasn't able to make it before I caught up to her.

Taking her by the arm, I stopped her hasty retreat. "Zandra, what the hell is going on?"

Her arm shook in my hand, letting me know she was very upset. "Just leave me alone," came her teary reply.

I wasn't about to just leave her alone like this. "I can't do that, baby. I love you, you know that." I pulled her quivering body around to face me then hugged her tightly. "Please let me in. Tell me what's wrong?"

"I don't have a job anymore," she whimpered. "That was the manager, Rob. He told me that he heard I was looking for another job and that he didn't much like that. So he decided to let me go, to give me more time to find something else, he said. The asshole." She sniffled.

Kissing the top of her head, I rocked back and forth with her still in my arms. "Baby, that's actually great news. Now you have absolutely no reason not to take me up on my offer. Come live with me, let me take care of you just for a little bit. Let me pay for you to go to college. Please." I couldn't believe I was begging her to let me do so much for her, when so many people would jump at the opportunity. It felt crazy.

Her body went rigid, her hands fisted against my chest. "Let me go, Kane!"

"Baby." Nothing else could be said, as she hit me hard, square in the chest. I had to let her go, or she might hurt herself.

Glaring at me, she kept her fists balled at her sides as she took three steps back. "Kane, I don't want your pity. How come you can't see that?"

"It's love, not pity, Zandra. How come you can't see that?" I pulled my sunglasses off so she could see the concern in my eyes. "I love you. People who love each other do things for them. Do you see it as pity when I do things for Fox?"

"That's different." She put her face in her hands as she growled with frustration. "I'm nothing to you. He's your son."

"And you're his mother," I reminded her. "How can you think that you're nothing to me? You're just as important to me as he is. You gave him to me. Well, not that you wanted to, but you did. Even if I didn't love you and want to do this for you, I owe you everything for bringing that boy into this world. He made my life so much better than I knew it could be, and you I owe that to you."

Shaking her head, she pulled her tearstained face out of her hands, looking at me with such a sorrowful gaze. "I'm pathetic. There. I've been so afraid that you would find that out one day, and then this would all be over. But I want it out there for you now. I. Am. Pathetic. That's why I can't get a job. I couldn't even keep the one I had. I don't deserve you. I don't deserve Fox. I never fought to keep him the way I should have. Why should I get to have him in my life now?"

"You can't blame yourself for that, Zandra." I hated seeing her like this. She'd crumbled right in front of me, and I didn't know if I could help her feel better. "And don't ever call yourself pathetic again. You're anything but pathetic. Look at all that you've done for yourself."

"Yeah, I became a cocktail waitress. Woohoo!" She spun around in a circle as she pointed one finger in the air. "And now, I'm not even that."

"It's time for a change, baby. That's all. We all have to make changes. They're inevitable. You're hanging onto something when everything else is pulling you away from it, and it's hurting you right now." I took a step toward her, but she stepped right back, holding her hand up.

"Don't, Kane. Don't come and wrap your arms around me and try to make me change my mind." Her chest rose then fell as she sighed deeply. "I should've known this would never work. I should've never tried to be a part of your life, or Fox's. I'm no good for anyone. I never have been. I don't know what I was thinking." She looked up at me then back down at the ground. "You're so damn gorgeous. The way you touch me sends lightning through my veins. It's like a dream, but dreams don't last. Nothing like that can ever last."

"It can." I took a step closer. "And I feel the same way when you touch me, and you're gorgeous too, baby. And we created this fantastic little boy together. I want you and I to raise him together. From now on, baby. Don't say these things you're saying. I don't think you realize how much they hurt me."

Her lips trembled as she looked up at me. "I don't mean to hurt you. But I know I'll just end up disappointing you so badly if I stay around here. I know I'll disappoint Fox, too." Turning away from me, she walked to the door to her apartment. "I think it's best if I leave, Kane. I won't come back and bother you guys again. I love you and Fox too much to inflict myself on the two of you. I always just end up causing problems for people, and I'm not worth the trouble. Just let me leave. Let me just go back to what I've always done, taking care of myself the only way I know how." She looked so sad, and everything that she was saying was breaking my heart. But what she said next really shattered me. "I'm incapable of taking care of anyone else. My parents knew that, and that's why they made me give up Fox. I'm not meant to be loved—I don't deserve it."

I had never seen anyone look so broken. My heart felt like it had splintered, like it had burst apart into an abyss filled with sorrow. "Please don't go, baby," my words were little more than a whisper. "I love you. Please."

She didn't say a single word as she went into her apartment, closing the door behind her.

Shutting me out of her life.

CHAPTER 28

Zandra

NOTHING FELT RIGHT. My feet hit the tiled living room floor, but I didn't feel them taking me to my bedroom. When I fell on the bed, face-first, I didn't feel the impact of the mattress hitting the side of my face. I heard the air rush out of my lungs but didn't feel it.

I'd become numb.

The feeling was familiar. It was the exact same way I'd felt after my baby son was taken away from me. I'd closed myself off from everyone. I'd kept to myself, stayed alone as much as possible, only allowing myself to cry when I was alone.

I knew I couldn't risk being seen with tears in my eyes. Not after what had happened when Mom had caught me crying the day I came back from the hospital. "And what are those tears for, Zandra?"

Gasping, trying hard to catch my breath as the sobs had nearly robbed me of it, I said, "My son, Mother!" I'd held my side, the pain from crying making my whole body cramp.

"Your son?" She shook her head. "You don't have a son, Zandra. You had a bastard child. You brought evil into this world—what's made from sin will only bring more sin. Be glad we made you get rid of him. Let him be a problem for some other family." Her finger wagged in my face as she leaned over me as I lay in my bed, making me feel even more helpless than I'd felt when I was pregnant.

"Mark my words, Zandra, that child will bring nothing but pain and misery to the poor people who took him in. You sinned. You gave your virginity to a stranger. You had sexual relations out of wedlock. You didn't follow God's laws, and now you and the bastard child you bore will suffer for the rest of your eternal lives. Be glad your father and I didn't allow you to keep him. He would hate you for bringing this misery down on him anyway."

"Please, stop," I'd begged her as I felt the numbing sensation taking me over again. "Please don't wish anything bad for him. Please just let him live in peace. Please pray that the family who has him takes good care of him and loves him as much as I would have."

I sucked in a breath to replenish my lungs then closed my eyes, praying in silence inside my head so my parents couldn't hear me. I prayed as much as I could that my son was okay and that the people who had him would love him and give him a great life. A life I wouldn't have ever been able to give him.

How vividly I could recall her cackle as she left me there. My body felt as if it had been ripped apart from the emotional and physical trauma. She wouldn't allow me to take the pain medication the doctor had sent home with me, either. She'd thrown that out as soon as I got back home.

I only had my mind to ease the pain. Shutting everything off was the only thing that worked, and once that numbness overtook me, it worked well. Taking me over, putting me in a state that hardly felt like living. No, it couldn't be called living. I'd merely existed from that moment until the day I'd turned eighteen and left.

And I could go back to that state now that I'd given everything up again, I supposed. Then I opened my eyes as the sun shone in through the thin curtain. "I can't go back there."

There wasn't anyone putting a roof over my head this time around. I no longer had the luxury of simply going numb. Not anymore.

My chance encounter with Kane and Fox seemed to have been my undoing. I had known from the moment I met them, that it would only be a matter of time before it all fell apart. Life hadn't been great before, but it hadn't felt this bad in a very long time.

Rolling over, I got up and went to my dresser to pull out the bag I always put my tips in. Thanks to the busy weekends I had been able to save quite a bit of money. I had enough to get me somewhere else, to start somewhere new. I just didn't know where I wanted to go yet.

There was a clanking sound in the kitchen that drew my attention. I shoved the bag back into the drawer I'd pulled it out of then went to see what Taylor was up to.

She looked at me as I came into the kitchen. "What the hell has happened to you, Zandy?"

Wiping my eyes, I sat down with a thud at the dining table. "I've got to get the hell out of here, Taylor. I don't have a job anymore."

She yawned then took a bowl out of the cabinet. "I'm gonna make a bowl of cereal, want some? And what do you mean you don't have a job anymore?"

"Rob was waiting for me when I came home today after meeting Kane for lunch." I sniffled. "Oh, and we broke up, FYI."

The bowl dropped out of her hands, crashing onto the granite countertop and bursting into pieces. "What the fuck?" Her black-rimmed eyes stared at me with a stunned look. "Did he break up with you?"

"No." I shook my head then got up to help her clean up the mess, afraid she might cut herself. "I ended it all."

"Huh," she huffed. "Why would you do that?" She stepped back so I could move in and clean things up.

"Go sit." I pointed at the table. "I'll make you a new bowl of cereal."

Staggering to the table, she took the seat I'd vacated. Resting her chin in her hand, she asked, "So, tell me why you broke up with him."

"He offered to pay for me to go to college." I wiped the broken pieces of bowl onto a paper towel then tossed it all in the garbage can.

Opening the pantry, I looked at the boxes of cereal. "Frosted Flakes or Wheaties?"

"Flakes," she said, and then her hand hit the table hard, making me look at her. "There's got to be more, Zandy. Come on, tell me everything."

Pouring the cereal into the bowl, I put the box down on the countertop. "Look, it happened kind of fast. One minute I was sitting there, happily waiting for Kane to show up. And then he said some things that pissed me off. I left. He followed me, found out I'd been fired and tried to play the hero. I wouldn't let him. I don't need a hero."

The sound that came out of Taylor made me cringe, it sounded so guttural and instinctual. "Ha! The hell you don't, girl!"

"I don't!" When I opened the fridge to get the milk out, I saw a bottle of red wine and pulled it out.

May as well drown my sorrows.

"Shit, Zandy, every girl dreams of the day her knight in shining armor will show up in her life, sweep her off her feet, then take her away to the castle where she'll be his queen, and he'll be her king." She took the bowl I handed her. "Thank you," her brows went up high as she added, "Mom."

"Don't," I cautioned her. Turning away from her so she didn't see the tears that sprang to my eyes, I hated how that one word stabbed me like a dull knife right in the heart. "I can't be that boy's mother. He deserves someone better. Someone worthy of his love—someone who deserves him. Not me."

"You think you're unworthy of love?" she asked, then took a big bite of her cereal.

"I know I am." Filling a glass to the top with the wine, I took it and went to sit across the table from her. "If a person's parents can't love them, then who can?"

"Look, your parents were whack jobs," she informed me. "Sorry to say it like that, but it's true. And everyone deserves to be loved."

"Not me." I took a long drink, thinking it tasted dry and acidic, but not much caring. I just needed it to dull my inner pain.

I'd made a mess out of things. I'd made Fox and Kane think that I could be what they needed in their lives when I clearly couldn't. I had even let myself believe that I could do that.

What a loser.

"You're making the biggest mistake of your entire life, Zandra." She slurped up another bite of the cereal. "I mean it. And what about that poor boy? Fox is going to be so crushed if you walk out of his life when he just got you back."

"Look, you don't know the whole thing." I felt a mix of pain and anger at her words, knowing she was right, but also knowing there was nothing I could do to make things better.

I took another drink and noticed it didn't taste as bad this time. I was getting used to adjusting to things I didn't like. I could get used to being alone again. Not having love in my life again.

I've lived without it for twenty-six years. What's the big damn deal?

"Then tell me the whole story, Zandra." She picked up the bowl, draining the remaining milk. Setting it down on the table, she said, "You now have my undivided attention. And I have to warn you that I will be interrupting you when I have something to say."

"I know that." I rolled my eyes, taking another drink. "Okay, Kane asked me to let him pay for my college, and suggested I quit my job, move in with him, and let him take care of me."

The sarcasm in her voice told me she wasn't going to be very sympathetic. "What an asshole." Her eyes held mine, unmoving and stoic. "Now tell me the bad thing he did and help me understand why you broke things off with him."

"Well," I stopped to take another drink, holding up my finger for her to wait. "Ah. This wine ain't half bad. Anyway. I came home, and there was Rob."

"Yeah, you've already told me that," Taylor rudely interrupted.

"And he left me standing there, jobless and crying. Then Kane pulled up, and I tried to get inside before he could get to me." I paused to have another drink before carrying on. "But he caught me, and I had to listen to him tell me that he loved me and that he would take care of me. And I had to tell him that I was fine on my own. And

I also didn't want to be his charity case." I had to stop and take a breath, as I was talking so fast.

Taylor's eyes were wide, and she rubbed them with the backs of her hands, making her black mascara smudge even more. Now she really looked like a raccoon. "You're certifiable. You know that, right?"

"I might be, yes." I took another drink and found my glass empty. "Well, shit." Getting up, I refilled my glass. "All I know is that I don't know. You know?"

"No." Taylor shook her head. "I think this decision is too big to leave to you when you're obviously not in your right mind. Let me make it for you. Here's what you're gonna do. You call Kane and tell him that you accidentally took some pills of mine. You thought they were just aspirins and you had a headache. Only they must've been something else, 'cause they made you crazy for a little while. You really aren't ever that way and would like to apologize and accept his generous offer."

"I can't do that. I have to move away from here. I've gotta go, girl." I sat down then took a drink from my new glass of wine. "This shit is starting to actually taste good."

"You need to stop drinking and maybe take a bath and then a nap, and when you wake up, then you might not be so damn crazy." Taylor got up and went to put her bowl in the sink. As she stood there, washing it before putting it in the dishwasher, she said, "You need to think about how you would feel if you saw Kane and Fox with another woman. A woman who would be sleeping in Kane's bed with him, who would be getting the great fucking you've been getting. A woman who he would call baby the way he calls you baby. A woman who Fox would call Mom, the way he calls you Mom. You really need to think about that, Zandy. Because that's giving up an awful lot in exchange for nothing."

Jealousy shot through me. But I couldn't let raw emotion rule me right now.

"You don't understand," I whined. "One day, they'll both see through me. I'm just a stupid cocktail waitress who's never done anything good in her life. They'll see that soon."

"You haven't been putting on an act," she said as she came back to me, standing in front of me with her hands on her hips. "I've been around. I've been watching all of you. You haven't been putting on an act. You've been changing, but it's all real, Zandy. You're growing up, you have things to aspire to, people to take care of—and people who want to take care of you. You've found your long-lost family, and you're taking your role in it. Just let it happen the way it has been. Let it all just happen, girl. Don't fight it now. Not when life has just started going your way. You do deserve this. You deserve your family. Take them. They want you. And you want them."

She made it sound so easy. I wished she was right.

Shaking my head, I picked up my glass. "You're a kid. You can't understand this at all."

"I'm a kid?" she asked, looking injured as she put her hand to her throat. "I can understand things, Zandy. I'm not a moron, but I'm beginning to think you might be." She looked up as if listening to someone else. "No, strike that. You're not a moron. What you are is so much worse than that. You're inconsiderate. You're unappreciative. And I can't believe I have to say this to you, as I've never thought this way about you until right now, but you're uncaring. You don't care that your leaving will kill that little boy. You don't care that your leaving will wound Kane. You just don't care." And with that, she turned and left me sitting there as she cried all the way back to her room, where she slammed the door shut behind her.

I didn't know how to react. And I didn't have anyone around to react to.

So I went to my bedroom and fell asleep. I slept for hours and hours, and only woke up because of the sound of my cell phone going off. It was the ringtone I'd set to Fox's name.

Picking it up, I fought against the pain in my pounding head. "Stupid wine." I swiped the screen. "Hi, Fox."

"Hi, Mom. It's Friday, and I know you're busy at work, but it's nine fifteen and Aunt Nancy's not gonna let me stay up much longer, so I called you to say goodnight."

Kane hasn't told him.

"Oh. Well, I'm not at work. I stayed home," I said as I rubbed my temple to help stop the headache. "I'm glad you called. I was asleep. I'm, uh, sick."

"Gosh, I hope you're better by Sunday when I get back home. I want to tell you all about my weekend adventure with Aunt Nancy and Uncle James."

He's got plans with me already.

I didn't know what to say. I couldn't tell him that I wouldn't be there. I couldn't tell him that I would be leaving as soon as I could.

"Mom?"

"Um, I'll see if I'm feeling better by then, Fox," I had no idea what else to say.

"If you're not better by then, can I come over to see you?" he asked, sounding a little worried.

"We'll see." I chewed my lower lip.

"I hope so." He waited a beat. "I love you, Mom. Goodnight. I hope you get better soon."

"I love you too. Goodnight." I ended the call and the tears flooded my eyes once more.

What am I going to do?

CHAPTER 29

Kane

NEVER IN MY life had I dealt with anyone like Zandra Larkin. A woman who'd gone through so much had many layers, and I hadn't even begun to peel them away.

That just meant I didn't know how to handle all the layers yet, but I was determined to stick it out and learn. Even if she didn't feel like listening just yet.

Being a doctor, I thought I should've been more informed about what possible effects could arise when a woman has to give up her child. I knew there had to be some pretty bad ones but hadn't taken the time to do any research.

Now that some of the effects were showing, I knew the time had come to do some research, before Fox and I lost her again.

What I found surprised me. It seemed PTSD was the best diagnosis for what Zandra was going through. My heart ached for her, and it just made me more determined that Fox and I would be the ones to help her through this.

He and I were the best medicine for her. She'd been through a tragedy eleven years ago, and that would never leave her, from what the research showed. But getting to live with her child, raise him, love him, and be loved by him would help make the future look brighter for her.

The fact she didn't want any help from me stemmed from the fact that she didn't easily trust people. Just one more thing to thank her parents for. If you couldn't trust your parents to do what's best for you, then who could you trust?

I understood that. And I knew it would take time for her to realize that she could trust Fox and me as well. Our love for her would never end, no matter what she thought about herself.

The lack of self-worth was also a common effect of having to give up a baby. Even women and men who were able to make the decision themselves suffered with those emotions. Giving up a baby, even if it was for the good of a child, deeply and profoundly affected the parents, my research showed me.

I hadn't been through that. I'd gotten to have my son. And I'd failed to think too much about Zandra during those years. I'd never thought about how much she must've been suffering. I'd never seriously thought to try to find her and let her know I had our boy.

But I had her now, and she knew our son, and she knew she had a part in his life forever now.

Or did she?

Did she worry that, just like with the baby, one day I too would be taken away from her? Maybe she feared that another woman would come along and that I would forget about her and move on to the next girl.

Maybe she was afraid that she would do something that would make me stop loving her, and that I'd start pulling away from her

She might even think that I would try to take Fox away from her again. That I'd make her give him up all over again.

There were so many things that could've been plaguing her. And I hadn't thought about any of them.

All I had thought about was how great she was, and how wonderful it was to have her in my life. I thought about how fantastic it was that Fox had his mother, his real mother, in his life. I'd told her that I loved her and that I thought she was incredible, but those words were only the tip of the iceberg if I wanted to help soothe her worst fears and insecurities.

She needs help.

At least now I realized what she needed, and I knew where to start looking for help for her. Many psychiatrists and therapists specialized in treating PTSD. There were plenty of places we could go to for help out there. And I would see that she got as much as she needed.

But first I had to get her to let me in, at least a little bit.

She'd shut me out. But I wasn't going to let that get me down. I loved the woman, and I would fight for her.

And I had to take responsibility for getting her pregnant, too. She'd been carrying that burden alone on her conscience for much too long, it seemed. And I had to be there for her now the way I hadn't been back then.

There had been times when I'd thought about asking my parents for help in getting to Zandra, to let her know what my family and I were doing to get our son. But I never asked.

And now I was thinking that that had been a giant mistake. I had blame to take, and it was time to take it. It was time to own up to my part in the tragedy that Zandra had suffered.

She thought of herself as damaged goods. Well, if that was true, then I was the one who'd damaged her first. Her parents, who I was coming to despise more and more every day, had finished the act.

It was up to me to do what I could to mend her broken soul. And I knew I could do it. I could do everything I could to help her myself, and I could make sure she got the professional help she needed, too.

She needed me more than she let herself believe. I held the key to helping her live a better life. And I couldn't let her walk away or run away. I had to grab her and make her stay. I had to make her understand that I wouldn't take no for an answer.

Once I set my mind on something, I always got it. I was a determined man, and I rarely, if ever, failed. And I wanted Zandra Larkin to get better. I wanted that woman to know love and accept it as her due. I wanted her to have the family we had created when we'd been foolish teens with no idea what life was all about.

And I would give her what she deserved. Even if I had to force-feed it to her in the beginning, then that would just be the way it went.

Zandra had everything she needed to make her happy right in front of her. She thought she was unlovable, but we already loved her. She thought no one would want her as their family, but we already wanted her.

By God, how I wanted her. And I wanted her forever. I would never let her go.

Now, how to make it all happen.

CHAPTER 30

Zandra

Tossing and turning the rest of the night after my call with Fox, I was restless and agitated. The sun broke through my window, making it impossible for me to even try to sleep anymore.

Being Saturday, I knew there would be very little I could do about finding a new job or place to move to. But I had to do something. I needed to get the hell out of Charleston before I changed my mind.

Lying in the bed, I looked up at the ceiling. My eyes burned from all the crying I'd done, and my skin felt dry too. I didn't feel good at all. Not emotionally, and not physically.

Pulling my body out of bed, I went straight to the bathroom. A long hot bath with bubbles should help me get my head straight and feel a little bit better about life in general.

The numbness still filled me as I soaked in the tub. I didn't even try to shake it off. It had helped me get through hard times before. It had helped me do what I'd had to.

A huge part of me wanted to stay right where I was, in Charleston. That part of me wanted to believe that my life didn't have to always be so bad. With Kane and Fox, I'd never felt more alive and happy.

And that scared the crap out of me.

I had never dared to let myself feel happy, loved, or even hopeful that life could turn out great for me. Not ever.

Maybe part of that came from being brought up by people who used the Bible as a weapon. I didn't know exactly what the main reason was that I felt like there could be no long-term happiness or love in my life.

Had I always felt that way, or had that only started after the pregnancy? God knew my mother had done a great job of convincing me that I was only destined for misery in my future, to make up for the sins of my past.

My mind wandered to Fox. My little boy was a perfect angel; there was nothing evil or sinful about him. He did well in school. His grades were much higher than mine ever were. I'd skirted by in school. But then I'd had no one pushing me to do much better. All my parents had asked of me was that I pass my classes.

Sometimes I thought they didn't expect more out of me because they knew I wasn't capable of more. That I just wasn't that smart.

Thinking that I wasn't smart, I'd only ever gone for the easiest thing I could find. When I did well at it, that was enough for me—I never tried to aspire for more. Being a cocktail waitress didn't take much mental work, so I could handle that just fine. I couldn't be good at anything else, I just wasn't smart enough, I'd always thought.

But Fox had managed to get his father's brain and physical abilities, thank God. My son played his little baseball games like he was playing in the big leagues. He took his games and practices very seriously. And he was a real team player, too. That was something else he certainly didn't get from me.

Not that I'd ever been asked to be on any teams. Or more accurately put, I'd never wanted to participate on any teams. I liked to be alone. Scratch that—I felt more comfortable being alone.

Like some unseen specter, I'd watched the others play, socialize, interact with the other kids in school. Every once in a while, a kid would call out to me to come and join them. I would pretend I didn't feel well so I could stay on my own.

After a while, no one asked me to join in. They all knew what my answer would be. They left me alone, the way I wanted them to.

Will Kane and Fox just leave me alone?

Kane would be easier to push away than Fox. If I could bring myself to even do that to my son—the baby I'd mourned for ten long years.

Even as I thought that, Kane's handsome face filled my mind.

Why do you want to push Kane away?

And why did I sometimes talk to myself in second person?

I supposed it was because at times I didn't feel as if I was a whole being. I felt split sometimes. Maybe I was crazy. No, I was crazy. That was just reality.

Fox didn't deserve to have to live with a crazy mother. Kane didn't deserve to be with a crazy woman. I didn't deserve either of them.

The sound of the doorbell ringing pulled me out of my internal dialogue. I didn't bother to get out of the bath, though, which grew colder with each passing minute.

Maybe I would just stay in the tub and freeze to death. Not likely, in a home with a thermostat that was set at a constant seventy-five degrees. No, I wouldn't find an out that easily.

And why was I even contemplating finding an out when I finally had so much good spread out in front of me?

Oh, yeah. 'Cause I'm crazy, that's why.

A knock came at my bedroom door, and I heard Taylor call out. "Get up, Zandy. You've got a surprise out here."

Ignoring her, I slumped down further, letting my head go under the now-cold water.

Maybe I just won't come up for air. That would do the trick.

But when my lungs began to burn, I pushed my head up out of the water, taking a deep breath. "What am I doing?"

It took everything I had, but I pulled my ass out of that tub. Slowly but surely, I dried off my body, put on a pair of shorts and a T-shirt, not bothering with a bra or panties. All I was going to do was lie around in my room anyway.

My hair was a wet mess, my clothes made me look homeless, and all I could do was stare at the loser in the mirror.

The doorbell sounded again. Taylor cussed, "Shit! Who is it now?" The sound of her bare feet padding across the living room floor made me look at my door, instead of the mirror over the dresser. "More?" she asked whoever was at the door. "My God!"

Waiting, I listened to what came next. Then her feet padded to my door, where she knocked again. "Hey, Zandy, get your ass up and come out here."

Biting my lip, I didn't answer her. I just looked back at my reflection. This time I found it intolerable.

Pulling off my clothes, I went back into the bathroom and took a proper shower. I washed my hair, shaved my legs and underarms, and put in some creamy leave-in-conditioner to tame my hair.

Something began to come to life inside of me again. The numbness was being pushed away, forced out by something else. I wasn't sure what the hell it was. Usually, when the darkness found me, it took a lot longer for me to get through it.

The sound of the doorbell ringing off and on, along with Taylor calling out to me to come out and see what the hell was going on, made me feel something really odd.

Hope.

Hope for what, I had no clue.

But there it was anyway. It pulled me out of the shower and made me want to put on a bit of makeup so I could look presentable. For what, again, I didn't know.

I dried my hair and put it up in a ponytail then dressed more appropriately. Bra, panties, a pair of slacks, a blouse that matched, and some flats too. I finally started to feel more alive, more human.

My eyes were still puffy, but I felt like that would go down if I could move around a bit and drink some water to rehydrate myself. I didn't know what I was getting myself ready for, but I felt like I needed to be prepared. It felt like something outside my body was pushing me to do it all. Another entity had entered my body, forcing it to do what it felt was necessary.

At least I was there, somewhere, not fighting it at all. For once.

Most of my life I'd felt like I was fighting a battle within me. Part of me wanted to get out and enjoy things the way others did. The other part of me wanted to hide.

With Kane and Fox, the part of me who wanted to join the world of the living—who wanted to have fun, and go on adventures, and feel love—took over. I wanted to be a part of their world. And I'd never been happier.

Running my hands along my waist as I looked into the mirror again, I found a much better version of myself than I'd been looking at earlier.

"So what the hell are you doing, Zandra Larkin?" I whispered to myself.

Running away, as usual.

Shaking my head, I knew I had to change things up. "You have a son now, Zandra. You have prayed and wondered about that boy since that horrible day you watched him being taken out of that delivery room. You have mourned him for what seems like forever. You don't have to mourn him anymore. He's right there. And he wants you in his life. He wants you to be his mother."

Looking at myself, I felt that familiar burn of tears behind my eyes. "No." Shaking my head, I pushed that crying shit away. "No more."

I didn't know what I was going to do, but I wasn't going to be running. Not again.

The truth was, I hadn't put as much into finding another job as I'd told myself I had. The truth was, I hadn't really let myself fall head over heels in love with Kane, or even Fox. And that was because I was still guarding my bruised heart, mind, and even my soul.

Fear of losing someone dear to me again had made me put my shields up, making sure I would find myself alone. And I'd lied to myself, telling myself that I was blissfully alone.

I wasn't blissfully anything. I was barely treading water.

And I had to stop with that and start something new.

Telling Kane that I hadn't been entirely truthful when I'd told him I loved him would be a start. I was too broken as it was to know how to give my love to him, but I was going to fix that. I just needed time, and I prayed he would be patient with me.

I wouldn't tell Fox the same thing. Mostly because I had loved Fox from the moment I found out I was pregnant with him. That love had never died. It gotten buried under grief, guilt, and remorse, but it had never been extinguished.

Another doorbell and another shout from Taylor told me something strange was happening and that I should go see what the hell it was. "Coming," I finally shouted back to her.

"Thank God!" came her exasperated reply. "I'd like to get some damn sleep, Zandy. I didn't get home until five this morning, unlike you who slept half the day yesterday and all damn night. You can deal with the bombardment from now on."

The overwhelming smell of flowers hit me as soon as I opened my door. Turning the corner to go into the living room, I found at least a dozen vases filled with assorted flowers all around the room. On the kitchen table there were boxes of what I thought must be candy. And a stack of pink envelopes, too.

Going over to the first vase, I pulled off the card. It read: *To Zandra, the mother of my child, the light of my life, you will always be in my heart.*

There wasn't any signature, but I knew they were from Kane. I knew that everything was from Kane. The stack of envelopes drew me to them. On the front of each one, *Happy Mother's Day* was written.

Opening the first one, I saw that Fox had handwritten a little note inside: *Happy first Mother's Day Mom. I wish I could've spent it with you. But we have many more to come, and I will spend each one with you. Love, Fox.*

All nine of the other cards had similar notes in them, each one written by my son. He wanted a future that included me in it, of that I was sure. And I wanted a future that included him, too.

But how could I ever make myself into someone who didn't turn into a basket case on occasion?

When things got hard, I lost it. No one's life was perfect, and I didn't expect mine would never get hard from time to time. How would I combat my inner demons to be the mother my son needed me to be?

How would Kane take it when I confessed that I had said the words, "I love you" to him without really meaning them?

He would probably hate me. He would call me a liar. He would tell me that he didn't want anything else to do with me, and he would tell me to get the hell out of his and his son's life.

Fox was still only Kane's. I had no legal right to my son. And I never would. I'd signed that right away before I'd even given birth to him.

Putting the last pink Mother's Day card back into the matching envelope, feeling my elation disappear as those negative thoughts kept coming, my whole body jerked when the doorbell rang again. Something flashed through me.

A sense of destiny.

It was weird, and I shook my head to send the odd sensation away as I walked toward the door. I didn't bother looking through the peephole. I figured it was a delivery person with more flowers or something like that.

Opening the door, I found Fox and Kane there. Both wore black suits with blue ties and white shirts, along with broad smiles. They both looked so beautiful and precious to me.

Fox tugged the hem of my blouse. "Hi, Mom."

Caressing his cheek, I said, "Hi, Fox."

Kane didn't say a thing. But when he started going down on one knee, I gasped and covered my mouth with my hands. That action spoke louder than words, and I couldn't believe what he was doing.

Pulling a ring out of his pocket, he held it up to me. "Zandra Larkin, you are the mother of my son. You are the reason for my happiness. You gave me a life worth living. Now let me give you one, too. Marry me and become my wife and Fox's mother and stay with us forever, the way you were meant to from the very beginning."

Blackness closed in around me from every side.

This cannot be real.

CHAPTER 31

Kane

"Fox, GRAB HER!" I shouted as Zandra started to sway, her eyes going so wide I could see the whites all around the iris.

My little boy grabbed his mother's arm and the contact pulled her out of whatever was happening to her. I stood up and put my arms around her, holding her close. "Baby, are you okay?"

"No." Her nails curled into my back as she held onto me like she'd never let me go.

I prayed that word meant that she wasn't okay and wasn't the answer to my marriage proposal.

"No?" I moved into the apartment with her, still holding until I got her into a chair. Looking at her, I saw her pupils were wide, and there was a lot of fear behind those pretty blue eyes. "It's okay, Zandra. It really is."

"How?" Her eyes moved back and forth rapidly as if searching mine for an answer.

"Because I'm here, and so is Fox." I knelt in front of her, the diamond engagement ring on my pinky finger. I took her hands in mine while Fox stood quietly beside me. "Baby, I haven't exactly done my best by you. I've failed you in many ways. I want the chance to make that right. I know you have some emotional scars that will never heal all the way. I know that you've got open wounds that need to be tended to. I can help you. Fox and I are the best medicine for you. No one else can do for you what we can."

"Yeah, Mom." Fox went to sit next to his mother, putting his little arm around her. "We want you to be a real part of our family. Please say yes to Dad."

She watched Fox as he spoke to her then her eyes came to mine once more. "I need to tell you the truth, Kane."

"Go ahead." I rubbed her knuckles with my fingertips as I held her hands.

She gulped then said, "When I told you that I loved you, they were only words. I'm not sure I meant them. I didn't lie, though. I just didn't have as much feeling behind them as I think I should've."

I'd figured she'd say something like that, so it didn't hurt as much as one would think. "I believe that you will come to love me in time. And I will come to love you more in time, too. If you come be a part of this family that we created so long ago, I promise that you will learn how to love and be loved again, as you deserve to. We already love you so much. As my wife, you will be Fox's mother in every aspect of the word. We'll fill out all the paperwork to make it official. He'll be yours once again."

I knew her heart had skipped a beat by the way she looked at our son. "He would, wouldn't he?"

Fox smiled, then kissed her cheek. "I don't need no paper to tell me that I'm your kid, Mom. But if you need one, then it sounds like marrying Dad would make that all a lot easier."

She caressed his cheek. "You're such a wise little man, Fox."

Turning her head to look at me, she caressed my cheek next. "You still want to marry me? I thought you'd hate me when I told you that. Even though you saw me break down, you still want to marry me? I don't know which one of us is crazier."

"Neither of us are, Zandra. We're just products of our lives." Pulling our clasped hands up, I kissed the backs of hers. "Tell me that you'll marry me and make me the happiest man alive."

Her lips stayed tightly shut. Her eyes closed. And she said nothing for so long that I wondered if she'd fallen asleep.

Fox and I looked at one another until we finally heard her soft reply. "I would love to marry you, Kane Price."

Sighs of relief came out of both Fox and me. "Thank goodness," he exclaimed, making Zandra and me both chuckle.

When Zandra opened her eyes, she said, "I think I need help. Lots of help, Kane."

"And I will make sure you get it. You will never have to worry again. We can help each other heal the wounds from the past, together, so that we can have the best future possible for all of us. Fox and I need you as much as you need us." I'd never said truer words in my life.

After a long group hug, Fox said, "Okay, now we go to leave me with Aunt Nancy and Uncle James while you guys go get married."

Zandra laughed. "It takes a little more time than that for a wedding, Fox."

"No, it doesn't." I got up off my knees and pulled her up with me. "You and I are taking a private jet to Vegas. We're getting married stat, and then we'll stick around to enjoy a short honeymoon there. Later, we can plan a longer honeymoon together. Anywhere you want and for as long as you want."

Fox took his mother's hand. "And when you guys come back, you're moving into our home. It'll be our home. And we will be a real family."

"This is a dream, isn't it?" she asked me.

"Nope." I kissed her cheek as I pulled her toward her bedroom. "It's not. Now get your purse, and make sure you've got your identification so we can get hitched." In all the excitement, I'd yet to put the engagement ring on her finger. "Oh, let me get this on you."

"Huh?" she asked as I turned her around to face me. As I slipped the ring on her finger, she gasped, one tear falling down her cheek. "Kane, it's beautiful."

"I had to pick out something that would match your beauty, Zandra." Kissing the ring on her finger, I felt my heart swell. "I love you."

She looked at me for a long time before she said, "I really do love you too, Kane Price. I really do."

Shrugging, I said, "Yeah, I know you do. You may not have thought you meant those words, but I knew deep down that you did. You just didn't want to believe in yourself that you were capable of that love. And you probably didn't want to believe that I really love you, but it's true."

"Yeah, from me too, Mom," Fox chimed in. "And I know you love me too, 'cause I can see it in your eyes."

"Oh, hell," she whimpered as more tears started trickling down her pink cheeks. "I mean, heck. Sorry." She pulled her hands out of mine. "Let me go freshen up, grab my things, and I'll be ready to go."

She rushed away as I called out, "Take only what you really need. I'll be buying you everything else."

I heard her sob as she closed the bedroom door. Fox looked up at me with a grin. "Is this what I should expect when I ask a girl to marry me, Dad?"

"I sure hope not." I ran my hand over his head. "I hope you don't put the cart before the horse the way I did. I hope you find a girl and you both fall in love and only experience happiness when you pop the question and for the rest of your lives."

With a nod, he said, "Yep. I think you're right, Dad."

When Zandra came back out, she'd changed into a beautiful light blue dress that flowed around her, all the way to her ankles. Her hair was pinned up prettily, and she looked every bit the part of a mother and wife. "You look amazing."

Fox laughed. "Wow, Mom!"

She spun around, letting the lightweight fabric flow around her. "Thank you, guys. I'm ready to start my life now."

Putting my arm around her waist, I led her out to the car. "Me too."

Fox climbed into the backseat. "Yeah, me too."

As we all laughed, I felt the air lighten around us. Things would be okay. I knew there would be hard times, but there would be more good times than bad.

I would make sure of it.

CHAPTER 32

Zandra

HIS STEADY HAND on my back as we walked down the short aisle together gave me goosebumps. Kane had never looked more handsome to me as he did when he walked by my side on our way to become man and wife.

Not in a million years did I ever see this coming for me.

Just before the wedding, I'd called my parents. Mom answered the phone, "Hello? Who is this?"

"Mom, it's me, Zandra. I'm just calling to say that I'm marrying Kane Price today. He's the father of the son I put up for adoption. I've got my son back, and his father and I are making a life for our family now." I took a deep breath to steady myself for the next part. "Mom, I've blamed you and Dad for what I did. I blamed you both for the loss of my son for the last eleven years. But the truth is, I played a part in it too. My lack of self-confidence stopped me from standing up for what I wanted and for what was right. I'm sorry."

"I don't know what to say," she muttered.

"I don't need you to say a word. I just needed to say my piece. Bye, now." I hesitated, then added, "I love you and Dad both, Mom." Then I ended the call.

Kane's smile told me I'd done the right thing. I hadn't let go of the resentment completely, but saying it out loud felt like a huge step toward healing.

The sweet kiss he gave me as I handed him back his phone made my heart fill up with love.

After the preacher had us say the vows that would connect us forever, we put platinum wedding bands on each other's fingers and then shared our first kiss as a married couple.

He rested his forehead against mine then whispered, "I love you, Zandra Price, and I always will."

"I love you, Dr. Price, and I always will, too."

Although I'd never seen any of this coming, the surprise of it all was appreciated.

And a little bit later, when Kane and I were in our honeymoon suite, I let myself feel adored by my husband. He moved his hands all over my naked body as I lay on the bed, showing me with his body how much he loved me, and how worthy I was of his love.

Starting at my toes, he kissed my entire body before kissing my lips. I ran my hands through his hair as he pushed my legs apart then eased his hard cock into me.

On the jet ride to Vegas, he and I had made an agreement. No more birth control. We wanted to have another baby as soon as possible.

Sure, things were happening fast, but we were both so sure. It had actually surprised me how easily I'd agreed to try for another baby. Especially since I'd made a solemn vow to myself all those years ago to never have another child.

But sometimes life took unpredictable turns, and we had to be ready to embrace those unexpected changes. My life had taken me places I had never imagined, and it had turned out so much better for it.

His cock moving slowly in and out of me, Kane pulled his lips away from mine, looking at me with desire in his eyes. "I can't wait to get to experience pregnancy with you, baby," he said.

I ran my fingertips across his cheek. "Me too, Kane. To get to share that experience with you will be amazing. I know it will. And giving Fox a sibling will make him happy too."

Kane ground his cock into me deeply. "Let's give him more than one. What do you say to a couple of them?"

I had to laugh lightly. "Can we get this one out before we even think about more?"

"I suppose so," he conceded. His mouth took mine again as he moved faster.

Passion took us over, like a fire spreading through our bodies, and we did what we had always done best. We shared our bodies the way God had intended all along.

Sin was a dirty word my parents had used far too much. Our son wasn't conceived in a sinful act. Kane and I might not have known it at that time, but we were always meant to be together.

No legal document needed to be signed and dated to make that true. No preacher had been needed to make our union real. And no one could have stopped what had inevitably happen.

It was simply fate.

Giving my virginity to Kane had been written in the stars long before our time. We were never the sinners I had let myself believe we were when I was force-fed those ideas by my parents. We were always meant to be.

And I would make sure I did my part to always live up to what we were supposed to be to each other. Lovers, partners, parents, teachers, followers, friends, and companions. Life would be sure that we had the opportunity to be all that and more to one another.

My body undulated with his as we made love for the first time as a married couple. But our bodies had belonged to the other forever. Our hearts had never been our own—I had found my heart when I found Kane, and I thought he'd found his in me.

Feeling his cock go stiff inside of me, I opened my eyes to look into his as he spilled his seed inside of me. Gripping the back of his neck, I felt my body spiral into an orgasm that milked everything it could get from him. "Give me all you've got, Kane."

"I will." He kissed my lips. "As long as you give me all you've got. I will always give you everything I have."

A light glowed from behind him. One I must not have noticed before. I gasped as the heat of his seed filled me, making my heart pound and my body feel as if we were floating in the air, instead of lying on a hotel bed.

When our bodies quit pulling what they needed from each other, he rested his head on my chest, leaving only part of his weight on me. "No matter what happens, Zandra Price, I will love you forever."

Running my hand through his hair, I told him the same. "And I too will love you forever, no matter what happens, Kane Price."

Our happily ever after had finally come. No one was more surprised than me.

The End.

Did you like this book? Then you'll LOVE The Virgin's Baby: A Forced Marriage Romance (The Sons of Sin 2)

Having a stranger's baby wasn't a thing I'd ever dreamt of doing...
As a busy college student, I didn't have time for the opposite sex.
The center of my world was my approaching career.
Until he came along.
Stimulating. Virile. Obsessive.
I was supposed to have his baby and nothing more.
Only, he wanted much more than I could give.
His slightest touch turned me into a puddle of melting flesh.
If I allowed it, he would own me—body and soul.
I would give him his heir, but never my heart.

Start reading The Virgin's Baby NOW!

ABOUT THE AUTHOR

Mrs. Love writes about smart, sexy women and the hot alpha billionaires who love them. She has found her own happily ever after with her dream husband and adorable 6 and 2 year old kids. Currently, Michelle is hard at work on the next book in the series, and trying to stay off the Internet.
"Thank you for supporting an indie author. Anything you can do, whether it be writing a review, or even simply telling a fellow reader that you enjoyed this. Thanks

❀ Created with Vellum